BAIT FOR
THE SHAPE-CHANGERS

In hawk-shape, Morgon burned a golden path into the sky and shot toward Isig Mountain.

The shape-changers melted out of the trees and flew after him. For a while, he raced ahead of them in a surge of speed. But as the sun set, they caught up with him. Their eyes and talons were of flame. Their sharp beaks were bone-white. They surrounded him, dove at him, snapping and tearing, until his wings grew ragged and his breast was flecked with blood.

He faltered; they flung themselves at him, blinding him with their wings, until he gave one piercing, despairing cry. He took his own shape then, in midair, and simply fell. The forests whirled up to meet him. Something cracked across his mind before he reached the ground.

He spun into darkness.

Harpist in the Wind

Patricia A. McKillip

A Del Rey Book

BALLANTINE BOOKS • NEW YORK

A Del Rey Book
Published by Ballantine Books

Library of Congress Catalog Card Number: 78-11410

ISBN 0-345-32440-4

This edition published by arrangement with Atheneum

Manufactured in the United States of America

First Ballantine Books Edition: April 1980
Seventh Printing: January 1985

Cover art and frontispiece by Darrell K. Sweet

For all who waited, and especially
for STEVE DONALDSON,
who always called at the right time

for GAIL,
who reminded me of the difference
between logic and grace

and for KATHY,
who waited the longest.

MAP BY KATHY MC KILLIP

Notes on people and places may be found beginning on page 258.

1

THE STAR-BEARER AND RAEDERLE OF AN SAT ON the crown of the highest of the seven towers of Anuin. The white stone fell endlessly away from them, down to the summer-green slope the great house sat on. The city itself spilled away from the slope to the sea. The sky revolved above them, a bright, changeless blue, its expression broken only by the occasional spiral of a hawk. Morgon had not moved for hours. The morning sun had struck his profile on the side of the embrasure he sat in and shifted his shadow without his notice to the other side. He was aware of Raederle only as some portion of the land around him, of the light wind, and the crows sketching gleaming black lines through the green orchards in the distance: something peaceful and remote, whose beauty stirred every once in a while through his thoughts.

His mind was spinning endless threads of conjecture that snarled constantly around his ignorance. Stars, children with faces of stone, the fiery, broken shards of a bowl he had smashed in Astrin's hut, dead cities, a dark-haired shape-changer, a harpist, all resolved under his probing into answerless riddles. He gazed back at his own life, at the history of the realm, and picked at facts like potshards, trying to piece them together.

Nothing fit; nothing held; he was cast constantly out of his memories into the soft summer air.

He moved finally, stiffly as a stone deciding to move, and slid his hands over his eyes. Flickering shapes like ancient beasts without names winged into light behind his eyelids. He cleared his mind again, let images drift and flow into thought until they floundered once again on the shoals of impossibility.

The vast blue sky broke into his vision, and the swirling maze of streets and houses below. He could think no longer; he leaned against his shadow. The silence within the slab of ancient stone eased through him; his thoughts, worn meaningless, became quiet again.

He saw a soft leather shoe then and a flicker of leaf-green cloth. He turned his head and found Raederle sitting cross-legged on the ledge beside him.

He leaned over precariously and drew her against him. He laid his face against her long windblown hair and saw the burning strands beneath his closed eyes. He was silent for a time, holding her tightly, as if he sensed a wind coming that might sweep them out of their high, dangerous resting place.

She stirred a little; her face lifting to kiss him, and his arms loosened reluctantly. "I didn't realize you were here," he said, when she let him speak.

"I guessed that, somehow, after the first hour or so. What were you thinking about?"

"Everything." He nudged a chip of mortar out of a crack and flicked it into the trees below. A handful of crows startled up, complaining. "I keep battering my brains against my past, and I always come to the same conclusion. I don't know what in Hel's name I am doing."

She shifted, drawing her knees up, and leaned back against the stone beside her to face him. Her eyes filled with light, like sea-polished amber, and his throat constricted suddenly, too full of words. "Answering riddles. You told me that that is the only thing you can keep doing, blind and deaf and dumb, and not knowing where you are going."

"I know." He searched more mortar out of the crack and threw it so hard he nearly lost his balance. "I know. But I have been here in Anuin with you for seven days, and I can't find one reason or one riddle to compel me out of this house. Except that if we stay here much longer, we will both die."

"That's one," she said soberly.

"I don't know why my life is in danger because of three stars on my face. I don't know where the High One is. I don't know what the shape-changers are, or how I can help a cairn of children who have turned into stone at the bottom of a mountain. I know of only one place to begin finding answers. And the prospect is hardly appealing."

"Where?"

"In Ghisteslwchlohm's mind."

She stared at him, swallowing, and then frowned down at the sun-warmed stone, "Well." Her voice shook almost imperceptibly. "I didn't think we could stay here forever. But, Morgon—"

"You could stay here."

Her head lifted. With the sun catching in her eyes again, he could not read their expression. But her voice was stiff. "I am not going to leave you. I refused even the wealth of Hel and all the pigs in it for your sake. You are going to have to learn to live with me."

"It's difficult enough just trying to live," he murmured, without thinking, then flushed. But her mouth twitched. He reached across to her, took her hand. "For one silver boar bristle, I would take you to Hed and spend the rest of my life raising plow horses in east Hed."

"I'll find you a boar bristle."

"How do I marry you, in this land?"

"You can't," she said calmly, and his hand slackened.

"What?"

"Only the king has the power to bind his heirs in marriage. And my father is not here. So we'll have to forget about that until he finds the time to return home."

"But, Raederle—"

She pitched a sliver of mortar across the tail feathers of a passing crow, causing it to veer with a squawk. "But what?" she said darkly.

"I can't . . . I can't walk into your father's land, trouble the dead as I have, nearly commit murder in his hall, then take you away with me to wander through the realm without even marrying you. What in Hel's name will your father think of me?"

"When he finally meets you, he'll let you know. What I think, which is more to the point, is that my father has meddled enough with my life. He may have foreseen our meeting, and maybe even our loving, but I don't think he should have his own way in every-thing. I'm not going to marry you just because he maybe foresaw that, too, in some dream."

"Do you think it was that, behind his strange vow about Peven's Tower?" he asked curiously. "Fore-knowledge?"

"You are changing the subject."

He eyed her a moment, considering the subject and her flushed face. "Well," he said softly, casting their future to the winds over the dizzying face of the tower, "if you refuse to marry me, I don't see what I can do about it. And if you choose to come with me—if that is what you really want—I am not going to stop you. I want you too much. But I'm terrified. I think we would have more hope of survival falling head first off this tower. And at least, doing that, we'd know where we were going."

Her hand lay on the stones between them. She lifted it, touched his face. "You have a name and a destiny. I can only believe that sooner or later you will stumble across some hope."

"I haven't seen any so far. Only you. Will you marry me in Hed?"

"No."

He was silent a little, holding her eyes. "Why?"

She looked away from him quickly; he sensed a sudden, strange turmoil in her. "For many reasons."

"Raederle—"

"No. And don't ask me again. And stop looking at me like that."

"All right," he said after a moment. He added, "I don't remember that you were so stubborn."

"Pig-headed."

"Pig-headed."

She looked at him again. Her mouth crooked into a reluctant smile. She shifted close to him, put her arm around his shoulders, and swung her feet over the sheer edge of nothingness. "I love you, Morgon of Hed. When we finally leave this house, where will we go first? Hed?"

"Yes. Hed . . ." The name touched his heart suddenly, like the word of a spell. "I have no business going home. I simply want to. For a few hours, at night . . . that might be safe." He thought of the sea, between them and his home, and his heart chilled. "I can't take you across the sea."

"In Hel's name, why not?" she said.

"It's far too dangerous."

"That makes no sense. Lungold is dangerous, and I'm going with you there."

"That's different. For one thing, no one I loved ever died in Lungold. Yet. For another thing—"

"Morgon, I am not going to die in the sea. I can probably shape water as well as fire."

"You don't know that. Do you?" The thought of her caught in the water as it heaved itself into faces and wet, gleaming forms made his voice rough. "You wouldn't even have time to learn."

"Morgon—"

"Raederle, I have been on a ship breaking apart in the sea. I don't want to risk your life that way."

"It's not your risk. It's mine. For another thing, I

have been on ships from Caithnard to Kyrth and back looking for you and nothing ever happened to me."

"You could stay at Caithnard. For only a few—"

"I am not going to stay at Caithnard," she said tersely. "I am going with you to Hed. I want to see the land you love. If you had your way, I would be sitting in a farmhouse in Hed shelling beans and waiting for you, just as I have waited for nearly two years."

"You don't shell beans."

"I don't. Not unless you are beside me helping."

He saw himself, a lean, shaggy-haired man with a worn, spare face, a great sword at his side and a starred harp at his back, sitting on the porch at Akren with a bowl of beans on his knees. He laughed suddenly. She smiled again, watching him, her argument forgotten.

"You haven't done that in seven days."

"No." He was still, his arm around her, and the smile died slowly in his eyes. He thought of Hed, gripped so defenselessly in the heart of the sea, with not even the illusion of the High One to protect it. He whispered, "I wish I could ring Hed with power, so that nothing of the turmoil of the mainland could touch it and it could stay innocent of fear."

"Ask Duac. He'll give you an army."

"I don't dare bring an army to Hed. That would be asking for disaster."

"Take a few wraiths," she suggested. "Duac would love to be rid of them."

"Wraiths." He lifted his eyes from the distant forests to stare at her. "In Hed."

"They're invisible. No one would see them to attack them." Then she shook her head a little at her own words. "What am I thinking? They would upset all the farmers in Hed."

"Not if the farmers didn't know they were there." His hands felt chilled, suddenly, linked around hers. He breathed, "What am I thinking?"

She drew back, searching his eyes. "Are you taking me seriously?"

"I think . . . I think so." He did not see her face then, but the faces of the dead, with all their frustrated power. "I could bind them. I understand them . . . their anger, their desire for revenge, their land-love. They can take that love to Hed and all their longing for war. . . . But your father . . . how can I wrest something out of the history of An and lead it to danger in Hed? I can't tamper with the land-law of An like that."

"Duac gave you permission. And for all my father is interested in land-law, he might as well be a wraith himself. But Morgon, what about Eliard?"

"Eliard?"

"I don't know him, but wouldn't he . . . wouldn't it disturb him maybe a little if you brought an army of the dead to Hed?"

He thought of the land-ruler of Hed, his brother, whose face he barely remembered. "A little," he said softly. "He must be used to being disturbed by me, even in his sleep, by now. I would bury my own heart under his feet if that would keep him and Hed safe. I would even face an argument with him over this—"

"What will he say?"

"I don't know . . . I don't even know him any more." The thought pained him, touching unhealed places within him. But he did not let her see that; he only moved reluctantly from their high place. "Come with me. I want to talk to Duac."

"TAKE THEM," DUAC SAID. "ALL OF THEM."

They had found him in the great hall, listening to complaints from farmers and messengers from Lords of An whose lands and lives were in turmoil over the restlessness and bickerings of the dead. When the hall finally cleared and Morgon could speak with him, he listened incredulously.

"You actually want them? But Morgon, they'll destroy the peace of Hed."

"No, they won't. I'll explain to them why they are there—"

"How? How do you explain anything to dead men who are fighting a centuries-old war in cow pastures and village market places?"

"I'll simply offer them what they want. Someone to fight. But, Duac, how will I explain to your father?"

"My father?" Duac glanced around the hall, then up at the rafters, and at each of the four corners. "I don't see him. Anywhere. And when I do see him, he will be so busy explaining himself to the living, he won't have time to count the heads of the dead. How many do you want?"

"As many as I can bind, of the kings and warriors who had some touch of compassion in them. They'll need that, to understand Hed. Rood would be able to help me—" He stopped suddenly and an unaccountable flush stained Duac's face. "Where is Rood? I haven't seen him for days."

"He hasn't been here for days." Duac cleared his throat. "You weren't noticing. So I waited until you asked. I sent him to find Deth."

Morgon was silent. The name flung him back seven days, as though he stood in the same pool of sunlight, his shadow splayed before him on the cracked stone floor. "Deth," he whispered, and the ambiguity of the name haunted him.

"I gave him instructions to bring the harpist back here; I sent fourteen armed men with him. You let him go, but he still has much to answer for to the land-rulers of the realm. I thought to imprison him here until the Masters at Caithnard could question him. That's not something I would attempt to do." He touched Morgon hesitantly. "You would never have known he was here. I'm only surprised Rood has not returned before this."

The color stirred back into Morgon's face. "I'm not

surprised," he said. "I wouldn't want to be in Rood's boots, trying to bring Deth back to Anuin. That harpist makes his own choices."

"Maybe."

"Rood will never bring him back here. You sent him into the chaos of the Three Portions for nothing."

"Well," Duac said resignedly, "you know the harpist better than I do. And Rood would have gone after him with or without my asking. He wanted answers too."

"You don't question that riddler with a sword. Rood should have known that." He heard the harsh edge that had crept into his voice then. He turned a little abruptly, out of the light, and sat down at one of the tables.

Duac said helplessly, "I'm sorry. This was something you didn't need to know."

"I do need to know. I just didn't want to think. Not yet." He spread his hands on the rich gold grain of oak and thought again of Akren, with its sunlit oak walls. "I'm going home." The words opened his heart, filled him with a sharp, sweet urgency. "Home . . . Duac, I need ships. Trade-ships."

"You're going to take the dead by water?" Raederle said amazedly. "Will they go?"

"How else can they get to Hed?" he asked reasonably. Then he thought a little, staring back at his vague reflection in the polished wood. "I don't dare take you on the same ship with them. So . . . we'll ride together to Caithnard and meet them there. All right?"

"You want to ride back through Hel?"

"We could fly instead," he suggested, but she shook her head quickly.

"No. I'll ride."

He eyed her, struck by an odd note in her voice. "It would be simple for you to take the crow-shape."

"One crow in the family is enough," she said darkly. "Morgon, Bri Corbett could find ships for you. And men to sail them."

"It will cost a small fortune to persuade them," Morgon said, but Duac only shrugged.

"The dead have already cost a great fortune in the destruction of crops and animals. Morgon, how in Hel's name will you control them in Hed?"

"They will not want to fight me," he said simply, and Duac was silent, gazing at him out of clear, sea-colored eyes.

"I wonder," he said slowly, "what you are. Man of Hed, who can control the dead of An . . . Star-Bearer."

Morgon looked at him with a curious gratitude. "I might have hated my own name in this hall, but for you." He stood up, mulling over the problem at hand. "Duac, I need to know names. I could spend days searching the cairns with my mind, but I won't know who I am rousing. I know many of the names of the Kings of the Three Portions, but I don't know the lesser dead."

"I don't either," Duac said.

"Well, I know where you can find out," Raederle sighed. "The place I almost lived in when I was a child. Our father's library."

She and Morgon spent the rest of the day and the evening there, among ancient books and dusty parchments, while Duac sent to the docks for Bri Corbett. By midnight, Morgon had tamped down in the deep of his mind endless names of warrior-lords, their sons and far-flung families, and legends of love, blood feuds and land wars that spanned the history of An. He left the house then, walked alone through the still summer night into the fields behind the king's house, which were the charnel house for the many who had died battling over Anuin. There he began his calling.

He spoke name after name, with the fragments of legend or poetry that he could remember, with his voice and his mind. The dead roused to their names, came out of the orchards and woods, out of the earth itself. Some rode at him with wild, eerie cries, their armor aflame with moonlight over bare bones. Others came silently: dark, grim figures revealing terrible death wounds. They sought to frighten him, but he only watched them out of eyes that had already seen all he needed to fear. They tried to fight him, but he opened his own mind to them, showed them glimpses of his power. He held them through all their challenging, until they stood ranged before him across an entire field, their awe and curiosity forcing them out of their memories to glimpse something of the world they had been loosed into.

Then he explained what he wanted. He did not expect them to understand Hed, but they understood him, his anger and despair and his land-love. They gave him fealty in a ritual as old as An, their moldering blades flashing greyly in the moonlight. Then they seeped slowly back into the night, into the earth, until he summoned them again.

He stood once again in a quiet field, his eyes on one still, dark figure who did not leave. He watched it curiously; then, when it did not move, he touched its mind. His thoughts were filled instantly with the living land-law of An.

His heart pounded sharply against his ribs. The King of An walked slowly toward him, a tall man robed and cowled like a master or a wraith. As he neared, Morgon could see him dimly in the moonlight, his dark brows slashing a tired, bitter face over eyes that were like Rood's hauntingly familiar. The king stopped in front of him, stood silently surveying him.

He smiled unexpectedly, the bitterness in his eyes yielding to a strange wonder. "I've seen you," he said, "in my dreams. Star-Bearer."

"Mathom." His throat was very dry. He bent his head to the king he had summoned out of the night of An. "You must . . . you must be wondering what I'm doing."

"No. You made that very clear, as you explained it to the army you raised. You do astounding things so quietly in my land."

"I asked Duac's permission."

"I'm sure Duac was grateful for the suggestion. You're going to sail with them to Hed? Is that what I heard?"

"I don't . . . I was thinking of riding with Raederle to Caithnard and meeting the ships there, but I think perhaps I should sail with the dead. It would make the living men on the ships feel easier, if I am with them."

"You're taking Raederle to Hed?"

"She won't . . . she won't listen to reason."

The king grunted. "Strange woman." His eyes were as sharp and curious as birds' eyes, searching beneath Morgon's words.

Morgon asked him suddenly, "What have you seen of me, in your dreams?"

"Pieces. Fragments. Little that will help you, and much more than is good for me. Long ago, I dreamed that you came out of a tower with a crown in your hand and three stars on your face . . . but no name. I saw you with a beautiful young woman, whom I knew was my daughter, but still, I never knew who you were. I saw. . . ." He shook his head a little, drawing his gaze back out of some perplexing, dangerous vision.

"What?"

"I am not sure."

"Mathom." He felt cold suddenly in the warm summer night. "Be careful. There are things in your mind that could cost you your life."

"Or my land-law?" His lean hand closed on Morgon's shoulder. "Perhaps. That is why I rarely explain my thoughts. Come to the house. There will be a minor tempest when I reappear, but if you can sit patiently through that, we will have time to talk afterward." He took a step, but Morgon did not move. "What is it?"

He swallowed. "There is something I have to tell you. Before I walk into your hall with you. Seven days ago, I walked into it to kill a harpist."

He heard the king draw a swift breath. "Deth came here."

"I didn't kill him."

"Somehow I am not surprised." His voice sounded husky, like a voice out of a barrow. He drew Morgon forward toward the great moonlit house. "Tell me."

Morgon told him much more than that before they reached the hall. He found himself talking a little about even the past seven days, which were so precious to him he wondered if they had even existed. Mathom said little, only making a faint noise deep in his throat now and then, like a blackbird's mutter. As they entered the inner courtyard, they saw horses, trembling and sweating, being led to the stables. Their saddle-cloths were purple and blue, the colors of the kings household guard. Mathom cursed mildly.

"Rood must be back. Empty-handed, furious, wraithridden, and unwashed." They entered the hall, which was a blaze of torchlight, and Rood, slumped over a cup of wine, stared at his father. Duac and Raederle were beside him, their heads turning, but he got to his feet first, drowning their voices.

"Where in Hel's name have you been?"

"Don't shout at me," the king said testily. "If you had no more sense than to roam through this chaos searching for that harpist, I have no pity for you." He switched his gaze to Duac, as Rood, his mouth still open, dropped back into his chair. Duac eyed the king coldly, but his voice was controlled.

"Well. What brought you home? Dropping out of the sky like a bad spell. Surely not distress over the shambles you have made of your land-rule."

"No," Mathom said imperturbably, pouring wine. "You and Rood have done very well without me."

"We have done what very well without you?" Rood asked between his teeth. "Do you realize we are on the verge of war?"

"Yes. And An has armed itself for it in a remarkably

short time. Even you have turned, in less than three months, from a scholar into a warrior."

Rood drew an audible breath to answer. Duac's hand clamped suddenly down on his wrist, silencing him. "War." His face had lost color. "With whom?"

"Who else is armed?"

"Ymris?" He repeated it incredulously, "Ymris?"

Mathom swallowed wine. His face looked older than it had under the moonlight, grim and worn with travel. He sat down beside Raederle. "I have seen the war in Ymris," he said softly. "The rebels hold half the coastal lands. It's a strange, bloody, merciless war, and it is going to exhaust Heureu Ymris' forces. He can never hope to contain it within his own borders once the people he is fighting decide to take it beyond the borders of Ymris. I suspected that before, but even I could not ask the Three Portions to arm themselves without reason. And to give reason might have precipitated attack."

"You did that deliberately?" Duac breathed. "You left us so that we would arm ourselves?"

"It was extreme," Mathom admitted, "but it was effective." He cast an eye at Rood again, as he opened his mouth and spoke in a subdued voice.

"Where have you been? And are you planning to stay home awhile?"

"Here and there, satisfying my curiosity. And yes, I think I will stay home now. If you can refrain from shouting at me."

"If you weren't so pig-headed, I wouldn't shout."

Mathom looked skeptical. "You even have a warrior's hard head. What exactly were you planning to do with Deth if you had caught him?"

There was a short silence. Duac said simply, "I would have sent him to Caithnard eventually, on an armed ship, and let the Masters question him."

"The College at Caithnard is hardly a court of law."

Duac looked at him, a rare trace of temper in his eyes. "Then you tell me. What would you have done?

If it had been you instead of me here, watching Morgon . . . watching Morgon forced to exact his own justice from a man bound to no law in the realm, who betrayed everyone in the realm, what would you have done?"

"Justice," Mathom said softly. Morgon looked at him, waiting for his answer. He saw in the dark, tired eyes a distant, curious pain. "He is the High One's Harpist. I would let the High One judge him."

"Mathom?" Morgon said, wondering suddenly, imperatively, what the king was seeing. But Mathom did not answer him. Raederle was watching him, too; the king touched her hair lightly, but neither of them spoke.

"The High One," Rood said. The warrior's harshness had left his voice; the words were a riddle, full of bitterness and despair, a plea for answer. His eyes touched Morgon's with a familiar twist of self-mockery. "You heard my father. I'm no longer even a riddler. You'll have to answer that one, Riddle-Master."

"I will," he said wearily. "I don't seem to have any choice."

"You," Mathom said, "have stayed here far too long."

"I know. I couldn't leave. I'll leave . . ." He glanced at Duac. "Tomorrow? Will the ships be ready?"

Duac nodded. "Bri Corbett said they'll sail on the midnight tide. Actually, he said a great deal more when I told him what you wanted. But he knows men who would sail even a cargo of the dead for gold."

"Tomorrow," Mathom murmured. He glanced at Morgon and then at Raederle, who was staring silently at the pooling candle, her face set as for an argument. He seemed to make his own surmises behind his black, fathomless gaze. She lifted her eyes slowly, sensing his thoughts.

"I am going with Morgon, and I am not asking you to marry us. Aren't you even going to argue?"

He shook his head, sighing. "Argue with Morgon.

I'm too old and tired, and all I want from either of you is that somewhere in this troubled realm you find your peace."

She stared at him. Her face shook suddenly, and she reached out to him, tears burning down her face in the torchlight. "Oh, why were you gone so long?" she whispered, as he held her tightly. "I have needed you."

He talked with her and with Morgon until the candles buried themselves in their holders and the windows grew pale with dawn. They slept most of the next day, and then, late that evening, when the world was still again, Morgon summoned his army of the dead to the docks at Anuin.

Seven trade-ships were moored under the moonlight carrying light cargoes of fine cloth and spices. Morgon, his mind weltering with names, faces, memories out of the brains of the dead, watched the ranks slowly become half-visible on the shadowy docks. They were mounted, armed, silent, waiting to board. The city was dark behind them; the black fingers of masts in the harbor rose with the swell of the tide to touch the stars and withdrew. The gathering of the dead had been accomplished in a dreamlike silence, under the eyes of Duac and Bri Corbett and the fascinated, terrified skeleton crews on the ships. They were just ready to board when a horse thudded down the dock, breaking Morgon's concentration. He gazed at Raederle as she dismounted, wondering why she was not still asleep, his mind struggling with her presence as he was drawn back slowly into the night of the living. There was a single dock lamp lit near them; it gave her hair, slipping out of its jewelled pins, a luminous, fiery sheen. He could not see her face well.

"I'm coming with you to Hed," she said. His hand moved out of the vivid backwash of centuries to turn her face to the light. The annoyance in it cleared his mind.

"We discussed it," he said. "Not on these ships full of wraiths."

"You and my father discussed it. You forgot to tell me."

He ran his wrist across his forehead, realizing he was sweating. Bri Corbett was leaning over the side of the ship near them, an ear to their voices, one eye on the tide. "Lord," he called softly, "if we don't leave soon, there'll be seven ships full of the dead stuck in the harbor until morning."

"All right." He stretched to ease the burning knots of tension in his back. Raederle folded her arms; he caught a pin falling out of her hair. "It would be best if you ride up through Hel to meet me in Caithnard."

"You were going to ride with me. Not sail with wraiths to Hed."

"I can't lead an army of the dead by land to Caithnard and load them there at the docks under the eye of every trader—"

"That's not the point. The point is: However you are going to Hed, I'm going with you. The point is: You were going to sail straight to Hed and leave me waiting for you at Caithnard."

He stared at her. "I was not," he said indignantly.

"You would have thought of it," she said tersely, "halfway there, leaving me safe and foresworn at Caithnard. I have a pack on my horse; I'm ready to leave."

"No. Not a four day journey by sea with me and the dead of An."

"Yes."

"No."

"Yes."

"No." His hands were clenched; shadows wedged beneath the bones of his taut face as he gazed at her. The lamplight was exploring her face as he had explored it the past days. Light gathered in her eyes, and he remembered that she had stared into the eyes of a skull and had outfaced dead kings. "No," he repeated harshly. "I don't know what trail of power the dead will leave across the water. I don't know—"

"You don't know what you're doing. You don't know how safe you will be, even in Hed."

"Which is why I will not take you on these ships."

"Which is why I am going with you. At least I am born to understand the sea."

"And if it tears apart the wood beneath you and scatters planks and spice and the dead into the waves, what will you do? You'll drown, because no matter what shape I take, I won't be able to save you, and then what will I do?"

She was silent. The dead ranked behind her seemed to be looking at him with the same distant, implacable expression. He turned suddenly, his hands opening and closing again. He caught the mocking eyes of one of the kings and let his mind grow still. A name stirred shadows of memory behind the dead eyes. The wraith moved after a moment, blurring into air and darkness, and entered the ship.

He lost all sense of time again, as he filled the seven trade-ships with the last of their cargo. Centuries murmured through him, mingling with the slap of water and the sounds of Duac and Raederle talking in some far land. Finally, he reached the end of names and began to see.

The dark, silent vessels were growing restless in the tide. Ship-masters were giving subdued orders, as if they feared their voices might rouse the dead. Men moved as quietly across the decks, among the mooring cables. Raederle and Duac stood alone on the empty dock, silently, watching Morgon. He went to them, feeling a salt wind that had not been there before drying the sweat on his face.

He said to Duac, "Thank you. I don't know how grateful Eliard is going to be, but it's the best protection I can think of for Hed, and it will set my mind at ease. Tell Mathom . . . tell him—" He hesitated, groping. Duac dropped a hand on his shoulder.

"He knows. Just be careful."

"I will be." He turned his head, met Raederle's eyes. She did not move or speak, but she bound him wordless, lost again in memories. He broke their silence as if he were breaking a spell. "I'll meet you at Caithnard." He kissed her and turned quickly. He boarded the lead ship. The ramp slid up behind him; Bri Corbett stood beside an open hatch.

He said worriedly as Morgon climbed down the ladder into the lightless hold, "You'll be all right among the dead?"

Morgon nodded without speaking. Bri closed the hatch behind him. He stumbled a little around bolts of cloth and found a place to sit on sacks of spice. He felt the ship ease away from the dock, away from Anuin toward the open sea. He leaned against the side of the hull, heard water spray against the wood. The dead were silent, invisible around him, their minds growing quiescent as they sailed away from their past. Morgon found himself trying to trace their faces suddenly out of the total darkness. He drew his knees up, pushed his face against his arms and listened to the water. A few moments later, he heard the hatch open.

He drew a long, silent breath and loosed it. Lamplight flickered beyond his closed eyes. Someone climbed down the ladder, found a path through the cargo, and sat down beside him. Scents of pepper and ginger wafted up around him. The hatch dropped shut again.

He lifted his head, said to Raederle, who was no more than her breathing and the faint smell of sea air, "Are you planning to argue with me for the rest of our lives?"

"Yes," she said stiffly.

He dropped his head back against his knees. After a while he drew one arm free, shaped her wrist in the dark, and then her fingers. He gazed back at the night, holding her scarred left hand in both his hands against his heart.

2

THEY ARRIVED IN HED FOUR NIGHTS LATER. SIX OF
the trade-ships had turned westward in the channel to wait at Caithnard; Bri took his ship to
Tol. Morgon, worn out from listening for disaster, was
startled out of a catnap by the hull scudding a little
against the dock. He sat up, tense, and heard Bri curse
someone amiably. The hatch opened; lamplight blinded
him. He smelled earth.

His heart began to pound suddenly. Beside him,
Raederle, half-buried in furs, lifted her head sleepily.

"You're home," Bri said, smiling behind the light,
and Morgon got to his feet, climbed up onto the deck.
Tol was a handful of houses scattered beyond the
moon-shadow flung by the dark cliffs. The warm,
motionless air smelled familiarly of cows and grain.

He hardly realized he had spoken until Bri, dousing
the light, answered, "On the lee side of midnight. We
got here sooner than I expected."

A wave curled lazily onto the beach, spread a fret-
work of silver as it withdrew. The shore road wound
bone-white away from the dock to disappear into the
cliff shadow. Morgon picked out the faint line above
the cliff where it appeared again, to separate pastures
and fields until it stopped at the doorstep of Akren.

His hands tightened on the railing; he stared, blind, back at the twisted road that had brought him to Hed on a ship full of the dead, and the shore road to Akren seemed suddenly little more than one more twist into shadows.

Raederle said his name, and his hands loosened. He heard the ramp thud onto the dock. He said to Bri, "I'll be back before dawn." He touched the outline of the ship-master's shoulder. "Thank you."

He led Raederle off the dock, past the dreaming fishermen's houses and the worn, beached boats with gulls sleeping on them. He found his way by memory up the shadows to the top of the cliff. The fields flowed smoothly under the moonlight, swirled around hillocks and dips, to converge from every direction around Akren. The night was soundless; listening, he heard the slow, placid breathing of cows and the faint whimper of a dog dreaming. There was a light gleaming at Akren, Morgon thought from the porch, but as they drew closer, he realized it came from within the house. Raederle walked silently beside him, her eyes flickering over field walls, bean rows, half-ripe wheat. She broke her silence finally as they drew near enough to Akren to see the lines of the roof slanting against the stars.

"Such a small house," she said, surprised. He nodded.

"Smaller than I remember . . ." His throat was dry, tight. He saw a movement in one hall window, dim in the candlelight, and he wondered who was sitting up so late in the house, alone. Then the smell of damp earth and clinging roots caught at him unexpectedly; memory upon memory sent shoots and hair roots spreading through him of land-law until for one split second he no longer felt his body, and his mind branched dizzyingly through the rootwork of Hed.

He stopped, his breath catching. The figure at the window moved. Blocking the light, it stared out at the night: big, broad-shouldered, faceless. It turned abruptly, flicking across the windows in the hall. The doors of Akren banged open; a dog barked, once. Morgon heard footsteps. They crossed the yard and stopped at the angled shadow of the roof.

"Morgon?" The name sounded in the still air like a question. Then it became a shout, setting all the dogs barking as it echoed across the fields. "Morgon!"

Eliard had reached him almost before he could move again. He got an impression of butter-colored hair, shoulders burled with muscles, and a face under moonlight that was startlingly like their father's. Then Eliard knocked the breath out of him, hugging him, his fists pounding against Morgon's shoulder blades. "You took your time coming home," he said. He was crying. Morgon tried to speak, but his throat was too dry; he dropped his burning eyes against Eliard's massive shoulder.

"You great mountain," he whispered. "Will you quiet down?"

Eliard pushed him away, started shaking him. "I felt your mind in mine just then, the way I felt it in my dreams when you were in that mountain." Tears were furrowing down his face. "Morgon, I'm sorry, I'm sorry, I'm sorry—"

"Eliard . . ."

"I knew you were in trouble, but I never did any-thing—I didn't know what to do—and then you died, and the land-rule came to me. And now you're back, and I have everything that belongs to you. Morgon, I swear if there was a way, I would take the land-rule out of myself and give it back to you—" Morgon's hands locked in a sudden, fierce grip on his arms and he stopped.

"Don't say that to me again. Ever." Eliard stared at him wordlessly, and Morgon felt, holding him, that he held all the strength and innocence of Hed. He said more quietly, his fingers tightening on the innocence, "You belong here. And I have needed you to be here taking care of Hed almost more than anything."

"But Morgon. . . you belong here. This is your home, you've come home—"

"Yes. Until dawn."

"No!" His fingers clamped on Morgon's shoulders again. "I don't know what you're running from, but I'm not watching you leave again. You stay here; we can fight for you, with pitchforks and harrow teeth. I'll borrow an army from somebody—"

"Eliard—"

"Shut up! You may have a grip like a bench vise, but you can't throw me into Tristan's rosebushes anymore. You're staying here, where you belong."

"Eliard, will you stop shouting!" He shook Eliard a little, astonishing him into silence. Then a small whirlwind of Tristan and dogs broke against them, shouting and barking. Tristan leaped at Morgon from a dead run, her arms clamped around his neck, her face buried at his collarbone. He kissed what he could find of it, then pushed her away, lifted her face between his hands. He barely recognized it. Something in his expression made her face crumple; she flung her arms around him again. Then she saw Raederle and reached out to her, and the dogs swarmed at Morgon. A couple of lights sparked in the windows of distant farmhouses. Morgon felt a moment's panic. Then he simply grew still, still as the motionless pour of the road under his feet, the moonlit air. The dogs dropped away from him; Tristan and Raederle stopped talking to look at him. Eliard stood quietly, bound unconsciously to his stillness.

"What's wrong?" he asked uneasily. Morgon moved after a moment to his side, dropped an arm wearily over his shoulders.

"So much," he said. "Eliard, I'm putting you in danger just standing here, talking to you. Let's go in the house at least."

"All right." But he did not move, his face turned away from Morgon to where Raederle stood, her face a blur of misty lines and shadows, jewelled pins here and there in her dishevelled hair flecking it with fire. She smiled, and Morgon heard Eliard swallow. "Raederle of An?" he said tentatively, and she nodded.

"Yes." She held out her hand, and Eliard took it as if it were made of chaff and might blow away. He seemed tongue-tied.

Tristan said proudly, "We sailed all the way to Isig and back, looking for Morgon. Where were you? Where did you—" Her voice faltered suddenly, oddly. "Where did you sail from?"

"Anuin," Morgon said. He caught the uncertain flicker of her dark eyes and read her thoughts. He said again, tiredly, "Let's go in the house; you can ask me."

She slid her hand into his free hand, walked with him, without speaking, to Akren.

She went down to the kitchens to find food for them, while Eliard lit torches and brushed a tangle of harness off the benches so they could sit.

He stood looking down at Morgon, kicking the bench moodily, then said abruptly, "Tell me so I can understand. Why you can't stay. Where do you have to get to so badly now?"

"I don't know. Nowhere. Anywhere but where I am. It's death to stand still."

Eliard scarred the bench with his boot. "Why?" he said explosively, and Morgon drew his hands over his face, murmuring.

"I'm trying to find out," he said. "Answer the unanswered—" He broke off at the expression on Eliard's face. "I know. If I had stayed home in the first place instead of going to Caithnard, I wouldn't be sitting here in the middle of the night wanting to hold dawn back with my hands and afraid to tell you what cargo I brought with me to Hed."

Eliard sat down slowly, blinking a little. "What?" Tristan came back up the stairs then with a huge tray full of beer, milk, fresh bread and fruit, the cold remains of a roast goose, butter and cheese. She balanced it on a stool between them. Morgon shifted; she sat down beside him and poured beer. She handed a cup to Raederle, who tasted it tentatively. Morgon watched her pour; her face had grown leaner, the graceful, sturdy bones more pronounced.

She was scowling at the head on the beer, waiting for it to subside before she finished pouring. Her eyes flicked at him, then dropped, and he said softly, "I found Deth at Anuin. I didn't kill him."

The breath went out of her soundlessly. She rested the beer pitcher on one knee, the cup on the other, and looked at Morgon finally. "I didn't want to ask."

He reached out, touched her face; he saw her eyes follow the white vesta-scars on his palm as he dropped his hand again. Eliard stirred.

"It's none of my business," he said huskily. "But you only tracked him clear across the realm." An odd hope touched his face. "Was he . . . did he explain—"

"He explained nothing." He took the beer from Tristan and drank; he felt blood ease back into his face. He added, more quietly, "I followed Deth through An and caught up with him at Anuin twelve days ago. I stood before him in the king's hall and explained to him that I was going to kill him. Then I raised my sword with both hands to do just that, while he stood without moving, watching it rise." He checked. Eliard's face was rigid.

"And then what?"

"Then . . ." He searched for words, pulled back into memory. "I didn't kill him. There's an ancient riddle from Ymris: Who were Belu and Bilo, and how were they bound? Two Ymris princes who were born at the same moment, and whose deaths, it was foretold, would occur at the same moment. They grew to hate each other, but they were so bound that one could not kill the other without destroying himself."

Eliard was eyeing him strangely. "A riddle did that? It kept you from killing him?"

Morgon sat back. For a moment he sipped beer

without speaking, wondering if anything he had done in his life had ever made sense to Eliard. Then Eliard leaned forward, gripped his wrist gently.

"You told me once my brains were made of oak. Maybe so. But I'm glad you didn't kill him. I would have understood why, if you had. But I wouldn't have been certain, ever again, of what you might or might not do." He loosed Morgon and handed him a goose leg. "Eat."

Morgon looked at him. He said softly, "You have the makings of a fine riddler."

Eliard snorted, flushing. "You wouldn't catch me dead at Caithnard. Eat." He cut thin slices of bread and meat and cheese for Raederle and gave them to her. Meeting her eyes at last as she smiled, he found his tongue finally.

"Are you . . . are you married?"

She shook her head over a bite. "No."

"Then what—have you come to wait here?" He looked a little incredulous, but his voice was warm. "You would be very welcome."

"No." She was talking to Eliard, but she seemed, to Morgon, to be answering his own hopes. "I am doing no more waiting."

"Then what are you going to do?" Eliard said, bewildered. "Where will you live?" His eyes moved to Morgon. "What are you going to do? When you leave at dawn? Do you have any idea?"

He nodded. "A vague idea. I need help. And I need answers. According to rumor, the last of the wizards are gathering at Lungold to challenge Ghisteslwchlohm. From the wizards, I can get help. From the Founder, I can get some answers."

Eliard stared at him. He heaved himself to his feet suddenly. "Why didn't you just ask him while you were at Erlenstar Mountain? It would have saved you the bother of going to Lungold. You're going to ask him questions. Morgon, I swear a cork in a beer keg has more sense than you do. What's he going to do? Stand there politely and answer them?"

"What do you want me to do?" Morgon stood, unexpectedly, his voice fierce, anguished, wondering if he was arguing with Eliard or with the implacable obtuseness of the island that suddenly held no more place for him. "Sit here, let him come knocking at your door to find me? Will you open your eyes and see me instead of the wraith of some memory you have of me? I am branded with stars on my face, with vesta-scars on my hands. I can take nearly any shape that has a word to name it. I have fought, I have killed, I intend to kill again. I have a name older than this realm, and I have no home except in memory. I asked a riddle two years ago, and now I am trapped in a maze of riddles, hardly knowing how to begin to find my way out. The heart of that maze is war. Look beyond Hed for once in your life. Try drinking some fear along with that beer. This realm is on the verge of war. There is no protection for Hed."

"War. What are you talking about? There's some fighting in Ymris, but Yrmis is always at war."

"Do you have any idea who Heureu Ymris is fighting?"

"No."

"Neither does he. Eliard, I saw the rebel army as I passed through Ymris. There are men in it who have already died, who are still fighting, with their bodies possessed by nothing human. If they choose to attack Hed, what protection do you have against them?"

Eliard made a sound in his throat. "The High One," he said. Then the blood ran completely out of his face. "Morgon," he whispered, and Morgon's hands clenched.

"Yes. I have been called a man of peace by dead children, but I think I've brought nothing but chaos. Eliard, at Anuin I talked with Duac about some way to protect Hed. He offered to send men and war-ships."

"Is that what you brought?"

He said steadily, "The trade-ship at Tol that brought us carried, along with regular cargo, armed kings and lords, great warriors of the Three Portions—" Eliard's fingers closed slowly on his arm.

"Kings?"

"They understand land-love, and they understand war. They won't understand Hed, but they'll fight for it. They are—"

"You brought wraiths of An to Hed?" Eliard whispered. "They're at Tol?"

"There are six more ships at Caithnard, waiting—"

"Morgon of Hed, are you out of your mind!" His fingers bit to the bone of Morgon's arm, and Morgon tensed. But Eliard swung away from him abruptly. His fist fell like a mallet on the tray, sending food and crockery flying, except for the milk pitcher, which Tristan had just lifted. She sat hugging it against her, white, while Eliard shouted.

"Morgon, I've heard tales of the chaos in An! How animals are run to death at night and the crops rot in the fields because no one dares harvest. And you want me to take that into my land! How can you ask that of me?"

"Eliard, I don't have to ask!" Their eyes locked. Morgon continued relentlessly, watching himself change shape in Eliard's eyes, sensing something precious, elusive, slipping farther and farther away from him. "If I wanted the land-rule of Hed, I could take it back. When Ghisteslwchlohm took it from me, piece by piece, I realized that the power of land-law has structure and definition, and I know to the last hair root on a hop vine the structure of the land-law of Hed. If I wanted to force this on you, I could, just as I learned to force the ancient dead of the Three Portions to come here—"

Eliard, backed against the hearthstones, breathing through his mouth, shuddered suddenly. "What are you?"

"I don't know." His voice shook uncontrollably. "It's time you asked."

There was a moment's silence: the peaceful, unbroken voice of the night of Hed. Then Eliard shrugged himself away from the hearth, stepped past Morgon, kicking shards out of the way. He leaned over a table, his hands flat on it, his head bowed. He said, his voice muffled a little, "Morgon, they're dead."

Morgon dropped his forearm against the mantel, leaned his face on it. "Then they have that advantage over the living in a battle."

"Couldn't you have just brought a living army? It would have been simpler."

"The moment you bring armed men to this island, you'll ask for attack. And you'll get it."

"Are you sure? Are you so sure they'll dare attack Hed? You might be seeing things that aren't there."

"I might be." His words seemed lost against the worn stones. "I'm not sure, anymore, of anything. I'm just afraid for everything I love. Do you know the one simple, vital thing I could never learn from Ghisteslwchlohm in Erlenstar Mountain? How to see in the dark."

Eliard turned. He was crying again as he pulled Morgon away from the stones. "I'm sorry. Morgon, I may yell at you, but if you pulled the land-rule out of me by the roots, I would still trust you blindly. Will you stay here? Will you please stay? Let the wizards come to you. Let Ghisteslwchlohm come. You'll just be killed if you leave Hed again."

"No. I won't die." He crooked an arm around Eliard's neck, hugged him tightly. "I'm too curious. The dead won't trouble your farmers. I swear it. You will scarcely notice them. They are bound to me. I showed them something of the history and peace of Hed, and they are sworn to defend that peace."

"You bound them."

"Mathom loosed his own hold over them, otherwise I would never have considered it."

"How do you bind dead Kings of An?"

"I see out of their eyes. I understand them. Maybe too well."

Eliard eyed him. "You're a wizard," he said, but Morgon shook his head.

"No wizard but Ghisteslwchlohm ever touched land-law. I'm simply powerful and desperate." He looked down at Raederle. Inured as she was to the occasional uproar in her father's house, her eyes held a strained, haunted expression. Tristan was staring silently into the milk pitcher. Morgon touched her dark hair; her face lifted, colorless, frozen.

"I'm sorry," he whispered. "I'm sorry. I didn't mean to come home and start a battle."

"It's all right," she said after a moment. "At least that's one familiar thing you can still do." She put the milk pitcher down and got to her feet. "I'll get a broom."

"I will."

That brought the flash of a smile into her eyes. "All right. You can sweep. I'll get more food." She touched his scarred palm hesitantly. "Then tell me how you change shape."

He told them after he swept up the mess, and he watched Eliard's face fill with an incredulous wonder as he explained how it felt to become a tree. He racked his brain for other things to tell them that might help them forget for a moment the terrible side of his journey. He talked about racing across the northlands in vesta-shape, when the world was nothing but wind and snow and stars. He told them of the marvellous beauty of Isig Pass and of the wolf-king's court, with its wild animals wandering in and out, and of the mists and sudden stones and marshes of Herun. And for a little while, he forgot his own torment as he found in himself an unexpected love of the wild, harsh, and beautiful places of the realm. He forgot the time, too, until he saw the moon beginning its descent, peering into the top of one of the windows. He broke off abruptly, saw apprehension replace the smile in Eliard's eyes.

"I forgot about the dead."

Eliard controlled a reply visibly. "It's not dawn, yet. The moon hasn't even set."

"I know. But the ships will come to Tol one by one from Caithnard, when I give the word. I want them away from Hed completely before I leave. Don't worry. You won't see the dead, but you should be there when they enter Hed."

Eliard rose reluctantly. His face was chalky under his tan. "You'll be with me?"

"Yes."

They all went back down the road to Tol that lay bare as a blade between the dark fields of corn. Morgon, walking beside Raederle, his fingers linked in hers, felt the tension still in her and the weariness of the long, dangerous voyage. She sensed his thoughts and smiled at him as they neared Tol.

"I left one pig-headed family for another . . ."

The moon, three-quarters full, seemed angled, as if it were peering down at Tol. Across the black channel were two flaming, slitted eyes: the warning fires on the horns of the Caithnard harbor. Nets hung in silvery webs on the sand; water licked against the small moored boats as they walked down the dock.

Bri Corbett, hanging over the ship's railing, called down softly, "Now?"

"Now," Morgon said, and Eliard muttered between his teeth.

"I wish you knew what you were doing." Then the ramp slid down off the empty deck, and he stepped back, so close to the dock edge he nearly fell off. Morgon felt his mind again.

The stubbornness, the inflexibility that lay near the heart of Hed seemed to slam like a bar across the end of the ramp. It clenched around Morgon's thoughts; he eased through it, filling Eliard's mind with images, rich, brilliant, and erratic, that he had

gleaned from the history of the Three Portions out of
the minds of the dead. Slowly, as Eliard's mind
opened, something emptied out of the ship, absorbed
itself into Hed.

Eliard shivered suddenly.

"They're quiet," he said, surprised. Morgon's hand
closed above his elbow.

"Bri will leave for Caithnard now and send the next
ship. There are six more. Bri will bring the last one
himself, and Raederle and I will leave on that one."

"No—"

"I'll come back."

Eliard was silent. From the ship came the groan of
rope and wood, and Bri Corbett's low, precise orders.
The ship eased away from the dockside, its dark canvas stretched full to catch the frail wind. It moved,
huge, black, soundless through the moon-spangled water into the night, leaving a shimmering wake that
curled away and slowly disappeared.

Eliard said, watching it, "You will never come back
to stay."

Six more ships came as slowly, as silently through
the night. Once, just before the moon set, Morgon saw
shadows flung across the water of armed, crowned figures. The moon sank, shrivelled and weary, into the
stars; the last ship moored at the dockside. Tristan
was leaning against Morgon, shifting from one foot to
another; he held her to keep her warm. Raederle was
blurred against the starlit water; her face was a dark
profile between the warning fires. Morgon's eyes
moved to the ship. The dead were leaving it; the dark
maw of its hold would remain open to take him away
from Hed. His mind tangled suddenly with a thousand
things he wanted to say to Eliard, but none of them
had the power to dispel that ship. Finally, he realized,
they were alone again on the dock; the dead were
dispersed into Hed, and there was nothing left for him
to do but leave.

He turned to Eliard. The sky was growing very dark

in the final, interminable hour before dawn. A low wind moaned among the breakers. He could not see Eliard's face, only sense his massiveness and the vague mass of land behind him. He said softly, his heart aching, the image of the land drenched gold under the summer sun in his mind's eye, "I'll find a way back to Hed. Somehow. Somewhere."

Eliard, reaching into the darkness, touched his face with a gentleness that had been their father's. Tristan was still clinging to him; Morgon held her tightly, kissed the top of her hair. Then he stepped back, stood suddenly alone in the night feeling the wood shiver under his feet in the roiling water.

He turned, found his way blindly up the ship's ramp, back down into the black hull.

3

T HE SHIP FOUND A QUIET BERTH IN THE CAITHNARD
harbor near dawn. Morgon heard the anchor
splash in still water and saw through the lattice
of the hatch covers squares of pearl-grey sky. Raederle
was asleep. He looked at her a moment with an odd
mixture of weariness and peace, as if he had brought
some great treasure safely out of danger. Then he
sagged down on the spice sacks and went to sleep. The
clamor on the docks at midmorning, the stifling noon
heat in the hold hardly troubled his dreams. He woke
finally at late afternoon and found Raederle watching
him, covered with floating spangles of sunlight.

He sat up slowly, trying to remember where he
was. She said, "Caithnard." Her arms were crooked
around her knees; her cheek was crosshatched with
weave from the sacking. Her eyes held an odd expression he had to puzzle over, until he realized that it was
simply fear. His throat made a dry, questioning sound.
She answered him softly.

"Now what?"

He leaned back against the side, gripped her wrist
lightly a moment, then rubbed his eyes. "Bri Corbett
said he would find horses for us. You'll have to take
the pins out of your hair."

"What? Morgon, are you still asleep?"

"No." His eyes fell to her feet. "And look at your shoes."

She looked. "What's the matter with them?"

"They're beautiful. So are you. Can you change shape?"

"Into what?" she asked bewilderedly. "A hoary old hag?"

"No. You have a shape-changer's blood in you; you should be able to—"

The expression in her eyes, of fear, torment, loathing, stopped him. She said distinctly, "No."

He drew breath, fully awake, cursing himself silently. The long road sweeping across the realm, straight towards the setting sun, touched him, too, then, with an edge of panic. He was silent, trying to think, but the stale air in the hold seemed to fill his brain with chaff. He said, "We'll be on the road to Lungold for a long time, if we ride. I thought to keep the horses just until I could teach you some shape."

"You change shape. I'll ride."

"Raederle, look at yourself," he said helplessly. "Traders from all over the realm will be on that road. They haven't seen me for over a year, but they'll recognize you, and they won't have to ask who the man beside you is."

"So." She kicked her shoes off, pulled the pins out of her hair and shook it down her back. "Find me another pair of shoes."

He looked at her wordlessly as she sat in a billow of wrinkled, richly embroidered cloth, the fine, dishevelled mass of her hair framing a high-boned face that, even tired and white, looked like something out of an ancient ballad. He sighed, pushing himself up.

"All right. Wait for me."

Her voice checked him briefly as he climbed the ladder. "This time."

He spoke to Bri Corbett, who had been waiting patiently all day for them to wake. The horses Bri had

found were on the dock; there were some supplies
packed on them. They were placid, heavy-hooved
farmhorses, restless at being tethered so long. Bri, as
the fact and implications of the long journey began
filling his mind, gave Morgon varied, impassioned arguments, to which he responded patiently. Bri ended
by offering to come with them.

Morgon said wearily, "Only if you can change
shape."

Bri gave up. He left the ship, returned an hour later
with a bundle of clothes, which he tossed down the
hatch to Morgon. Raederle examined them expres-
sionlessly, then put them on. There was a dark skirt,
a linen shift, and a shapeless over-tunic that went to
her knees. The boots were of soft leather, good but
plain. She coiled her hair up under the crown of a
broad-brimmed straw hat. She stood still resignedly
for Morgon's inspection.

He said, "Pull the hat brim down."

She gave it a wrench. "Stop laughing at me."

"I'm not," he said soberly. "Wait till you see what
you have to ride."

"You aren't exactly inconspicuous. You may be
dressed like a poor farmer, but you walk like a land-
ruler, and your eyes could quarry stone."

"Watch," he said. He let himself grow still, his
thoughts shaping themselves to his surroundings: wood,
pitch, the vague murmur of water and indistinct rum-
blings of the harbor. His name seemed to flow away
from him into the heat. His face held no discernible
expression; for a moment his eyes were vague, blank
as the summer sky.

"If you aren't aware of yourself, few people will be
aware of you. That's one of a hundred ways I kept
myself alive crossing the realm."

She looked startled. "I almost couldn't recognize
you. Is it illusion?"

"Very little of it. It's survival."

She was silent. He saw the conflict of her thoughts

in her face. She turned away without speaking and climbed up the ladder to the deck.

The sun was burning into night at the far edge of the realm as they bade farewell to Bri and began to ride. Great shadows from masts and piled cargo loomed in their path across the docks. The city, a haze of late light and shadow, seemed suddenly unfamiliar to Morgon, as if, on the verge of taking a strange road, he became a stranger to himself. He led Raederle through the twists of streets, past shops and taverns he had known once, toward the west edge of the city, down one cobbled street that widened as it left the city, wore out of its cobblestones, widened again, rutted with centuries of cartwheels, widened again and ran ahead of them through hundreds of miles of no-man's-land, until it angled northward at the edge of the known realm towards Lungold.

They stopped their horses, looking down it. Tangled shadows of oak faded as the sun set; the road lay tired, grey, and endless in the dusk. The oak fanned over their heads, branches nearly joined across the road. They looked weary, their leaves dulled with a patina of dust kicked up by the cartwheels. The evening was very quiet; the late traffic had already wound its way into the city. The forests blurred grey in the distance, and then dark. From the greyness an owl woke and sang a riddle.

They began to ride again. The sky turned black, and the moon rose, spilling a milky light through the forest. They rode the moon high, until their shadows rode beneath them on a tangle of black leaves. Then Morgon found the leaves blurring together into one vast darkness under his eyes. He reined; Raederle stopped beside him.

There was the sound of water not far away. Morgon, his face coated with a mask of dust, said tiredly, "I remember. I crossed a river, coming south out of Wind Plain. It must follow the road." He turned his horse off the road. "We can camp there."

They found it not far from the road, a shallow
streak of silver in the moonlight. Raederle sank down
at the foot of a tree while Morgon unsaddled the
horses and let them drink. He brought their packs and
blankets to a clear space among the fern. Then he sat
down beside Raederle, dropped his head in his arms.

"I'm not used to riding, either," he said. She took
her hat off, rested her head against him.

"A plow horse," she murmured. She fell asleep
where she sat. Morgon put his arm around her. For a
while he stayed awake, listening. But he heard only
the secret noises of hunting animals, the breath of
owl's wings, and as the moon set, his eyes closed.

They woke to the blaze of the summer sun and the
tortured groan of cartwheels. By the time they had
eaten, washed, and made their way back to the road,
it was filled with carts, traders on horseback with their
packs, farmers taking produce or animals from outly-
ing farms into Caithnard, men and women with reti-
nues and packhorses making the long journey, for
indiscernible reasons, across the realm to Lungold.
Morgon and Raederle eased their horses into the slow,
rhythmic pace that would wear the monotonous, six-
weeks journey to its ending. Riding in traffic varying
between pigs and rich lords, they were not conspicuous. Morgon discouraged traders' idle conversation,
responding grumpily to their overtures. Once he startled Raederle by cursing a rich merchant who commented on her face. The man looked angry a moment,
his hand tightening on his riding crop; then, glancing
at Morgon's patched boots and the sweat beading his
dusty face, he laughed, nodded to Raederle, and
passed on. Raederle rode in silence, her head bowed,
her reins bunched in one fist. Morgon, wondering
what she was thinking, reached across and touched her
lightly. She looked at him, her face filmed with dust
and weariness.

He said softly, "This is your choice."

She met his eyes without answering. She sighed finally, and her grip on the reins loosened. "Do you know the ninety-nine curses the witch Madir set on a man for stealing one of her pigs?"

"No."

"I'll teach you. In six weeks you might run out of curses."

"Raederle—"

"Stop asking me to be reasonable."

"I didn't ask you!"

"You asked me with your eyes."

He swept a hand through his hair. "You are so unreasonable sometimes that you remind me of me. Teach me the ninety-nine curses. I'll have something to think about while I'm eating road dust all the way to Lungold."

She was silent again, her face hidden under the shadow of her hat brim. "I'm sorry," she said. "The merchant frightened me. He might have hurt you. I know I am a danger to you, but I didn't realize it before. But Morgon, I can't . . . I can't—"

"So. Run from your shadow. Maybe you'll succeed better than I did." Her face turned away from him. He rode without speaking, watching the sun burn across bands of metal on wine barrels ahead of them. He put a hand over his eyes finally, to shut out the hot flare of light. "Raederle," he said in the darkness, "I don't care. Not for myself. If there is a way to keep you safely with me, I'll find it. You are real, beside me. I can touch you. I can love you. For a year, in that mountain, I never touched anyone. There is nothing I can see ahead of me that I could love. Even the children who named me are dead. If you had chosen to wait for me in Anuin, I would be wondering what the wait would be worth for either of us. But you're with me, and you drag my thoughts out of a hopeless future always back to this moment, back to you—so that I can find some perverse contentment even in swallowing road dust." He looked at her. "Teach me the ninety-nine curses."

"I can't." He could barely hear her voice. "You made me forget how to curse."

But he coaxed them from her later, to while away the long afternoon. She taught him sixty-four curses before twilight fell, a varied, detailed list that covered the pig thief from hair to toenails, and eventually transformed him into a boar. They left the road then, found the river fifty yards from it. There were no inns or villages nearby, so the travellers moving at the same pace down the long road were camped all around them. The evening was full of distant laughter, music, the smell of wood burning, meat roasting. Morgon went upriver a way, caught fish with his hands. He cleaned them, stuffed them with wild onions, and brought them back to their camp. Raederle had bathed and started a fire; she sat beside it, combing her wet hair. Seeing her in the circle of her light, stepping into it himself and watching her lower her comb and smile, he felt ninety-nine curses at his own ungentleness march into his throat. She saw it in his face, her expression changing as he knelt beside her. He set the fish, wrapped in leaves, at her feet like an offering. Her fingers traced his cheekbone and his mouth.

He whispered, "I'm sorry."

"For what? Being right? What did you bring me?" She opened a leaf wonderingly. "Fish." He cursed himself again, silently. She lifted his face in her hands and kissed him again and again, until the dust and weariness of the day vanished from his mind, and the long road burned like a streak of light among his memories.

Later, after they had eaten, they lay watching the fire, and she taught him the rest of the curses. They had transformed the legendary thief into a boar, all but for his ears and eyeteeth and ankles, the last three curses, when a slow, tentative harping rippled across the night, mingling with the river's murmuring. Morgon, listening to it, did not realize Raederle was speaking to him until she put her hand on his shoulder. He jumped.

"Morgon."

He rose abruptly, stood at the edge of the firelight, staring into the night. His eyes grew accustomed to the moonlight; he saw random fires lighting the great, tormented faces of oak. The air was still, the voices and music frail in the silence. He quelled a sudden, imperative impulse to snap the harp strings with a thought, let peace fall again over the night.

Raederle said behind him, "You never harp."

He did not answer. The harping ceased after a while; he drew a slow breath and moved again. He turned to find Raederle sitting beside the fire, watching him. She said nothing until he dropped down beside her. Then she said again, "You never harp."

"I can't harp here. Not on this road."

"Not on the road, not on that ship when you did nothing for four days—"

"Someone might have heard it."

"Not in Hed, not in Anuin, where you were safe—"

"I'm never safe."

"Morgon," she breathed incredulously. "When are you going to learn to use that harp? It holds your name, maybe your destiny; it's the most beautiful harp in the realm, and you have never even shown it to me."

He looked at her finally. "I'll learn to play it again when you learn to change shape." He lay back. He did not see what she did to the fire, but it vanished abruptly, as if the night had dropped on it like a stone.

He slept uneasily, always aware of her turning beside him. He woke once, wanting to shake her awake, explain, argue with her, but her face, remote in the moonlight, stopped him. He turned, pushed one arm against his eyes, and fell asleep again. He woke again abruptly, for no reason, though something he had heard or sensed, a fragment of a dream before he woke, told him there was reason. He saw the moon drifting deeper into the night. Then something rose before him, blotting out the moon.

He shouted. A hand came down over his mouth. He kicked out and heard an anguished grunt. He rolled to his feet. Something smacked against his face, spun him jarringly into a tree trunk. He heard Raederle cry out in pain and fear, and he snapped a streak of fire into the embers.

The light flared over half a dozen burly figures dressed like traders. One of them held Raederle's wrists; she looked frightened, bewildered in the sudden light. The horses were stirring, nickering, shadows moving about them, untethering them. Morgon moved toward them quickly. An elbow slammed into his ribs; he hunched over himself, muttering the fifty-ninth curse with the last rag of his breath. The thief gripping him, wrenching him straight, shouted hoarsely in shock and shambled away in the trees. The man behind Raederle dropped her wrists with a sudden gasp. She whirled, touching him, and his beard flamed. Morgon got a glimpse of his face before he dove toward the river. The horses were beginning to panic. He caught at their minds, fed them a bond of moonlit stillness until they stood rock still, oblivious to the men pulling at them. They were cursing ineffectually. One of them mounted, kicked furiously at the horse, but it did not even quiver. Morgon flicked a silent shout through his mind, and the man fell backwards off the horse. The others scattered, then turned on him again, furious and uneasy. He cleared his mind for another shout, picked up threads of their thoughts. Then something came at him from behind, the man out of the river, drove into his back and knocked him to the ground. He twisted as he hit the earth, then froze.

The face was the same, yet not the same. The eyes he knew, but from another place, another struggle. Memory fought against his sight. The face was heavy, wet, the beard singed, but the eyes were too still, too calculating. A boot drove into Morgon's shoulder from behind. He rolled belatedly. Something ripped across the back of his skull, or across his mind, he was not sure which. Then a Great Shout broke like a thunderclap over them all. He put his face in the bracken and clung to a rocking earth, holding his binding over the horses like the one firm point in the world.

The shout echoed away slowly. He lifted his head. They were alone again; the horses stood placidly, undisturbed by the turmoil of voices and squealing animals in the darkness around them. Raederle dropped down beside him, her brows pinched in pain.

He said, "Did they hurt you?"

"No." She touched his cheek, and he winced. "That shout did. From a man of Hed, that was a marvellous shout."

He stared at her, frozen again. "You shouted."

"I didn't shout," she whispered. "You did."

"I didn't." He sat up, then settled his skull into place with his hands. "Who in Hel's name shouted?"

She shivered suddenly, her eyes moving through the night. "Someone watching, maybe still watching. . . . How strange. Morgon, were they only men wanting to steal our horses?"

"I don't know." He searched the back of his head with his fingers. "I don't know. They were men trying to steal our horses, yes, which was why it was so hard for me to fight them. There were too many to fight, but they were too harmless to kill. And I didn't want to use much power, to attract attention."

"You gave that one man boar bristles all over his body."

Morgon's hand slid to his ribs. "He earned it," he said dourly. "But that last man coming out of the water—"

"The one whose beard I set on fire."

"I don't know." He pushed his hands over his eyes, trying to remember. "That's what I don't know. If the man coming back out of the river was the same one who ran into it."

"Morgon," she whispered.

"He might have used power; I'm not sure. I don't know. Maybe I was just seeing what I expected to see."

"If it was a shape-changer, why didn't he try to kill you?"

"Maybe he was unsure of me. They haven't seen me since I disappeared into Erlenstar Mountain. I was that careful, crossing the realm. They wouldn't expect me to be riding a plow horse in broad daylight down Trader's Road."

"But if he suspected—Morgon, you were using power over the horses."

"It was a simple binding of silence, peace; he wouldn't have suspected that."

"He wouldn't have run from a Great Shout, either. Would he? Unless he left for help. Morgon—" She was trying suddenly to tug him to his feet. "What are we doing sitting here? Waiting for another attack, this time maybe from shape-changers?"

He pulled his arm away from her. "Don't do that; I'm sore."

"Would you rather be dead?"

"No." He brooded a moment, his eyes on the swift, shadowy flow of the river. A thought ran through his mind, chilling him. "Wind Plain. It lies just north of us . . . where Heureu Ymris is fighting his war against men and half-men . . . there might be an army of shape-changers across the river."

"Let's go. Now."

"We would only attract attention, riding in the middle of the night. We can move our camp. Then I want to look for whoever it was that shouted."

They shifted their horses and gear as quietly as they could, away from the river and closer to a cluster of traders' carts. Then Morgon left Raederle, to search the night for a stranger.

Raederle argued, not wanting him to go alone; he said patiently, "Can you walk across dry leaves so gently they don't stir? Can you stand so still animals pass you without noticing you? Besides, someone has to guard the horses."

"What if those men return?"

"What if they do? I've seen what you can do to a wraith."

She sat down under a tree, muttering something. He hesitated, for she looked powerless and vulnerable.

He shaped his sword, keeping the stars hidden under his hand, and laid it in front of her. It disappeared again; he told her softly, "It's there if you need it, bound under illusion. If you have to touch it, I'll know."

He turned, slipped soundlessly into the silence between the trees.

The forest had quieted again after the shout. He drifted from camp to camp around them, looking for someone still awake. But travellers were sleeping peacefully in carts or tents, or curled under blankets beside their firebeds. The moon cast a grey-black haze over the world; trees and bracken were fragmented oddly with chips and streaks of shadow. There was not a breath of wind. Single sprays of leaves, a coil of bramble etched black in the light seemed whittled out of silence. The oak stood as still. He put his hand on one, slid his mind beneath its bark, and sensed its ancient, gnarled dreaming. He moved towards the river, skirted their old camp. Nothing moved. Listening through the river's voice, his mind gathering its various tones, defining and discarding them one by one, he heard no human voices. He went farther down the river, making little more noise than his own controlled breathing. He eased into the surface he walked on, adjusting his thoughts to the frail weight of leaves, the tension in a dry twig. The sky darkened slowly, until he could scarcely see, and he knew he should turn back. But he lingered at the river's edge, facing Wind Plain, listening as if he could hear the shards of battle noises in the broken dreams of Heureu's army.

He turned finally, began to move back upriver. He took three soundless steps and stopped with an animal's fluid shift from movement into stillness. Someone was standing among the trees with no discernible face or coloring, a broad half-shadow, half-faded, as Morgon was, into the night. Morgon waited, but the shadow did not move. Eventually, as he hovered between decisions on the river bank, it simply merged into the night. Morgon, his mouth dry, and blood beating hollowly into his thoughts, formed himself around a curve of air and flew, with an owl's silence, a night hunter's vision, back through the trees to the camp.

He startled Raederle, changing shape in front of her. She reached for the sword; he stilled her, squatting down and taking her hand. He whispered, "Raederle."

"You're frightened," she breathed.

"I don't know. I still don't know. We'll have to be very careful." He settled beside her, shaped the sword, and held it loosely. He put his other arm around her. "You sleep. I'll watch."

"For what?"

"I don't know. I'll wake you before sunrise. We'll have to be careful."

"How?" she asked helplessly, "if they know where to find you: somewhere on Trader's Road, riding to Lungold?" He did not answer her. He shifted, holding her more closely; she leaned her head against him. He thought, listening to her breathing, that she had fallen asleep. But she spoke after a long silence, and he knew that she, too, had been staring into the night.

"All right," she said tightly. "Teach me to change shape."

4

HE TRIED TO TEACH HER WHEN SHE WOKE AT dawn. The sun had not yet risen; the forest was cool, silent around them. She listened quietly while he explained the essential simplicity of it, while he woke and snared a falcon from the high trees. The falcon complained piercingly on his wrist; it was hungry and wanted to hunt. He quieted it patiently with his mind. Then he saw the dark, haunted expression that had crept into Raederle's eyes, and he tossed the falcon free.

"You can't shape-change unless you want to."

"I want to," she protested.

"No, you don't."

"Morgon . . ."

He turned, picked up a saddle and heaved it onto one of the horses. He said, pulling the cinch tight, "It's all right."

"It's not all right," she said angrily. "You didn't even try. I asked you to teach me, and you said you would. I'm trying to keep us safe." She moved to stand in front of him as he lifted the other saddle. "Morgon."

"It's all right," he said soothingly, trying to believe it. "I'll think of something."

47

She did not speak to him for hours. They rode quickly through the early morning, until the easier pace of the traffic made them conspicuous. The road seemed full of animals: sheep, pigs, young white bullocks being driven from isolated farms to Caithnard. They blocked traffic and made the horses skittish. Traders' carts were irritatingly slow; farmers' wagons full of turnips and cabbages careened at a slow, drunken pace in front of them at odd moments. The noon heat pounded the road into a dry powder that they breathed and swallowed. The noise and smell of animals seemed inescapable. Raederle's hair, limp with dust and sweat, kept sliding down, clinging to her face. She stopped her horse once, stuck her hat between her teeth, wound her hair into a knot in the plain view of an old woman driving a pig to market, and jammed her hat back on her head. Morgon, looking at her, checked a comment. Her silence began to wear at him subtly, like the heat and the constant interruptions of their pace. He searched back, wondering if he had been wrong, wondering if she wanted him to speak or keep quiet, wondering if she regretted ever setting foot out of Anuin. He envisioned the journey without her; he would have been halfway across Ymris, taking a crow's path to Lungold, a silent night flight across the backlands to a strange city, to face Ghisteslwchlohm again. Her silence began to build stone by stone around his memories, forming a night smelling of limestone, broken only by the faint, faroff trickle of water running away from him.

He blinked away the darkness, saw the world again, dust and bedraggled green, sun thumping rhythmically off brass kettles on a peddlar's cart. He wiped sweat off his face. Raederle chipped at the wall of her own silence stiffly.

"What did I do wrong? I was just listening to you."

He said wearily, "You said yes with your voice and no with your mind. Your mind does the work."

She was silent again, frowning at him. "What's wrong?"

"Nothing."

"You're sorry I came with you."

He wrenched at his reins. "Will you stop? You're twisting my heart. It's you who are sorry."

She stopped her own horse; he saw the sudden despair in her face. They looked at one another, bewildered, frustrated. A mule brayed behind them, and they were riding again, suddenly, in the familiar, sweltering silence, with no way out of it, seemingly, like a tower without a door.

Then Morgon stopped both their horses abruptly, led them off the road to drink. The noise dwindled; the air was clear and gentle with bird calls. He knelt at the river's edge and drank of the cold, swift water, then splashed it over his face and hair. Raederle stood beside him, her reflection stiff even in the rippling water. He sank back on his heels, gazing at its blurred lines and colors. He turned his head slowly, looked up at her face.

How long he gazed at her, he did not know, only that her face suddenly shook, and she knelt beside him, holding him. "How can you look at me like that?"

"I was just remembering," he said. Her hat fell off; he stroked her hair. "I thought about you so often in the past two years. Now all I have to do is turn my head to find you beside me. It still surprises me sometimes, like a piece of wizardry I'm not used to doing."

"Morgon, what are we going to do? I'm afraid— I'm so afraid of that power I have."

"Trust yourself."

"I can't. You saw what I did with it at Anuin. I was hardly even myself, then; I was the shadow of another heritage—one that is trying to destroy you."

He gathered her tightly. "You touched me into shape," he whispered. He held her quietly a long time.

Then he said tentatively, "Can you stand it if I tell you a riddle?"

Shet shifted to look at him, smiling a little. "Maybe."

"There was a woman of Herun, a hill woman named Arya, who collected animals. One day she found a tiny black beast she couldn't name. She brought it into her house, fed it, cared for it. And it grew. And it grew. Until all her other animals fled from the house, and it lived alone with her, dark, enormous, nameless, stalking her from room to room while she lived in terror, unfree, not knowing what to do with it, not daring to challenge it—"

Her hand lifted, came down over his mouth. She dropped her head against him; he felt her heartbeat. She whispered finally, "All right. What did she do?"

"What will you do?"

He listened for her answer, but if she gave him one, the river carried it away before he heard it.

The road was quieter when they returned to it. Late shadows striped it; the sun was hovering in the grip of oak boughs. The dust had settled; most of the carts were well ahead of them. Morgon felt a touch of uneasiness at their isolation. He said nothing to Raederle, but he was relieved when, an hour later, they caught up with most of the traders. Their carts and horses were outside of an inn, an ancient building big as a barn, with stables and a smithy attached to it. From the sound of the laughter rumbling from it, it was well-stocked and its business was good. Morgon led the horses to the trough outside the stable. He longed for beer, but he was wary of showing himself in the inn. The shadows faded on the road as they went back to it; dusk hung like a wraith ahead of them.

They rode into it. The birds stilled; their horses made the only noise on the empty road. A couple of times, Morgon passed gatherings of horse traders camped around vast fires, their livestock penned and guarded for the night. He might have been safe in their vicinity, but he was seized by a sudden reluctance to stop. The voices faded behind them; they pushed deeper into the twilight. Raederle was uneasy, he sensed, but he could not stop. She reached across, touched him finally, and he looked at her. Her face was turned back toward the road behind them, and he reined sharply.

A group of horsemen a mile or so behind them dipped down into a hollow of road. The twilight blurred them as they appeared again, riding no more quickly than the late hour justified. Morgon watched them for a moment, his lips parted. He shook his head wordlessly, answering a question in Raederle's mind.

"I don't know . . ." He turned his horse abruptly off the road into the trees.

They followed the river until it was almost too dark to see. Then they made a camp without a fire, eating bread and dried meat for supper. The river was deep and slow where they stopped, barely murmuring. Morgon could hear clearly through the night; the horsemen never passed them. His thoughts drifted back to the silent figure he had seen among the trees, to the mysterious shout that had come so aptly out of nowhere. He drew his sword then, soundlessly.

Raederle said, "Morgon, you were awake most of last night. I'll watch."

"I'm used to it," he said. But he gave her the sword and stretched out on a blanket. He did not sleep; he lay listening, watching patterns of stars slowly shift across the night. He heard again the faint, hesitant harping coming out of the blackness like a mockery of his memories.

He sat up incredulously. He could see no campfires among the trees; he heard no voices, only the awkward harping. The strings were finely tuned; the harp gave a gentle, mellow tone, but the harpist tripped continually over his notes. Morgon linked his fingers over his eyes.

"Who in Hel's name . . ." He rolled to his feet abruptly.

Raederle said softly, "Morgon, there are other harpists in the world."

"He's playing in the dark."

"How do you know it's a man? Maybe it's a woman, or a young boy with his first harp, travelling alone to Lungold. If you want to destroy all the harps in the world, you'd better start with the one at your back, because that's the one that will never give you peace." He did not answer. She added equivocally to his silence, "Can you bear it if I tell you a riddle?"

He turned, found the dim, moon-struck lines of her, the blade glittering faintly in her hands. "No," he said. He sat down beside her after a while, his mind worn from straining for the notes of a familiar Ymris ballad the harpist kept missing. "I wish," he muttered savagely, "I could be haunted by a better harpist." He took the sword from her. "I'll watch."

"Don't leave me," she pleaded, reading his mind. He sighed.

"All right." He angled the sword on his knees, stared down at it while the high moon tempered it to cold fire, until at last the harping stopped and he could think again.

THE NEXT NIGHT, AND THE NEXT, AND THE NEXT, Morgon heard the harping. It came at odd hours of the night, usually when he sat awake listening. He heard it at the far edges of his awareness; Raederle slept undisturbed by it. Sometimes he heard it in his dreams and it woke him, numb and sweating, blinking out of a dream of darkness into darkness, both haunted by the same inescapable harping. He searched for the harpist one night, but he only got lost among the trees. Returning wearily near dawn in the shape of a wolf, he scared the horses, and Raederle flung a circle of fire around them and herself that nearly singed his pelt. They discussed matters furiously for a few moments, until the sight of their weary, flushed, bedraggled faces made them both break into laughter.

The longer they rode, the longer the road seemed to stretch itself, mile after mile through changeless forest. Morgon's mind milled constantly through scraps of conversations, expressions on faces they passed, noises ahead and behind them, the occasional mute imagery behind the eyes of a bird flying overhead. He grew preoccupied, trying to see ahead and behind them at the same time, watching for harpists, for horse thieves, for shape-changers. He scarcely heard Raederle when she spoke. When she stopped speaking to him altogether once, he did not realize it for hours. As they grew farther from Caithnard, the traffic lessened; they had isolated miles, now and then, of silence. But the heat was constant, and every stranger appearing behind them after a quiet mile looked suspicious. Except for the harping, though, their nights were peaceful. On the day that Morgon finally began to feel secure, they lost their horses.

They had camped early that day, for they were both exhausted. Morgon left Raederle washing her hair in the river and walked half a mile to an inn they had passed to buy a few supplies and pick up news. The inn was crowded with travellers: traders exchanging gossip; impoverished musicians playing every instrument but a harp for the price of a meal; merchants; farmers; families who looked as if they had fled from their homes, carrying all their possessions on their backs.

The air was heavy with wine-whetted rumors. Morgon, picking a rich, heavy voice at random from a far table, followed it as though he were following an instrument's voice. "Twenty years," the man said. "For twenty years I lived across from it. I sold fine cloth and furs from all parts of the realm in my shop, and I never saw so much as a shadow out of place in the ruins of the ancient school. Then, late one night while I was checking my accounts, I saw lights here and there in the broken windows. No man ever walks across those grounds, not even for the wealth of it: the place reeks of disaster. So that was enough for me. I took every bolt of cloth out of that shop, left messages for my buyers to bring what they had for me to Caithnard, and I fled. If there is going to be another wizard's war in that city, I intend to be on the other side of the realm."

"In Caithnard?" another merchant answered incredulously. "With half the Ymris coastline to the north plagued with war? At least Lungold has wizards in it. Caithnard has nothing but fishwives and scholars. There's as much defense in a dead fish as in a book. I've left Caithnard. I'm heading for the backlands; I might come out again in fifty years."

Morgon let the voices fade back into the noise. He found the innkeeper hovering at his shoulder. "Lord?" he said briskly, and Morgon ordered beer. It was from Hed, and it washed a hundred miles of road dust down his throat. He dipped sporadically into other conversations; one word from a sour-looking trader caught his attention.

"It's that cursed war in Ymris. Half the farmers in Ruhn had their horses drafted into war—the descendants of Ruhn battle horses bred to the plow. The king is holding his own on Wind Plain, but he's paying a bloody price for stalemate. His warriors buy what horses they are offered—so do the farmers. No one asks any more where the horses come from. I've had an armed guard around my wagon teams every night since I left Caithnard."

Morgon set down an empty glass, worried suddenly about Raederle alone with their horses. A trader beside him asked a friendly question; he grunted a reply. He was about to leave when his own name caught his ear.

"Morgon of Hed? I heard a rumor that he was in Caithnard, disguised as a student. He vanished before the Masters even recognized him."

Morgon glanced around. A group of muscians had congregated around a jug of wine they were sharing. "He was in Anuin," a piper said, wiping spit out of his instrument. He looked at the silent faces around him. "You haven't heard that tale? He caught up with the High One's harpist finally in Anuin, in the king's own hall—"

"The High One's harpist," a gangling young man with a collection of small drums hanging about him said bitterly. "And what was the High One doing through all this? A man loses his land-rule, betrayed in the High One's name by a harpist who lied to every king in the realm, and the High One won't lift a finger—if he has one—to give him justice."

"If you ask me," a singer said abruptly, "the High One is nothing more than a lie. Invented by the Founder of Lungold."

There was a short silence. The singer blinked a little nervously at his own words, as if the High One might be standing at his shoulder sipping beer and listening. Another singer growled, "Nobody asked. Shut up, all of you. I want to hear what happened at Anuin."

Morgon turned abruptly. A hand stopped him. The trader who had spoken to him said slowly, perplexedly, "I know you. Your name hangs at the edge of my memory, I know it. . . . Something to do with rain . . ."

Morgon recognized him: the trader he had talked to long ago on a rainy autumn day in Hlurle, after he had ridden out of the Herun hills. He said brusquely, "I don't know what in Hel's name you're talking about. It hasn't rained for weeks. Do you want to keep your hand, or do I take it with me?"

"Lords, Lords," the innkeeper murmured. "No violence in my inn." The trader took two beers off his tray, set one down in front of Morgon.

"No offense." He was still puzzled, searching Morgon's face. "Talk with me a little. I haven't been home to Kraal in months, and I need some idle—"

Morgon jerked out of his hold. His elbow hit the beer, splashing it across the table into the lap of a horse trader, who rose, cursing. Something in Morgon's face, of power or despair, quelled his first impulse. "That's no way to treat fine beer," he said darkly. "Or the offer of it. How have you managed to live as long as you have, picking quarrels out of thin air?"

"I mind my own business," Morgon said curtly. He tossed a coin on the table and went back into the dusk. His own rudeness lay like a bad taste in his mouth. Memories stirred up by the singers hovered in the back of his mind: light gathering on his sword blade, the harpist's face turning upward to meet it. He walked quickly through the trees, cursing the length of the road, the dust on it, the stars on his face, and all the shadows of memory he could not outrun.

He nearly walked through their camp before he recognized it. He stopped, bewildered. Raederle and both the horses were gone. For a second he wondered if something he had done had offended her so badly that she decided to ride both horses back to Anuin. The packs and saddles lay where he had left them; there was no sign of a struggle, no flurries of dead leaves or singed oakroots. Then he heard her call him and saw her stumbling across a shallow section of the river.

There were tears on her face. "Morgon, I was beside the river getting water when two men rode past me. They nearly ran me down. I was so furious I didn't even realize they were riding our horses until they reached the far side. So I—"

"You ran after them?" he said incredulously.

"I thought they might slow down, through the trees. But they started to gallop. I'm sorry."

"They'll get a good price for them in Ymris," Morgon said grimly.

"Morgon, they're not a mile away. You could get them back easily."

He hesitated, looking at her angry, tired face. Then he turned away from her, picked up their food pack. "Heureu's army needs them more than we do."

He felt her sudden silence at his back like something tangible. He opened the pack and cursed himself again, realizing he had forgotten to buy their supplies.

She said softly, "Are you telling me we are going to walk all the way to Lungold?"

"If you want." His fingers were shaking slightly on the pack ties.

He heard her move finally. She went back down to the river to get their water skin. She said when she returned, her voice inflectionless, "Did you bring wine?"

"I forgot it. I forgot everything." He turned then, blazing into argument before she could speak. "And I can't go back. Not without getting into a tavern brawl."

"Did I ask you to? I wasn't even going to ask." She dropped down beside the fire, tossed a twig in it. "I lost the horses, you forgot the food. You didn't blame me." She dropped her face suddenly against her knees. "Morgon," she whispered. "I'm sorry. I will crawl to Lungold before I change shape."

He stood gazing down at her. He turned, paced a half-circle around the fire, and stared into the gnarled, haggard eye of a tree bole. He tilted his face against it, felt it gazing into him, at all the twisted origins of his own power. For a moment doubt bit into him, that he was wrong to demand such a thing of her, that even his own power, wrested out of himself by such dark circumstances, was suspect. The uncertainty died slowly, leaving, as always, the one thing he grasped with any certainty: the fragile, imperative structure of riddlery.

"You can't run from yourself."

"You are running. Maybe not from yourself, but from the riddle at your back that you never face."

He lifted his head wearily, looked at her. He moved after a moment, stirred the lagging fire. "I'll catch some fish. Tomorrow morning, I'll go back to the inn, get what we need. Maybe I can sell the saddles there. We can use the money. It's a long walk to Lungold."

They scarcely spoke at all the next day. The summer heat poured down at them, even when they walked among the trees beside the road. Morgon carried both their packs. He had not realized until then how heavy they were. The straps wore at his shoulders as their quarrelling chafed at his mind. Raederle offered to carry one, but he refused with something kin to anger, and she did not suggest it again. At noon, they ate with their feet in the river. The cold water soothed them, and they spoke a little. The road in the afternoon was fairly quiet; they could hear the creak of cartwheels long before the carts came into view. But the heat was intense, almost unbearable. Finally they gave up, trudged along the rough river bank until twilight.

They found a place to camp, then. Morgon left Raederle sitting with her feet in the river and went hunting in falcon-shape. He killed a hare dreaming in the last rays of the sun on a meadow. Returning, he found Raederle where he had left her. He cleaned the hare, hung it on a spit of green wood above the fire. He watched Raederle; she sat staring down at the water, not moving. He said her name finally.

She got up, stumbling a little on the bank. She joined him slowly, sitting down close to the fire, drawing her damp skirt tightly under her feet. In the firelight, he took a good look at her, forgetting to turn the spit. Her face was very still; there were tiny lines of pain under her eyes. He drew a sudden breath; her eyes met his, holding a clear and definite warning. But the worry in him blazed out in spite of her.

"Why didn't you tell me you were in that much pain? Let me see your feet."

"Leave me alone!" The fierceness in her voice startled him. She was huddled over herself. "I told you I would walk to Lungold, and I will."

"How?" He stood up, anger at himself beating in his throat. "I'll find a horse for you."

"With what? We couldn't sell the saddles."

"I'll change into one. You can ride on my back."

"No." Her voice was shaken with the same, strange anger. "You will not. I'm not going to ride you all the way to Lungold. I said I will walk."

"You can hardly walk ten feet!"

"I'll do it anyway. If you don't turn the spit, you'll burn our supper."

He did not move; she leaned forward and turned it herself. Her hand was trembling. As the lights and shadows melted over her, he wondered suddenly if he knew her at all. He pleaded, "Raederle, what in Hel's name will you do? You can't walk like that. You won't ride; you won't change shape. Do you want to go back to Anuin?"

"No." Her voice flinched on the word, as if he had hurt her. "Maybe I'm no good with riddles, but I do keep vows."

"How much of your honor can you place in Ylon's name when you give him and his heritage nothing but hatred?"

She bent again, to turn the spit, he thought, but instead she grasped a handful of fire. "He was King of An, once. There is some honor in that." Her voice was shaking badly. She shaped a wedge of fire, spun thread-thin strings down from it through her fingers. "I swore in his name I would never let you leave me." He realized suddenly what she was making. She finished it, held it out to him: a harp made of fire, eating at the darkness around her hand. "You're the riddler. If you have such faith in riddles, you show me. You

can't even face your own hatred, and you give me riddles to answer. There's a name for a man like you."

"Fool," he said without touching the harp. He
watched the light leap soundlessly down the strings.
"At least I know my name."

"You are the Star-Bearer. Why can't you leave
me alone to make my own choices? What I am doesn't
matter."

He stared at her over the flaming harp. Something
he said or thought without realizing it snapped the
harp to pieces in her hand. He reached across the fire,
gripped her shoulders, and pulled her to her feet.

"How can you say that to me? What in Hel's name
are you afraid of?"

"Morgon—"

"You're not going to change shape into something
neither of us will recognize!"

"Morgon." She was shaking him suddenly, trying to
make him see. "Do I have to say it? I'm not running
from something I hate, but something I want. The
power of that bastard heritage. I want it. The power
eating across Ymris, trying to destroy the realm and
you—I am drawn to it. Bound to it. And I love you.
The riddler. The Master. The man who must fight
everything of that heritage. You keep asking me for
things you will only hate."

He whispered, "No."

"The land-rulers, the wizards at Lungold—how can
I face them? How can I tell them I am kin to your
enemies? How will they ever trust me? How can I trust
myself, wanting such terrible power—"

"Raederle." He lifted one hand stiffly, touched her
face, brushing at the fire and tears on it, trying to see
clearly. But the uneasy shadows loomed across it,
molding her out of flame and darkness, someone he
had not quite seen before and could not quite see now.
Something was eluding him, vanishing as he touched
it. "I never asked anything from you but truth."

"You never knew what you were asking—"

"I never do know. I just ask." The fire was shaping itself between them into the answer his mind grasped at. He saw it suddenly, and he saw her again, at the same time, the woman men had died for in Peven's tower, who had shaped her mind to fire, who loved him and argued with him and was drawn to a power that might destroy him. For a moment pieces of the riddle struggled against each other in his mind. Then they slid together, and he saw the faces of shape-changers he knew: Eriel, the harpist Corrig, whom he had killed, the shape-changers in Isig he had killed. A chill of fear and wonder brushed through him. "If you see . . . if you see something of value in them," he whispered, "then what in Hel's name are they?"

She was silent, gripping him, her face gone still, fiery with tears. "I didn't say that."

"Yes, you did."

"No, I didn't. There's nothing of value in their power."

"Yes, there is. You sense it in you. That's what you want."

"Morgon—"

"Either you change shape in my mind, or they change shape. You, I know."

She let go of him slowly. She was uncertain. He held her, wondering what words would make her trust him. Slowly he realized what argument she would hear.

He loosed her and touched the harp into shape at his back. It filled his hands like a memory. He sat down while she watched him at the edge of the fire, not moving, not speaking. The stars on the harp's face, enigmatic, answerless, met his gaze. Then he turned it and began to play. For a while he thought of little but her, a shadowy figure at the edge of the light, drawn to his harping. His fingers remembered rhythms, patterns, drew hesitant fragments of song out of a year of silence. The ancient, flawless voice of

the harp, responsive to his power, touched him again
with unexpected wonder. She drew closer to him as
he played, until step by step she had reached his side.
She stood still again. With the fire behind her, he
could not see her face.

A harpist echoed him in the shadows of his memory. The more he played to drown the memory, the
more it haunted him: a distant, skilled, beautiful
harping, coming from beyond blackness, beyond the
smell of water that went nowhere and had gone nowhere for thousands of years. The fire beyond
Raederle grew small, a point of light that went farther and farther away from him, until the blackness
came down over his eyes like a hand. A voice startled
him, echoing over stones, fading away into harsh
cadences. He never saw the face. Reaching out in the
darkness, he touched only stone. The voice was always unexpected, no matter how hard he listened for
a footstep. He grew to listen constantly, lying on stone,
his muscles tensed with waiting. With the voice came
mind-work he could not fight, pain when he fought
with his fists, endless questions he would not answer
out of a desperate fury, until suddenly his fury turned
to terror as he felt the fragile, complex instincts for
land-law begin to die in him. He heard his own voice
answering, rising a little, answering, rising, no longer
able to answer. . . . He heard harping.

His hands had stopped. The bones of his face ached
against the harpwood. Raederle sat close to him, her
arm around his shoulders. The harping still sounded
raggedly through his mind. He stirred stiffly away
from it. It would not stop. Raederle's head turned;
he realized, the blood shocking through him, that she
was hearing it, too.

Then he recognized the familiar, hesitant harping.
He stood up, his face white, frozen, and caught a
brand out of the fire. Raederle said his name; he
could not answer. She tried to follow him, barefoot,
limping through the bracken, but he would not wait.

He tracked the harpist through the trees, across the road to the other side, where he startled a trader sleeping under his cart; through brambles and under-brush, while the harping grew louder and seemed to circle him. The torch, flaring over dead leaves, lit a figure finally, sitting under a tree, bowed over his harp. Morgon stopped, breathing jerkily, words, questions, curses piling into his throat. The harpist lifted his face slowly to the light.

Morgon's breath stopped. There was not a sound anywhere in the black night beyond the torchlight. The harpist, staring back at Morgon, still played softly, awkwardly, his hands gnarled like oak root, twisted beyond all use.

5

M ORGON WHISPERED, "DETH."

The harpist's hands stilled. His face was so worn and haggard there was little familiar in it but the fine cast of his bones and the expression in his eyes. He had no horse or pack, no possessions that Morgon could see besides a dark harp, adorned by nothing but its lean, elegant lines. His broken hands rested a moment on the strings, then slid down to tilt the harp to the ground beside him.

"Morgon." His voice was husky with weariness and surprise. He added, so gently that he left Morgon floundering wordlessly in his own turmoil, "I didn't mean to disturb you."

Morgon stood motionlessly, even the flame in his hand was drawn still in the windless night. The deadly, flawless harping that ran always in some dark place beneath his thoughts tangled suddenly with the hesitant, stumbling efforts he had heard the past nights. He hung at the edge of his own light, wanting to shout with fury, wanting to turn without speaking and go, wanting even more to take one step forward and ask a question. He did, finally, so noiselessly he scarcely realized he had moved.

"What happened to you?" His own voice sounded

strange, flinching a little away from its calm. The harpist glanced down at his hands, lying at his sides like weights.

"I had an argument," he said, "with Ghisteslwch-lohm."

"You never lose arguments." He had taken another step forward, still tense, soundless as an animal.

"I didn't lose this one. If I had, there would be one less harpist in the realm."

"You don't die easily."

"No." He watched Morgon move another step, and Morgon, sensing it, stilled. The harpist met his eyes clearly, acknowledging everything, asking nothing. Morgon shifted the brand in his hand. It was burning close to his skin; he dropped it, started a small blaze in the dead leaves. The change of light shadowed Deth's face; Morgon saw it as behind other fires, in earlier days. He was silent, hovering again within the harpist's silence. It drew him forward, as across a bridge, narrow as a blade, slung across the gulf of his anger and confusion. He squatted finally beside the fire, traced a circle around it, keeping it small with his mind in the warm night.

He asked, after a while, "Where are you going?"

"Back, to where I was born. Lungold. I have no place else to go."

"You're walking to Lungold?"

He shrugged slightly, his hands shifting. "I can't ride."

"What will you do in Lungold? You can't harp."

"I don't know. Beg."

Morgon was silent again, looking at him. His fingers, burrowing, found an acorn cap and flicked it into the fire. "You served Ghisteslwchlohm for six hundred years. You gave me to him. Is he that ungrateful?"

"No," Deth said dispassionately. "He was suspicious. You let me walk out of Anuin alive."

Morgon's hand froze among the dead leaves. Something ran through him, then, like a faint, wild scent of a wind that had burned across the northern wastes, across the realm, to bring only the hint of its existence to the still summer night. He let his hand move after a moment; a twig snapped between his fingers. He added the pieces to the fire and felt his way into his questioning, as if he were beginning a riddle-game with someone whose skill he did not know.

"Ghisteslwchlohm was in An?"

"He had been in the backlands, strengthening his power after you broke free of him. He did not know where you were, but since my mind is always open to him, he found me easily, in Hel."

Morgon's eyes rose. "Are your minds still linked?"

"I assume so. He no longer has any use for me, but you may be in danger."

"He didn't come to Anuin looking for me."

"He met me seven days after I left Anuin. It seemed unlikely that you would still be there."

"I was there." He added a handful of twigs to the fire, watched them turn bright then twist and curl away from the heat. His eyes slid suddenly to the harpist's twisted fingers. "What in Hel's name did he do to you?"

"He made a harp for me, since you destroyed mine, and I had none." A light flicked through the harpist's eyes, like a memory of pain, or a distant, cold amusement. The flame receded, and his head bent slightly, leaving his face in shadow. He continued dispassionately, "The harp was of black fire. Down the face of it were three burning, white-hot stars."

Morgon's throat closed. "You played it," he whispered.

"He instructed me to. While I was still conscious, I felt his mind drawing out of mine memories of the events at Anuin, of the months you and I travelled together, of the years and centuries I served him, and before. . . . The harp had a strange, tormented voice, like the voices I heard in the night as I rode through Hel."

"He let you live."

He leaned his head back against the tree, meeting Morgon's eyes. "He found no reason not to."

Morgon was silent. The flame snapped twigs like small bones in front of him. He felt cold suddenly, even in the warm air, and he shifted closer to the fire. Some animal drawn from the brush turned lucent, burning eyes toward him, then blinked and vanished. The silence around him was haunted with a thousand riddles he knew he should ask, and he knew the harpist would only answer them with other riddles. He rested a moment in the void of the silence, cupping light in his hands.

"Poor pay for six centuries," he said at last. "What did you expect from him when you entered his service in the first place?"

"I told him that I needed a master, and no king deluded by his lies would suffice. We suited one another. He created an illusion; I upheld it."

"That was a dangerous illusion. He was never afraid of the High One?"

"What cause has the High One given him to be afraid?"

Morgon moved a leaf in the fire with his fingers. "None." He let his hand lay flat, burning in the heart of the flame, while memories gathered in his mind. "None," he whispered. The fire roared suddenly, noiselessly under his hand as his awareness of it lapsed. He flinched away from it, tears springing into his eyes. Through the blur, he saw the harpist's hands, knotted, flame-ridden, clinging, even in torment, to his silence. He hunched over his own hand, swallowing curses. "That was careless."

"Morgon, I have no water—"

"I noticed." His voice was harsh with pain. "You have no food, you have no water, you have no power of law or wealth, or even enough wizardry to keep

yourself from getting burned. You can hardly use
the one thing you do possess. For a man who walked
away from death twice in seven days, you create a
great illusion of powerlessness." He drew his knees
up, rested his face against them. For a while he was
quiet, not expecting the harpist to speak, and no
longer caring. The fire spoke between them, in an
ancient language that needed no riddles. He thought
of Raederle and knew he should leave, but he did not
move. The harpist sat with an aged, worn stillness, the
stillness of old roots or weathered stone. The fire,
loosed from Morgon's control, was dying. He watched
the light recede between the angles of his arms. He
stirred finally, lifting his head. The flame drifted
among its ashes; the harpist's face was dark.

He stood up, his burned fist cradled in his palm. He
heard the faint, dry shift of the harpist's movement
and knew, somehow, that if he had stayed all night
beside that fire, the harpist would have been there,
silent and sleepless, at dawn. He shook his head
wordlessly over his own confusion of impulses.

"You drag me out of my dreams with your harping,
and I come and crouch like a dog in your stillness. I
wish I knew whether to trust you or kill you or run
from you because you play a game more skillful and
deadly than any riddler I have ever known. Do you
need food? We can spare some."

It was a long time before Deth answered him; the
answer itself was nearly inaudible. "No."

"All right." He lingered, both hands clenched, still
hoping in spite of himself for one cracked, marrow-
less bone of truth. He turned finally, abruptly, smoke
from the charred embers burning in his eyes. He
walked three steps in the dark, and the fourth into a
blue fire that snapped out of nothingness around
him, grew brighter and brighter, twisting through him
until he cried out, falling into light.

He woke at dawn, sprawled on the ground where
he had fallen, his face gritty with dirt and broken

leaves. Someone slid a foot under his shoulder, rolled him on his back. He saw the harpist again, still sitting beneath the tree, with a circle of ash in front of him. Then he saw who reached down to grip the throat of his tunic and pull him to his feet.

He drew breath to shout, in agony and fury; Ghisteslwchlohm's hand cut sharply across his mouth, silencing him. He saw the harpist's eyes then, night-dark, still as the black, motionless water at the bottom of Erlenstar Mountain, and something in them challenged him, checked the bitterness in his throat. The harpist rose with a stiff, awkward movement that told Morgon he had been sitting there all night. He laid his harp with a curious deliberateness across the ashes of their fire. Then he turned his head, and Morgon followed his gaze to where Raederle stood, white and silent in the eye of the rising sun.

A silent, despairing cry swelled and broke in Morgon's chest. She heard it; she stared back at him with the same despair. She looked dishevelled and very tired, but unharmed.

Ghisteslwchlohm said brusquely, "If you touch my mind, I will kill her. Do you understand?" He shook Morgon roughly, pulling his gaze away from her. "Do you understand?"

"Yes," Morgon said. He attacked the Founder promptly with his hands. A white fire slapped back at him, seared through his bones, and he slid across the ground, blinking away sweat, gripping at stones and twigs to keep sounds from breaking out of him. Raederle had moved; he felt her arm around him, helping him to his feet.

He shook his head, trying to push her out of the way of the wizard's fire, but she only held him more tightly, and said, "Stop it."

"Sound advice," the Founder said. "Take it." He looked weary in the sudden, hot light. Morgon saw hollows and sharp angles worn into the mask of serenity he had assumed for centuries. He was poorly dressed, in a rough, shapeless robe that gave his age an illusion of frailty. It was very dusty, as if he had been walking down Trader's Road himself.

Morgon, fighting to get words beyond the fury and pain in him, said, "Couldn't you hear your harpist's harping, that you had to guess where I was along this road?"

"You left a trail across the realm for a blind man to follow. I suspected you would go to Hed, and I even tracked you there, but——" His uplifted hand checked Morgon's sudden movement. "You had come and gone. I have no war with farmers and cows; I disturbed nothing while I was there." He regarded Morgon silently a moment. "You took the wraiths of An to Hed. How?"

"How do you think? You taught me something of land-law."

"Not that much." Morgon felt his mind suddenly, probing for the knowledge. The touch blinded him, brought back memories of terror and helplessness. He was helpless again, with Raederle beside him, and tears of despair and rage gripped at his throat. The wizard, exploring the mind-link he had formed at Anuin with the dead, grunted softly and loosed him. The morning light drenched the ground again; he saw the harpist's shadow lying across the charred leaves. He stared at it; its stillness dragged at him, wore even his bewilderment into numbness. Then Ghisteslwch-lohm's words jarred in his mind and he lifted his eyes.

"What do you mean? Everything I know I learned from you."

The wizard gazed at him conjecturingly, as if he were a riddle on some dusty parchment. He did not answer; he said abruptly to Raederle, "Can you change shape?"

She eased a step closer to Morgon, shaking her head. "No."

"Half the kings in the history of An have taken the crow-shape at one time or another, and I learned from Deth that you have inherited a shape-changer's power. You'll learn fast."

The blood pushed up into her white face, but she did not look at the harpist. "I will not change shape," she said softly, and added with so little change of inflection it surprised both Morgon and the wizard, "I curse you, in my name and Madir's, with eyes small and fiery, to look no higher than a man's knee, and no lower than the mud beneath—" The wizard put his hand on her mouth and she stopped speaking. He blinked, as if his sight had blurred for a moment. His hand slid down her throat, and something began to tighten in Morgon to a fine, dangerous precision, like a harp string about to snap.

But the wizard said only, drily, "Spare me the next ninety-eight curses." He lifted his hand, and she cleared her throat. Morgon could feel her trembling.

She said again, "I am not going to change shape. I will die, first. I swear that, by my—" The wizard checked her again.

He contemplated her with mild interest, then said over his shoulder to Deth, "Take her across the backlands with you to Erlenstar Mountain. I don't have time for this. I will bind her mind; she won't attempt to escape. The Star-Bearer will come with me to Lungold and then to Erlenstar Mountain." He seemed to sense something in the stiff, black shadow across the bracken; he turned his head. "I'll find men to hunt for you and guard her."

"No."

The wizard swung around to one side of Morgon so that Morgon could not move without his knowledge. His brows were drawn; he held the harpist's eyes until Deth spoke again.

"I owe her. In Anuin, she would have let me walk away free before Morgon ever came. She protected me, unwittingly, from him with a small army of wraiths. I am no longer in your service, and you owe me for six hundred years of it. Let her go."

"I need her."

"You could take any one of the Lungold wizards and still hold Morgon powerless."

"The Lungold wizards are unpredictable and too powerful. Also, they are too apt to die for odd impulses. Suth proved that. I do owe you, if for nothing but your broken harping that brought the Star-Bearer to kneel at your feet. But ask something else of me."

"I want nothing else. Except a harp strung with wind, perhaps, for a man with no hands to play it."

Ghisteslwchlohm was silent. Morgon, the faint overtones of some riddle echoing through his memory, lifted his head slowly and looked at the harpist. His voice sounded dispassionate as always, but there was a hardness in his eyes Morgon had never seen before. Ghisteslwchlohm seemed to listen a moment to an ambiguity: some voice he did not quite catch beneath the voice of the morning wind.

He said finally, almost curiously, "So. Even your patience has its limits. I can heal your hands."

"No."

"Deth, you are being unreasonable. You know as well as I do what the stakes are in this game. Morgon is stumbling like a blind man into his power. I want him in Erlenstar Mountain, and I don't want to fight him to get him there."

"I'm not going back to Erlenstar Mountain," Morgon said involuntarily. The wizard ignored him; his eyes, intent, narrowed a little on Deth's face.

Deth said softly, "I am old and crippled and very tired. You left me little more than my life in Hel. Do you know what I did then? I walked my horse to Caithnard and found a trader who didn't spit when I spoke to him. I traded my horse to him for the last harp I will ever possess. And I tried to play it."

"I said I will—"

"There is not a court open to me in this realm to play in, even if you healed my hands."

"You accepted that risk six centuries ago," Ghisteslwchlohm said. His voice had thinned. "You could have chosen a lesser court than mine to harp in, some innocent, powerless place whose innocence will not survive this final struggle. You know that. You are too wise for recriminations, and you never had any lost innocence to regret. You can stay here and starve, or take Raederle of An to Erlenstar Mountain and help me finish this game. Then you can take what reward you want for your services, anywhere in this realm." He paused, then added roughly, "Or are you bound, in some hidden place I cannot reach, to the Star-Bearer?"

"I owe nothing to the Star-Bearer."

"That is not what I asked you."

"You asked me that question before. In Hel. Do you want another answer?" He checked, as if the sudden anger in his voice were unfamiliar even to himself, and he continued more quietly, "The Star-Bearer is the pivot point of a game. I did not know, any more than you, that he would be a young Prince of Hed, whom I might come dangerously close to loving. There is no more binding than that, and it is hardly important. I have betrayed him to you twice. But you will have to find someone else to betray Raederle of An. I am in her debt. Again, that is a small matter: she is no threat to you, and any land-ruler in the realm can serve in her place—"

"The Morgol?"

Deth was still, not breathing, not blinking, as if he were something honed into shape by wind and weather. Morgon, watching, brushed something off his face with the back of his hand; he realized in surprise that he was crying.

Deth said finally, very softly, "No."

"So." The wizard contemplated him, hair-thin lines of impatience and power deepening at the sides of his mouth. "There is something that is not such a small matter. I was beginning to wonder. If I can't hire you back into my service, perhaps I can persuade you. The

Morgol of Herun is camped outside of Lungold with two hundred of her guard. The guard is there, I assume, to protect the city; the Morgol, out of some incomprehensible impulse, is waiting for you. I will give you a choice. If you choose to leave Raederle here, I will bring the Morgol with me to Erlenstar Mountain, after I have subdued, with Morgon's help, the last of the Lungold wizards. Choose."

He waited. The harpist was motionless again; even the crooked bones in his hands seemed brittle. The wizard's voice whipped at him and he flinched. "Choose!"

Raederle's hands slid over her mouth. "Deth, I'll go," she whispered. "I'll follow Morgon anyway, or I will be foresworn."

The harpist did not speak. He moved finally, very slowly toward them, his eyes on Ghisteslwchlohm's face. He stopped a pace away from him and drew breath to speak. Then, in a swift, fluid movement, the back of his crippled hand cracked across the Founder's face.

Ghisteslwchlohm stepped back, his fingers driving to the bone on Morgon's arm, but he could not have moved. The harpist slid to his knees, hunched over the newly broken bones in his hand. He lifted his face, white, bruised with agony, asking nothing. For a moment Ghisteslwchlohm looked down at him silently, and Morgon saw in his eyes what might have been the broken memories of many centuries. Then his own hand rose. A lash of fire caught the harpist across the eyes, flung him backward across the bracken, where he lay still, staring blindly at the sun.

The wizard held Morgon with his hand and his eyes, until Morgon realized slowly that he was shaken with a dry, tearless sobbing and his muscles were locked to attack. The wizard touched his eyes briefly, as if the streak of fire torn out of his mind had given him a headache. "Why in Hel's name," he demanded, "are you wasting grief on him? Look at me. Look at me!"

"I don't know!" Morgon shouted back at him. He saw more fire snap through the air, across the harpist's body. It touched the dark harp and flamed. The air wailed with snapping strings. Raederle shimmered suddenly into sheer fire; the wizard pulled her relentlessly back into shape with his mind. She was still half-fire, and Morgon was struggling with an impulse of power that would have doomed her, when something in him froze. He whirled. Watching curiously among the trees were a dozen men. Their horses were the color of night, their garments all the wet, rippling colors of the sea.

"The world," one of them commented in the sudden silence, "is not a safe place for harpists." He bent his head to Morgon. "Star-Bearer." His pale, expressionless face seemed to flow a little with the breeze. From him came the smell of brine. "Ylon's child." His lucent eyes went to Ghisteslwchlohm. "High One."

Morgon stared at them. His mind, spinning through possibilities of action, went suddenly blank. They had no weapons; their black mounts were stone still, but any movement, he sensed, a shift of light, a bird call on the wrong note, could spring a merciless attack. They seemed suspended from motion, as on a breath of silence between two waves; whether by curiosity or simple uncertainty, he did not know. He felt Ghisteslwchlohm's hand grip his shoulder and was reassured oddly by the fact that the wizard wanted him alive.

The shape-changer who had spoken answered his question with a soft, equivocal mockery, "For thousands of years we have been waiting to meet the High One."

Morgon heard the wizard draw breath. "So. You are the spawn of the seas of Ymris and An—"

"No. We are not of the sea. We have shaped ourselves to its harping. You are careless of your harpist."

"The harpist is my business."

"He served you well. We watched him through the centuries, doing your bidding, wearing your mask,

waiting . . . as we waited, long before you set foot on
this earth of the High One's, Ghisteslwchlohm. Where
is the High One?" His horse snaked forward soundlessly, like a shadow, stopped three paces from Morgon. He resisted an impulse to step backward. The
Founder's voice, tired, impatient, made him marvel.
"I am not interested in riddle-games. Or in a fight.
You take your shapes out of dead men and seaweed;
you breathe, you harp and you die—that is all I know
or care to know about you. Back your mount or you
will be riding a pile of kelp."

The shape-changer backed it a step without a shift
of muscle. His eyes caught light like water; for an instant they seemed to smile. "Master Ohm," he said,
"do you know the riddle of the man who opened his
door at midnight and found not the black sky filling his
doorway but the black, black eye of some creature
who stretched beyond him to measureless dimension?
Look at us again. Then go, quietly, leaving the Star-
Bearer and our kinswoman."

"You look," the Founder said brusquely. Morgon,
still in his hold, was jolted by the strength that poured
out of him: energy that slapped at the shape-changers,
flattened an oak in its way and sent frightened birds
screaming into the air. The silent thunder of the fire
streaked towards their minds; Morgon felt it, but as at
a distance, for the wizard had shielded his mind. When
the trees had splintered and settled, the shape-changers
slowly reappeared out of the flock of birds that had
startled into the air. Their number had doubled, for
half of them had been the motionless horses. They
took their previous shapes leisurely, while Ghisteslwchlohm watched, puzzled, Morgon sensed, about the ex-
tent of their power. His grip had slackened. A twig in a
bush rustled slightly, for no discernible reason, and the
shape-changers attacked.

There was a wave of black pelt, soundless, shell-
black hooves rolling toward them so fast that Morgon
barely had time to react. He worked an illusion of

nothingness over himself that he suspected only Raederle noticed; she gasped when he gripped her wrist. Something struck him: a horse's hoof, or the hilt of a shadowy blade, and he wavered an instant in and out of visibility. He felt his muscles tense for a death blow. But nothing touched him, only wind, for a few broken moments. He flung his mind forward, miles ahead along the road, where a trader driving a wagon-load of cloth was whistling away his boredom. He filled Raederle's mind with the same awareness and gripping her hard, pulled her forward into it.

A moment later he was lying with her at the bottom of the big covered cart, bleeding onto a bolt of embroidered linen.

6

RAEDERLE WAS SOBBING. HE TRIED TO QUIET HER, gathering her to him as he listened, but she could not stop. He heard beneath her weeping the grind of wheels in the dust and the driver's whistling, muffled by the bolts of cloth piled behind him and the canvas covering the wagon. The road was quiet; he heard no sounds of disturbance behind them. His head was aching; he leaned it against the linen. His eyes closed. A darkness thundered soundlessly toward him again. Then a cartwheel banged into a pothole, jarring him, and Raederle twisted out of his hold and sat up. She pushed her hair out of her eyes.

"Morgon, he came for me at night, and I was barefoot—I couldn't even run. I thought it was you. I don't even have shoes on. What in Hel's name was that harpist doing? I don't understand him. I don't—" She stopped suddenly, staring at him, as if he were a shape-changer she had found beside her. She put one hand over her mouth, and touched his face with the other. "Morgon . . ."

He put his hand to his forehead, looked at the blood on his fingers, and made a surprised sound. The side of his face, from temple to jaw, was burning. His shoulder hurt; his tunic fell apart when he touched it. A raw, wide gash, like the scrape of a sharp hoof,

continued from his face to his shoulder and halfway
down his chest.

He straightened slowly, looking at the bloodstains
he had left on the floor of the wagon, on the trader's
fine cloth. He shuddered suddenly, violently, and
pushed his face against his knees.

"I walked straight into that one." He began to curse
himself, vividly and methodically, until he heard her
rise. He caught her wrist, pulled her down again.
"No."

"Will you let go of me? I'm going to tell the trader to
stop. If you don't let go, I'll shout."

"No. Raederle, listen. Will you listen! We are only a
few miles west of where we were captured. The shape-
changers will search for us. So will Ghisteslwchlohm,
if he isn't dead. We have to outrun them."

"I don't even have shoes on! And if you tell me to
change shape, I will curse you." Then she touched his
cheek again, swallowing. "Morgon, can you stop crying?"

"Haven't I stopped?"

"No." Her own eyes filled again. "You look like a
wraith out of Hel. Please let the trader help you."

"No." The wagon jerked to a stop suddenly, and he
groaned. He got to his feet unsteadily, drew her up.
The trader's startled face peered back at them between
the falls of his canvas.

"What in the name of the wolf-king's eyes are you
doing back there?" He shifted the curtains so the light
fell on them. "Look at the mess you made on that embroidered cloth! Do you realize how much that costs?
And that white velvet . . ."

Morgon heard Raederle draw breath to respond. He
gripped her hand and sent his mind forward, like an
anchor flung on its line across water, disappearing into
the shallows to fall to a resting place. He found a quiet,
sunlit portion of the road ahead of them, with only a
musician on it singing to himself as he rode toward

Lungold. Holding Raederle's mind, halting her in mid-sentence, Morgon stepped toward the singing.

They stood in the road only a minute, while the singer moved obliviously away from them. The unexpected light spun around Morgon dizzily. Raederle was struggling against his mind-hold with a startling intensity. She was angry, he sensed, and beneath that, panicked. She could break his hold, he knew suddenly as he glimpsed the vast resource of power in her, but she was too frightened to control her thoughts. His thoughts, shapeless, open, soared over the road again, touched the minds of horses, a hawk, crows feeding around a dead campfire. A farmer's son, leaving his heritage behind him, riding an ancient plow horse to seek his fortune in Lungold, anchored Morgon's mind again. He stepped forward. As they stood in the dust raised by the plow horse, Morgon heard his own harsh, exhausted breathing. Something slapped painfully across his mind, and he nearly fought back at it until he realized it was Raederle's mind-shout. He stilled both their minds and searched far down the road.

A smith who travelled from village to village along the road, shoeing horses and patching cauldrons, sat half-asleep in his cart, dreaming idly of beer. Morgon, dreaming his dream, followed him through the hot morning. Raederle was oddly still. He wanted to speak to her then, desperately, but he did not dare break his concentration. He threw his mind open again, until he heard traders laughing. He let his mind fill with their laughter until it was next to him among the trees. Then his sense of Raederle's mind drained out of him. He groped for it, startled, but touched only the vague thoughts of trees or animals. He could not find her with his mind. His concentration broken, he saw her standing in front of him.

She was breathing quickly, silently, staring at him, her body tensed to shout or strike or cry. He said, his face so stiff he could hardly speak, "Once more. Please. The river."

She nodded, after a moment. He touched her hand, and then her mind. He felt through the sunlight for cool minds: fish, water birds, river animals. The river appeared before them; they stood on the bank in a soft grassy clearing among the ferns.

He let go of Raederle, fell to his hands and knees and drank. The water's voice soothed the sear of the sun across his mind. He looked up at Raederle and tried to speak. He could not see her. He slumped down, laid his face in the river and fell asleep.

He woke again in the middle of the night, found Raederle sitting beside him, watching him by the gentle light of her fire. They gazed at one another for a long time without speaking, as if they were looking out of their memories. Then Raederle touched his face. Her face was drawn; there was an expression in her eyes that he had never seen before.

An odd sorrow caught at his throat. He whispered, "I'm sorry. I was desperate."

"It's all right." She checked the bandages across his chest; he recognized strips of her shift. "I found herbs the pig-woman—I mean Nun—taught me to use on wounded pigs. I hope they work on you."

He caught her hands, folded them between his fingers. "Please. Say it."

"I don't know what to say. No one ever controlled my mind before. I was so angry with you, all I wanted to do was break free of you and go back to Anuin. Then . . . I broke free. And I stayed with you because you understand . . . you understand power. So do the shape-changers who called me kinswoman, but you I trust." She was silent; he waited, seeing her oddly, feverishly in the firelight, the tangled mass of her hair like harvested kelp, her skin pale as shell, her expressions changing like light changing over the sea. Her face twisted away from him suddenly. "Stop seeing me like that!"

"I'm sorry," he said again. "You looked so beautiful.

Do you realize what kind of power it takes to break one of my bindings?"

"Yes. A shape-changer's power. That's what I have."

He was silent, staring at her. A light, chill shudder ran through him. "They have that much power." He sat up abruptly, scarcely noticing the drag of pain down his shoulder. "Why don't they use it? They never use it. They should have killed me long ago. In Herun, the shape-changer Corrig could have killed me as I slept; instead he only harped. He challenged me to kill him. In Isig—three shape-changers could not kill one farmer-prince of Hed who had never used a sword in his life? What in Hel's name are they? What do they want of me? What does Ghisteslwchlohm want?"

"Do you think they killed him?"

"I don't know. He would have had sense enough to run. I'm surprised we didn't find him in the wagon with us."

"They'll look for you in Lungold."

"I know." He slid his palms over his face. "I know. Maybe with the wizards' help, I can draw them away from the city. I've got to get there quickly. I've got to—"

"I know." She drew a deep breath and loosed it wearily. "Morgon, teach me the crow-shape. At least it's a shape of the Kings of An. And it's faster than walking barefoot."

He lifted his head. He lay back down after a moment, drew her down with him, searching for some way to speak at once all the thoughts crowding into his head. He said finally, "I'll learn to harp," and he felt her smile against his breast. Then all his thoughts froze into a single memory of a halting harping out of the dark. He did not realize he was crying again until he lifted his hand to touch his eyes. Raederle was silent, holding him gently. He said, after a long time, when her fire had died down, "I sat with Deth in the night not because I was hoping to understand him, but because he drew me there, he wanted me there. And he didn't keep me there with his harping or his words, but something powerful enough to bind me across all my anger. I came because he wanted me. He wanted me, so I came. Do you understand that?"

"Morgon, you loved him," she whispered. "That was the binding."

He was silent again, thinking back to the still, shadowed face beyond the flame, listening to the harpist's silence until he could almost hear the sound of riddles spun like spider's web in the darkness in a vast, secret game that made his death itself a riddle. Finally some herb Raederle had laid against his cheek breathed across his mind and he slept again.

He taught her the crow-shape the next morning when they woke at dawn. He went into her mind, found deep in it crow-images, tales of them, memories she scarcely knew were there: her father's unreadable crow-black eyes, crows among the oak trees surrounding Raith's pigherds, crows flying through the history of An, carrion-eaters, message-bearers, cairn-guardians, their voices full of mockery, bitter warnings, poetry.

"Where did they all come from?" she murmured, amazed.

"They are of the land-law of An. The power and heart of An. Nothing more."

He called a sleepy crow out of one of the trees around them; it landed on his wrist. "Can you go into my mind? See behind my eyes, into my thoughts?"

"I don't know."

"Try. It won't be hard for you." He opened his mind to the crow-mind, drew its brain-workings into his own, until he saw his blurred, nameless face out of its eyes. He heard movements, precise and isolated as flute notes, under dead leaves, under oak roots. He began to understand its language. It gave a squawk, more curious than impatient. His mind filled then with a sense of Raederle, as if she were within him, touching him gently, filling him like light. His throat ached with wonder. For a moment the three minds drew from one another, fearlessly, tentatively. Then the crow cried; its wings soared blackly over Morgon's vision. He was left alone in his mind, groping for something that had gone out of him. A crow fluttered up, landed on his shoulder. He looked into its eyes.

He smiled slowly. The crow, its wings beating awkwardly, swooped to a high branch. It missed its perch landing. Then it caught itself, and the fine balance of instinct and knowledge within it wavered. The crow became Raederle, dodging leaves as she changed shape.

She looked down at Morgon, breathless and astonished. "Stop laughing. Morgon, I flew. Now, how in Hel's name do I get down?"

"Fly."

"I've forgotten how!"

He flew up beside her, one wing stiff with his half-healed wound. He changed shape again. The branch creaked a warning under his weight, and she gasped. "We'll fall in the river! Morgon, it's breaking—" She fluttered up again with a squawk. Morgon joined her. They streaked the sunrise with black, soared high above the woods until they saw the hundreds of miles of endless forest and the great road hewn through it, crossing the realm. They rose until traders' wagons were only tiny lumbering insects crawling down a ribbon of dust. They dropped slowly, spiralling together, their wings beating the same slow rhythm, winding lesser and lesser rings through the sunlight until they traced one last black circle above the river. They landed among ferns on the bank, changed shape. They gazed at one another wordlessly in the morning. Raederle whispered,

"Your eyes are full of wings."

"Your eyes are full of the sun."

THEY FLEW IN CROW-SHAPE FOR THE NEXT TWO weeks. The silent golden oak forest melted away at the edge of the backlands. The road turned, pushed north-

ward through rich, dark forests of pine whose silence
seemed undisturbed by the passage of centuries. It
wound up dry rocky hills pounded the color of brass
by the noon sun, bridged chasms through which silvery veins of water flowing down from the Lungold
Lakes flashed and roared against sheer walls of stone.
Trees blurred endlessly together in the crows' vision,
ebbed toward a faint blue mist of mountains bordering the remote western edges of the backlands. By
day the sun fired the sky a flawless, metallic blue.
The night shook stars from one horizon to another,
down to the rim of the world. The voices of the backlands, of land and stone and ancient untamed wind,
were too loud for sound. Beneath them lay a silence
implacable as granite. Morgon felt it as he flew; he
breathed it into his bones, sensed its strange, cold
touch in his heart. He would grope away from it at
first, reach into Raederle's mind to share a vague,
inarticulate language. Then the silence wore slowly
into the rhythm of his flight and finally into a song.
At last, when he scarcely remembered his own language and knew Raederle only as a dark, wind-
sculpted shape, he saw the interminable trees part
before them. In the distance, the great city founded
by Ghisteslwchlohm sprawled against the shores of
the first of the Lungold Lakes, glinting of copper and
bronze and gold under the last rays of the sun.

The crows beat a final weary flight toward their
destination. The forest had been pushed back for
miles around the city to make room for fields, pastures, orchards. The cool scent of pine yielded to the
smell of harrowed earth and crops that teased at
Morgon's crow-instincts. Trader's Road, striped with
shadow, ran its last scarred mile into the mouth of the
city. The gateway was a fragile, soaring arch of dark
polished timber and white stone. The city walls were
immense, thick, buttressed with arms of timber and
stone that rose high above the buildings scattered beyond the old bounds of the city. Newer streets had

made inroads into the ancient walls; lesser gateways opened in it; houses and shops had grow against, and even on top of the walls, as if their builders had long forgotten the terror that had flung the walls up seven centuries before.

The crows reached the main gate, rested among the arches. The gates themselves looked as if they had not been closed for centuries. They were of thick slabs of oak, hinged and reinforced with bronze. Birds were nesting on the hinges in the shadows. Within the walls, a maze of cobbled streets wandered away in all directions, lined by brightly painted inns, trade-halls, merchants' and craftsmen's shops, houses with tapestries and flowers trailing from the windows. Morgon, sifting through his crow-vision, saw across the rooftops and chimneys to the north edge of the city. The setting sun struck the lake with a full, broad battery, spangling it with fire, until the hundred fishing-boats moored at the docks seemed to burn on the water.

He fluttered to the ground in the angle between the open gate and the wall and changed shape. Raederle followed him. They stood looking at one another, their faces thin, stamped with the wildness and silence of the backlands, half-unfamiliar. Then Morgon, remembering he had an arm, put it around Raederle's shoulders and kissed her almost tentatively. The expression began to come back into her face.

"What in Hel's name did we do?" she whispered. "Morgon, I feel as if I have been dreaming for a hundred years."

"Only a couple of weeks. We're in Lungold."

"Let's go home." Then a strange look came into her eyes. "What have we been eating?"

"Don't think about it." He listened. The traffic through the gate had almost stopped; he heard only one slow horseman preceding the twilight into the city. He took her hand. "Let's go."

"Where?"

"Can't you smell it? It's there, at the edge of my mind. A stench of power . . ."

It drew him through the twisting streets. The city was quiet, for it was supper hour; the succulent smells out of inns they passed made them both murmur. But they had no money, and with Morgon's torn clothing and Raederle's bare feet, they looked almost like beggars. The sense of decayed, misused power pulled Morgon toward the heart of the city, through wide streets full of fine shops and wealthy traders' houses. The streets sloped upward at the center of the city. The rich buildings dwindled away at the crown of the rising. The streets ended abruptly. On an immense, scarred stretch of land rose the shell of the ancient school, fashioned of the power and art of wizardry, its open, empty walls gleaming in the last of the light.

Morgon stopped. An odd longing ached in him, as at a glimpse of something he could never have and never knew before that he might have wanted. He said incredulously, "No wonder they came. He made it so beautiful . . ."

Huge rooms, broken open, half-destroyed, revealed the wealth of the realm. Shattered windows with jagged panes the colors of jewels were framed in gold. Inner walls blackened with fire held remnants of pale ash and ebony, of oak and cedar. Here and there, a scarred, fallen beam glinted with a joint work of copper and bronze. Long arched windows, through which prisms of refracted light passed, suggested the illusion of peace that had lulled the restless, driven minds drawn into the school. From across seven centuries Morgon felt its illusion and its promise: the gathering of the most powerful minds of the realm to share knowledge, to explore and discipline their powers. The obscure longing bruised his heart again; he could not put a name to it. He stood gazing at the silent, ruined school until Raederle touched him.

"What is it?"

"I don't know. I wish . . . I wish I could have

studied here. The only power I have ever known is
Ghisteslwchlohm's."

"The wizards will help you," she said, but he found
no reassurance in that. He looked at her.

"Will you do something for me? Go back into crow-
shape. I'll take you on my shoulder while I search for
them. I don't know what traps or bindings might still
linger here."

She nodded tiredly, without comment, and changed
shape. She tucked herself under his ear, and he
stepped onto the grounds of the school. No trees grew
anywhere on them; the grass struggled only patchily
around white furrows of scorched earth. Shattered
stones lay where they had fallen, still burning deep
within them with a memory of power. Nothing had
been touched for centuries. Morgon felt it as he drew
near the school itself. The terrible sense of destruction
hung like a warning over the wealth. He moved
quietly, his mind open, scenting, into the silent buildings.

The rooms stank with a familiar name. In most, he
found bones crushed beneath a cairn of broken walls.
Memories of hope or energy, of despair, collected
about him like wraiths. He began to sweat lightly,
struck by shadows, faint and fine as ancient dust, of
a devastating, hopeless battle. As he entered a great
circular hall in the center of the buildings, he felt the
reverberations still beating within the walls of a terrible explosion of hatred and despair. He heard the
crow mutter harshly in its throat; its claws were prick-
ling his shoulder. He picked his way across the ceiling,
which was lying in pieces on the floor, toward a door
in the back of the room. The door, hanging in splinters
on its hinges, opened into a vast library. A priceless
treasure of books lay torn and charred on the floor.
Fire had raged across the shelves, leaving little more
than the backbones and skeletons of ancient books of
wizardry. The smell of burned leather still hung in

the room, as if nothing had moved through the air itself in seven centuries.

He moved through empty room after empty room. He found in one melted pools of gold and silver, precious metals and shattered jewels the students had worked with; in another, the broken bones of small animals. In another, he found beds. The bones of a child were crouched under the covers of one of them. At that point, he turned and groped through the torn wall back into the evening. But the air was filled with silent cries, and the earth beneath his feet was dead.

He sat down on a pile of stone blown out of the corner of the building. Down the barren crest of the hill, the maze of rooftops spilled toward the crumbling walls. They were all of timber. He saw vividly a sheet of fire spreading across the entire city, burning crops and orchards, billowing along the lake edge into the forests under the hot summer sky, with no hope of rain for months to quench it. He dropped his face against his fists, whispered, "What in Hel's name do I think I'm doing here? He destroyed Lungold once; now he and I will destroy it again. The wizards haven't come back here to challenge him; they've come back to die."

The crow murmured something. He stood up again, gazing at the huge, ruined mass looming darkly against the translucent wake of the sunset. Scenting with his mind, he touched only memories. Listening, he heard only the echoes of a name cursed silently for all centuries. His shoulders slumped. "If they're here, they've guarded themselves well . . . I don't know how to look for them."

Raederle's voice broke through the crow-mind with a brief, mental comment. He turned his head, met the black, probing eye. "All right. I know I can find them. I can see through their illusions and break their bindings. But, Raederle . . . they are great wizards. They came into their power through curiosity, discipline, integrity . . . maybe even joy. They did not get it

screaming at the bottom of Erlenstar Mountain. They
never meddled with land-law, or hunted a harpist
from one end of the realm to the other to kill him.
They may need me to fight for them here, but I wonder if they will trust me . . ." The crow was silent; he
brushed a finger down its breast. "I know. There is
only one way to find out."

He went back into the ruins. This time, he opened
himself completely to all the torment of the destruction and the lingering memories of a forgotten peace.
His mind, like a faceted jewel, reflected all the shades
of lingering power—from cracked stones, from an un-
touched page out of a spell book, from various ancient instruments he found near the dead: rings,
strangely carved staffs, crystals with light frozen in
them, skeletons of winged animals he could not name.
He sorted through all the various levels of power,
found the source of each. Once, tracing a smoldering
fire to its bed deep in a pool of melted iron, he deto-
nated it accidentally and realized the iron itself had
been some crucible of knowledge. The blast blew the
crow six feet in the air and shook stones down from
the ceiling. He had melted into the force automatically, not fighting it; the crow, squawking nervously,
watched him shape himself back out of the solid stone
he had blown himself into. He took it into his hands
to soothe it, marveling at the intricacies of ancient
wizardry. Everything his mind touched—wood, glass,
gold, parchment, bone—held within it an ember of
power. He explored patiently, exhaustingly, lighting a
sliver of roof beam when it grew too dark to see.
Finally, near midnight, when the crow was dozing on
his shoulder, his mind strayed across the face of a
door that did not exist.

It was a powerful illusion; he had looked at the
door before and not seen through it, or felt an urge
to open it. It was of thick oak and iron, barred and
bolted. He would have to pick his way over a pile
of broken stone and charred timber to open it. The

walls were crumbled almost to the ground around the
door; it seemed bolted against nothing but the battle-
seared ground between two ruined buildings. But it
had been created out of a living power, for some purpose. He clambered over the rubble to reach it and
laid his hand flat against it. Some mind barred his
passage, gave him a feel of wood grain under his fingers. He paused before he broke it, disturbed once
more by the ambiguity of his own great power. Then
he walked forward, becoming, for a breath, worm-
eaten oak, rusted locks, and encompassing the power
that bound them there.

He stepped downward abruptly into darkness. Steps
that lay hidden under an illusion of parched ground
led down under the earth. His fire wavered, grew
smaller and smaller until he realized what force was
working against it. He held the flame clear, steady,
burning out of fire deep in his mind.

The worn stone steps sloped sharply down a narrow passageway. Gradually they levelled, and a blank,
empty face of darkness loomed beyond Morgon's
shadow, smelling of rotting timbers and damp stone.
He let his brand burn brighter; it probed feebly
at the vastness. A chill, like a mountain chill, shivered through him. The crow made a harsh noise. He
felt it begin to change shape, and he shook his head
quickly. It subsided under his hair. As he drew the
fire brighter and brighter, searching for some limit to
the darkness, something began to seep into his
thoughts. He sensed a power very near him that had
nothing to do with a vast, underground chasm. Puzzling over it, he wondered if the chasm itself were an
illusion.

He drew breath softly and held it. Only one possibility suggested itself to him: a paradox of wizardry.
He had no other choice, except to turn and leave. He
dropped his torch on the ground, let it dwindle into
blackness. How long he stood wrestling with the dark,
he did not know. The more he strained to see, the

more he realized his blindness. He lifted his hands finally, linked them across his eyes. He was shivering again; the darkness seemed to squat over his head like some immense, bulky creature. But he could not leave; he stood silently, stubbornly, hoping for help.

A voice said, almost next to him, "Night is not something to endure until dawn. It is an element, like wind or fire. Darkness is its own kingdom; it moves to its own laws and many living things dwell in it. You are trying to separate your mind from it. That is futile. Accept the strictures of darkness."

"I can't." His hands had dropped, clenched; he waited, very still.

"Try."

His hands tightened; sweat stung his eyes. "I can fight the Founder, but I never learned from him how to fight this."

"You broke through my illusion as if it scarcely existed." The voice was tranquil, yet sinewy. "I held it with all the power that I still possess. There are only two others who could have broken it. And you are more powerful than either. Star-Bearer, I am Iff." He pronounced his full name then, a series of harsh syllables with a flowing, musical inflection. "You freed me from the Founder's power, and I place myself in your service, to my life's end. Can you see me?"

"No," Morgon whispered. "I want to."

Stars of torch fire ringed him, upholding an arch of light. The sense of vastness melted away. The gentle, wordless awareness of something not quite real, like a memory haunting the edge of his mind, was very strong. Then he saw a death's head gazing at him quizzically, and another, amid a tangle of assorted bones. The chamber he stood in was circular; the damp walls of living earth were full of deep slits. The hair prickled on the nape of his neck. He was standing in a tomb, hidden beneath the great school, and he had interrupted the last living wizards of Lungold burying their dead.

7

E RECOGNIZED NUN IMMEDIATELY: A TALL, THIN woman with long grey hair and a shrewd, angular face. She was smoking a little jewelled pipe; her eyes, studying him with an odd mixture of wonder and worry, were a shade darker than her smoke. Behind her, in the torchlight, stood a big, spare wizard whose broad, fine-boned face was carved and battered with battle like a king's. His dead hair was flecked with silver and gold; his eyes were vivid, smoldering with blue flame. He was gazing at Morgon out of the past, as if three stars had burned for a moment across his vision sometime in the darkness of forgotten centuries. Kneeling next to one of the crevices in the wall was a dark-eyed wizard with a spare face like a bird of prey. He seemed fierce, humorless, until Morgon met his eyes and saw a faint smile, as at some incongruity. Morgon turned a little to the tall, frail wizard beside him, with the voice of a Caithnard Master. His face was worn, ascetic, but Morgon, watching him step forward, sensed the unexpected strength in his lean body.

He said tentatively, "Iff?"

"Yes." His hand slid very gently up Morgon's shoulder, taking the crow, and Morgon thought suddenly of the books the Morgol of Herun had brought to Caithnard with drawings of wildflowers down their precise margins.

"You are the scholar who loves wild things."

The wizard glanced up from the crow, his still face surprised, suddenly vulnerable. The crow was staring at him darkly, not a feather moving. The hawk-faced wizard slid the skull he was holding into a crevice and crossed the room.

"We sent a crow much like that back to Anuin, not long ago." His spare, restless voice was like his eyes, at once fierce and patient.

Nun exclaimed, "Raederle!" Her voice slid pleasantly in and out of her pigherder's accent. "What in Hel's name are you doing here?"

Iff looked startled. He put the crow back on Morgon's shoulder and said to it, "I beg your pardon." He added to Morgon, "Your wife?"

"No. She won't marry me. She won't go home, either. But she is capable of taking care of herself."

"Against Ghisteslwchlohm?" A hawk's eyes met the crow's a full moment, then the crow shifted nervously back under Morgon's ear. He wanted suddenly to take the bird and hide it in his tunic next to his heart. The wizard's thin brows were puckered curiously. "I served the Kings of An and Aum for centuries. After the destruction of Lungold, I became a falcon, constantly caught, growing old and escaping to grow young again. I have worn jesses and bells and circled the wind to return to the hands of Kings of Anuin for centuries. None of them, not even Mathom of An, had the power even to see behind my eyes. There is great, restless power in her. . . . She reminds me of someone, a falcon-memory . . ."

Morgon touched the crow gently, uncertain in its silence. "She'll tell you," he said at last, and the expression on the aged, proud face changed.

"Is she afraid of us? For what conceivable reason? In falcon-shape, I took meat from her father's bare hand."

"You are Talies," Morgon said suddenly, and the wizard nodded. "The historian. At Caithnard, I read what you wrote about Hed."

"Well." The sharp eyes were almost smiling again. "I wrote that many centuries ago. No doubt Hed has changed since then, to produce the Star-Bearer along with plow horses and beer."

"No. If you went back, you would recognize it." He remembered the wraiths of An, then, and his voice caught slightly. He turned to the wizard built like a Ymris warrior. "And you are Aloil. The poet. You wrote love poems to—" His voice stuck again, this time in embarrassment. But Nun was smiling.

"Imagine anyone bothering to remember all that after a thousand years and more. You were well-educated at that College."

"The writings of the Lungold wizards—those that were not destroyed here—formed the base of riddlery." He added, sensing a sudden question in Aloil's mind, "Part of your work is at Caithnard, and the rest in the king's library at Caerweddin. Astrin Ymris had most of your poetry."

"Poetry." The wizard swept a knotted hand through his hair. "It should have been destroyed here. It was worth little more than that. You come bearing memories into this place, tales of a realm that we will not live to see again. We came here to kill Ghisteslwchlohm or die."

"I didn't," Morgon said softly. "I came to ask the Founder some questions."

The wizard's inward gaze seemed to pull itself out of memory, turn toward him. "Questions!"

"It's proper," Nun said soothingly. "He is a riddle-master."

"What has riddlery to do with this?"

"Well." Then her teeth clamped back down on her pipe, and she sent up a stream of little, perturbed puffs without answering.

Iff asked practically, "Do you have the strength?"

"To kill him? Yes. To hold his mind and get what knowledge I need . . . I must. I'll find the power. He is no use to me dead. But I can't fight shape-changers at the same time. And I am not sure how powerful they are."

"You do complicate matters," Nun murmured. "We came here for such a simple purpose . . ."

"I need you alive."

"Well. It's nice to be needed. Look around you." The firelight seemed to follow her hand as she gestured. "There were twenty-nine wizards and over two hundred men and women of talent studying here seven centuries ago. Of those, we are burying two hundred and twenty-four. Twenty-three, not counting Suth. And you know how he died. You have walked through this place. It is a great cairn of wizardry. There is power still in the ancient bones, which is why we are burying them, so centuries from now the small witches and sorcerors of the realm will not come hunting thighbones and fingerbones for their spells. The dead of Lungold deserve some peace. I know you broke Ghisteslwchlohm's power to free us. But when you pursued that harpist instead of him, you gave him time to strengthen his powers. Are you so sure now that you can hold back a second destruction?"

"No. I am certain of nothing. Not even my own name, so I move from riddle to riddle. Ghisteslwchlohm built and destroyed Lungold because of these stars." He slid his hair back. "They drove me out of Hed into his hands—and I would have stayed in Hed forever, content to make beer and breed plow horses, never knowing you were alive, or that the High One in Erlenstar Mountain was a lie. I need to know what these stars are. Why Ghisteslwchlohm was not afraid of the High One. Why he wants me alive, powerful yet trapped. What power he is watching me stumble into. If I kill him, the realm will be rid of him, but I will still have questions no one will ever answer—like a starving man possessing gold in a land

where gold has no value. Do you understand?" he
asked Aloil suddenly, and saw in the burled shoulders, the hard, scrolled face, the great, twisted tree he
had been for seven centuries on King's Mouth Plain.

"I understand," the wizard said softly, "where I
have been for seven hundred years. Ask him your
questions. Then, if you die, or if you let him escape,
I will kill him or die. You understand revenge. As for
the stars on your face . . . I do not know how to begin to place any hope in them. I don't understand all
your actions. If we survive to walk out of Lungold
alive, I will find a need to understand them . . . especially the power and impulse that made you tamper
with the land-law of An. But for now . . . you freed
us, you dredged our names out of memory, you found
your way down here to stand with us among our dead
. . . you are a young, tired prince of Hed, with a
blood-stained tunic and a crow on your shoulder, and
a power behind your eyes straight out of Ghisteslwchlohm's heart. Was it because of you that I spent seven
centuries as an oak, staring into the sea wind? What
freedom or doom have you brought us back to?"

"I don't know." His throat ached. "I'll find you an
answer."

"You will." His voice changed then, wonderingly.
"You will, Riddle-Master. You do not promise hope."

"No. Truth. If I can find it."

There was a silence. Nun's pipe had gone out. Her
lips were parted a little, as if she were watching something blurred, uncertain begin to take shape before
her. "Almost," she whispered, "you make me hope.
But in Hel's name, for what?" Then she stirred out
of her thoughts and touched the rent in Morgon's tunic,
shifting it to examine the clean scar beneath. "You
had some trouble along the road. You didn't get that
in crow-shape."

"No." He stopped, reluctant to continue, but they
were waiting for an answer. He said softly, bitterly, to
the floor, "I followed Deth's harping one night and

walked straight into another betrayal." There was not
a sound around him. "Ghisteslwchlohm was looking
for me along Trader's Road. And he found me. He
trapped Raederle, so that I could not use power
against him. He was going to take me back to Erlenstar Mountain. But the shape-changers found us all. I
escaped from them"—he touched the scar on his
face—"by that much. I hid under illusion and escaped. I haven't seen any of them since we began to
fly. Maybe they all killed each other. Somehow I
doubt it." He added, feeling their silence like a spell,
compelling him, drawing words from him, "The High
One killed his harpist." He shook his head a little,
pulling back from their silence, unable to give them
more. He heard Iff draw breath, felt the wizard's
skilled, quieting touch.

Talies said abruptly, "Where was Yrth during all
this?"

Morgon's eyes moved from a splinter of bone on the
floor. "Yrth."

"He was with you on Trader's Road."

"No one was—" He stopped. A hint of night air
found its way past illusion, shivered through the chamber; the light fluttered like something trapped. "No
one was with us." Then he remembered the Great
Shout out of nowhere, and the mysterious, motionless
figure watching him in the night. He whispered incredulously, "Yrth?"

They looked at one another. Nun said, "He left
Lungold to find you, give you what help he could. You
never saw him?"

"Once—I might have, when I needed help. It must
have been Yrth. He never told me. He may have lost
me when we began to fly." He paused, thinking back.
"There was one moment, after the horse struck me,
when I could barely hold my own illusion. The shape-
changers could have killed me then. They should
have. I expected it. But nothing touched me. . . . He

may have been there, to save my life in that moment. But if he stayed there after I escaped—"

"He would have let us know, surely," Nun said, "if he needed help." She passed the back of a workworn hand over her brow worriedly. "But where is he, I wonder. An old man wandering up and down Trader's Road looking for you no doubt, along with the Founder and shape-changers. . . ."

"He should have told me. If he needed help, I could have fought for him; that's what I came for."

"You could have lost your life for his sake, too. No." She seemed to be answering her own doubt. "He'll come in his own time. Maybe he stayed to bury the harpist. Yrth taught him harp songs once, here in this college." She was silent again, while Morgon watched two battered faces of the dead against the far wall shift closer and closer together. He closed his eyes before they merged. He heard the crow cry from a distance; a painful grip on his shoulder kept him from falling. He opened his eyes to meet the hawk's stare and felt the sudden, cold sweat that had broken out on his face.

"I'm tired," he said.

"With reason." Iff loosened his hold. His face was seamed with a network of hair-fine lines. "There is venison on a spit in the kitchens—the only room left with four walls and a roof. We have been sleeping down here, but there are pallets beside the hearth. There will be a guard outside the door, watching the grounds."

"A guard?"

"One of the Morgol's guards. They provide for us, out of the Morgol's courtesy."

"Is the Morgol still here?"

"No. She resisted every argument we gave her to go home, until suddenly about two weeks ago, without explanation she went back to Herun." He raised his hand, pulled a torch out of air and darkness. "Come. I'll show you the way."

Morgon followed him silently back through his illu-

sion, through the broken rooms, down another winding
flight of stone steps into the kitchens. The smell of
meat cooling over the embers made even his bones
feel hollow. He sat down at the long, half-charred table, while Iff found a knife and some chipped goblets.

"There is wine, bread, cheese, fruit—the guards
keep us well-supplied." He paused, then smoothed a
feather on the crow's wing. "Morgon," he said softly,
"I have no idea what the dawn will bring. But if you
had not chosen to come here, we would be facing certain death. Whatever blind hope kept us alive for
seven centuries must have been rooted in you. You
may be afraid to hope, but I am not." His hand rested
briefly against Morgon's scarred cheek. "Thank you
for coming." He straightened. "I'll leave you here; we
work through the night and rarely sleep. If you need
us, call."

He tossed his torch into the hearth and left. Morgon
stared down at the table, at the still shadow of the
crow on the wood. He stirred finally, said its name. It
seemed about to change shape; its wings lifted to fly
down from his shoulder. Then the outer door to the
kitchens opened abruptly. The guard entered: a young,
dark-haired woman so familiar yet unfamiliar that
Morgon could only stare at her. She stopped dead,
halfway across the room, staring at him without blinking. He saw her swallow.

"Morgon?"

He stood up. "Lyra." She had grown; her body was
tall and supple in the short, dark tunic. Her face in
the shadows was half the child's he remembered and
half the Morgol's. She could not seem to move. So he
went to her. As he neared, he saw her hand shift on
her spear; he paused midstep and said, "It's me."

"I know." She swallowed again, her eyes still startled, very dark. "How did . . . how did you come into
the city? No one saw you."

"You have a guard on the walls?"

She gave a little jerky nod. "There's no other defense in the city. The Morgol sent for us."

"You. Her land-heir."

Her chin came up slightly in a gesture he remembered. "There is something I stayed here to do." Then, slowly, she came toward him, her expression changing in the wash of the firelight. She put her arms around him, her face bowed hard against his shoulder. He heard her spear clatter to the floor behind him. He held her tightly; something of her clear, proud mind brushing like a good wind through his mind. She loosed him finally, stepping back to look at him again. Her dark brows puckered at his scars.

"You should have had a guard along Trader's Road. I went with Raederle, searching for you last spring, but you were always a step ahead of us."

"I know."

"No wonder the guards didn't recognize you. You look—you look like—" She seemed to see the crow for the first time, motionless, watching from under his hair. "That's—is that Mathom?"

"Is he here?"

"He was, for a while. So was Har, but the wizards sent them both home."

His hands tightened on her shoulders. "Har?" he said incredulously. "In Hel's name, why did he come?"

"To help you. He stayed with the Morgol in her camp outside of Lungold until the wizards persuaded him to leave."

"Are they so sure he went? Have they checked the mind of every blue-eyed wolf around Lungold?"

"I don't know."

"Lyra, there are shape-changers coming. They know they can find me here."

She was silent; he watched her calculate. "The Morgol had us bring a supply of weapons for the traders; there were very few in the city. But the traders—Morgon, they're not fighters. The wall will crumble like old bread under attack. There are two hundred guards . . ." Her brows creased again, helplessly, and she looked suddenly young. "Do you know what they are? The shape-changers?"

"No." Something unfamiliar was building behind her eyes: the first hint of fear he had ever seen in her. He said, more harshly than he intended to, "Why?"

"Have you heard the news from Ymris?"

"No."

She drew breath. "Heureu Ymris lost Wind Plain. In a single afternoon. For months he held the rebel army back, at the edge of the plain. The Lords of Umber and Marcher had gathered an army to push the rebels back into the sea. It would have reached Wind Plain within two days. But suddenly an army greater than anything anyone knew existed swarmed out of Meremont and Tor across Wind Plain. Men who survived said they found themselves fighting— fighting men they swore they had already killed. The king's army was devastated. A trader was caught in the battlefield selling horses. He fled with the survivors into Rhun, and then into Lungold. He said—he said the plain was a nightmare of unburied dead. And Heureu Ymris has not been seen anywhere in Ymris since that day."

Morgon's lips moved soundlessly. "Is he dead?"

"Astrin Ymris says no. But even he can't find the king. Morgon, if I must fight shape-changers with two hundred guards, I will. But if you could just tell me what we are fighting? . . ."

"I don't know." He felt the crow's claws through his tunic. "We'll take this battle out of the city. I didn't come here to destroy Lungold a second time. I'll give the shape-changers no reason to fight here."

"Where will you go?"

"Into the forest, up a mountain—anywhere, as long as it's not here."

"I'm coming," she said.

"No. Absolutely—"

"The guard can stay here in the city, in case they

are needed. But I am coming with you. It's a matter of honor."

He looked at her silently, his eyes narrowed. She met them calmly. "What did you do?" he asked. "Did you take a vow?"

"No. I don't take vows. I make decisions. This one I made in Caerweddin, when I learned that you had lost the land-rule of Hed and you were still alive. I remembered, when you spoke of Hed in Herun, how much the land-rule meant to you. This time, you will have a guard."

"Lyra. I have a guard. Five wizards."

"And me."

"No. You are the land-heir of Herun. I have no intention of taking your body back to Crown City to give it to the Morgol."

She slipped out of his hold with a swift, light twist that left his hands gripping air. She swept her spear from the floor, held it upright beside her, standing at easy attention. "Morgon," she said softly, "I have made a decision. You fight with wizardry; I fight with a spear. It's the only way I know how. Either I fight here, or one day I will be forced to fight in Herun itself. When you met Ghisteslwchlohm again, I will be there." She turned, then remembered what she had come in for. She took an ancient torch out of its socket and dipped it into the fire. "I'm going to check the grounds. Then I'll come back and guard you until dawn."

"Lyra," he said wearily, "please just go home."

"No, I'm simply doing what I am trained to do. And so," she added without a suspicion of irony, "are you." Then her eyes moved back to the crow. "Is that something I should know to guard?"

He hesitated. The crow sat like a black thought on his shoulder, absolutely motionless. "No," he said finally. "Nothing will harm it. I swear that by my life."

Her dark eyes widened suddenly, going back to it.

She said softly, puzzled, after a moment, "Once we were friends."

She left him. He went to the fire, but thoughts lay hard, knotted in his belly, and he could not eat. He stilled the fire, sent it back into the embers. Then he lay down on one of the pallets, his face on his forearm, turned to look at the crow. It rested beside him on the stones. He reached out with his free hand, smoothed its feathers again and again.

"I will never teach you another shape," he whispered. "Raederle, what happened on Wind Plain has nothing to do with you. Nothing." He stroked it, talking to it, arguing, pleading without response until his eyes closed and he melted finally into its darkness.

Dawn broke into his dreams as the door swung open and shut with a bang. He startled up, his heart pounding, and saw the young, surprised face of a strange guard. She bent her head courteously.

"I'm sorry, Lord." She heaved a bucket of water and an earthen jar of fresh milk onto the table. "I didn't see you sleeping there."

"Where is Lyra?"

"On the north wall, overlooking the lake. There is a small army of some kind coming across the backlands. Goh rode out to check it." He got to his feet, murmuring. She added, "Lyra told me to ask you if you could come."

"I'll come." Nun, in a cloud of pipe smoke, drifted into the corner of his eye, and he started again. She put a soothing hand on his shoulder.

"You'll go where?"

"Some kind of an army is coming; maybe help, maybe not." He scooped water onto his face from the bucket and poured milk into a cracked goblet and drained it. Then his head swung back to the pallet he had been sleeping on. "Where—?" He took a step toward it, his eyes running frantically over the iron and brass pots on the wall, over the smoky roof beams. "Where in Hel's name . . ." He dropped to his knees, searched the trestles under the table, then the wood-box, and even the ashes on the grate. He straightened, still on his knees, stared, white, up at Nun. "She left me."

"Raederle?"

"She's gone. She wouldn't even talk to me. She flew away and left me." He got to his feet, slumped against the chimney stones. "It was that news out of Ymris. About the shape-changers."

"Shape-changers." Her voice sounded flat. "That's what was troubling her then? Her own power?"

He nodded. "She's afraid . . ." His hand dropped soundlessly against the stones. "I've got to find her. She's foresworn—and the ghost of Ylon is already troubling her."

Nun cursed the dead king with a pigherder's fluency. Then she put her fingers to her eyes. "No," she said tiredly, "I'll find her. Maybe she will talk to me. She used to. You see what that army is. I wish Yrth would come; he worries me. But I don't dare call either him or Raederle; my call might find its way straight into the Founder's mind. Now. Let me think. If I were a princess of An with a shape-changer's power, flying around like a crow, where would I go—"

"I know where I would go," Morgon murmured. "But she hates beer."

He went on foot through the city toward the docks, looking for a crow as he walked. The fishing-boats were all out on the broad lake, but there were other small craft, mining barges and flat-bottomed trading-vessels nosing out of the docks full of cargo to peddle among the trappers and herdsmen around the lake. He saw no crows on any of the masts. He found Lyra, finally, standing at a piece of sagging parapet to one side of a gate. Much of the north wall seemed to be underwater, supporting the docks; the rest was little more than broad, arched gates, with fish stalls set up against the wall between them. Morgon, ignoring the glassy-eyed stare of a fishwife, vanished in front of her and appeared at Lyra's side. She only blinked a little when she saw him, as if she had grown used to the unpredictable movements of wizards. She pointed east of the lake, and he saw tiny flecks of light in the distant forest.

"Can you see what it is?" she asked.

"I'll try." He caught the mind of a hawk circling the trees outside of the city. The noise of the city rumbled away to the back of his mind until he heard only the lazy morning breeze and the piercing cry of another hawk in the distance who had missed its kill. The hawk's circles grew wider under his prodding; he had a slow, sweeping vision of pine, hot sunlight on dried needles that slipped into shadows, through underbrush, then out into the light again onto hot, bare rock, where lizards under the hawk-shadow startled into crevices. The hawk-brain sorted every sound, every vague slink of shadow through the bracken. He urged it farther east, making a broad spiral of its circles. Finally, it swung across a line of warriors picking their way through the trees. He made the hawk return to the line again and again, until finally a movement in the full light below snapped its attention, and as it flung itself eastward, he shirred himself from its mind.

He slid down against the parapet. The sun struck him at an odd angle, much higher than he expected.

"They look like Ymris warriors," he said tiredly, "who have spent days crossing the backlands. They were unshorn, and their horses were balky. They didn't smell of the sea. They smelled of sweat."

Lyra studied him, her hands at her hips. "Should I trust them?"

"I don't know."

"Maybe Goh can tell. I gave her orders to watch them and listen to them and then to speak to them if she thought it wise. She has good sense."

"I'm sorry." He pulled himself to his feet. "I think they're men, but I am in no mood to trust anyone."

"Are you going to leave the city?"

"I don't know. Yrth is still missing, and now Raederle is gone. If I leave, she won't know where I am. If you sight nothing more dangerous, we can wait a little. If they are Ymris warriors, they can deploy themselves around this travesty of a defense wall and everyone here will feel much easier."

She was silent a moment, searching the breeze, as for a shadow of dark wings. "She'll come back," she said softly. "She has great courage."

He dropped his arm around her shoulders, hugged her briefly. "So do you. I wish you would go home."

"The Morgol placed her guard in the service of the Lungold merchants, to watch over the welfare of the city."

"She didn't place her land-heir in the service of the merchants. Did she?"

"Oh, Morgon, stop arguing. Can't you do something about this wall? It's useless and dangerous and dropping apart under my feet."

"All right. I'm not doing anything else worthwhile."

She turned her head, kissed his cheekbone. "Raederle is probably somewhere thinking. She'll come back to you." He opened his mouth; she shrugged out of his hold, her face suddenly averted. "Go fix the wall."

He spent hours repairing it, trying not to think. Ignoring the traffic passing around him—the farmers and merchants eying him uneasily, the traders who recognized him—he stood with his hands and his face against the ancient stones. His mind melded into their ponderous silence until he sensed their sagging, their precarious balance against the buttresses. He built illusions of stone within the archways, buttressing them with his mind. The blocked gates snarled carts and horses, started fights, and sent crowds to the city council chambers to be warned of the impending dangers. The traffic leaving through the main gate increased enormously. Street urchins gathered around him as he circled the city. They watched him work, followed at his heels, delighted, marvelling as non-existent stones built under his hands. In the late afternoon, laying his sweating face against the stones in an archway, he felt the touch of another power. He closed his eyes and traversed a silence he had learned well. For a long time, his mind moving deep into the stones, he heard nothing but the occasional, minute shift of a particle of mortar. Finally, edging onto the sunwarmed surface of the outer wall, he felt wedged against it a buttress of raw power. He touched it tentatively with his thoughts. It was a force pulled from the earth itself, rammed against the weakest point of the stone. He withdrew slowly, awed.

Someone was standing at his shoulder, saying his name over and over. He turned questioningly, found one of the Morgol's guards with a red-haired man in leather and mail beside her. The guard's broad, browned face was sweating, and she looked as tired as Morgon felt. Her gruff voice was patient, oddly pleasant.

"Lord, my name is Goh. This is Teril Umber, son of the High Lord Rork Umber of Ymris. I took the responsibility of guiding him and his warriors into the city." There was a faint tension in her voice and in her calm eyes. Morgon looked at the man silently. He was young but battle-hardened and very tired. He bent his head courteously to Morgon, oblivious of his suspicions.

"Lord, Heureu Ymris sent us out one day before . . . the day before he lost Wind Plain, apparently. We just heard the news from the Morgol's land-heir."

"Was your father at Wind Plain?" Morgon asked suddenly. "I remember him."

Teril Umber nodded wearily. "Yes. I have no idea if he survived or not." Then beneath the drag of his dusty mail, his shoulders straightened. "Well, the king was concerned about the defenselessness of the traders here; he sailed on trade-ships once himself. And of course, he wanted to put as many men as he could spare at your disposal. There are a hundred and fifty of us, to aid the Morgol's guard in defending the city, if there's need."

Morgon nodded. The lean, sweating face with its uncomfortable fringe of beard seemed beyond suspicion. He said, "I hope there's no need. It was generous of the king to spare you."

"Yes. He did exactly that, sending us out of Wind Plain."

"I'm sorry about your father. He was kind to me."

"He talked about you. . . ." He shook his head, running his fingers through his flaming hair. "He's come out of worse," he said without hope. "Well, I'd better talk to Lyra, get men situated before nightfall."

Morgon looked at Goh. The relief in her face told him how worried she had been. He said softly, "Please tell Lyra I'm nearly finished with the wall."

"Yes, Lord."

"Thank you."

She gave him a brief, shy nod, smiling suddenly. "Yes, Lord."

As his work around the wall progressed and the day burned toward a fiery end, he began to feel enclosed by power. The wizard working with him silently on the other side of the wall strengthened stones before he touched them, sealed broken places with grey, grainy illusions, balanced cracked walls against a weight of power. The walls lost their look of having grown battered by sunlight and hunched under winter winds. They stood firm again, patched, buttressed, rolling without a break around the city, challenging entrance.

Morgon wove a force from stone to stone to seal one last crack in some ancient mortar, then leaned against the wall wearily, his face in his arms. He could smell the twilight riding over the fields. The stillness of the last moments of the sunset, the peaceful, sleepy bird songs made him think for a moment of Hed. A distant crow call kept him from falling asleep against the wall. He roused himself and stepped into one of the two front gates he had left open. A man stood in the archway at the other end, with a crow on his shoulder.

He was a tall old man, with short grey hair and a battered, craggy face. He was talking in crow-language to the crow; Morgon understood some of it. As the crow answered, a hard fist of worry around Morgon's heart eased until his heart seemed to rest on some warm place, on the hand of the ancient wizard, perhaps, scarred as it was with vesta-horns. He went towards them quietly, his mind lulled by the sense of the wizard's great power, and by his kindness to Raederle.

But before he reached them, he saw the wizard break off mid-sentence and toss the crow into the air. He cried something at it that Morgon did not understand. Then he vanished. Morgon, his breathing dry, quick, saw the twilight moving down Trader's Road, surely, soundlessly; a wave of horsemen the color of the evening sky. Before he could move, a light the color of molten gold lit the archway around him. The wall lurched; stones, murmuring, undulating, shrugged off a blast of power into the street that exploded the cobblestones and slammed Morgon to his knees. He pulled himself up and turned.

The heart of the city was in flames.

8

TWO OF THE YMRIS WARRIORS WERE ALREADY struggling to close the main gates as he slipped back into the city. The hinges groaned, flaking rust as the slabs of oak shuddered, rising out of the ruts they had rested in for centuries. Morgon slapped them shut with a thought that nearly cost him his life. A mind, familiar, deadly, groped at the flash of power, gripped him across the distance. The dark air in front of him tore apart with a blue-white seam, so quick and strangely beautiful that he could only stand and watch it. Then his bones seemed to fly piecemeal in all directions, while his brain burned like a star. He felt stone behind him, dimly, and let his mind flow into it, grow blank, motionless. The power slid away. He gathered his bones back out of the night and realized vaguely that he was still alive. One of the warriors, his face bleeding, pulled him off the ground. The other man was dead.

"Lord—"

"I'm all right." He flung his thoughts out of the fraction of time he stood in. When the next flare of energy raked across the night, he stepped away from it, into another moment near the burning school. People were running down the streets toward the main gates: guards, armed Ymris warriors, traders, mer-

111

chants, and fishermen carrying their swords with a fierce, clumsy determination. Children stood at the edge of the school grounds, transfixed in the play of light, their faces turning red, gold, purple. Then the wall of a house behind them shattered, swept an arc of fiery stones toward them. They scattered, screaming.

Morgon gathered a memory of the fabric of energy out of his thoughts, fed it with a power he had never tapped before. He let it build through him, eating at all his thoughts and inner movements until it spat away from him, humming a high, dangerous language. It crackled luminously toward the source of power within the walls, disappeared within them, but it did not detonate. It reappeared before it struck, shooting back at Morgon with the same deadly intensity. He stared at it incredulously for a split second, then opened his mind to absorb it back. It imploded into darkness within him. It was followed, before he could even blink, by a blast of light and fire that jarred to the ground floor of his defenseless mind. It flung him flat on the cobblestones, blinded, gasping for air, while another surge of energy pounded into him. He let his awareness flow away from it, down into the cracks between the stones, into the dark, silent earth beneath them. A fragment of stone blasted to pieces near him, split his cheek, but he did not feel it. His body anchored to earth, he began to draw out of the mute, eyeless living things in it a silence that would shelter him. From moles and earthworms and tiny snakes, from the pale roots of grass, he wove a stillness into his mind. When he rose finally, the world seemed dark around him, flecked by minute, soundless flashes of light. He moved with an earthworm's blind instinct into darkness.

The mind-disguise took him safely across the grounds into the school. Fire had kindled the ancient power still locked within the stones; cold, brilliant flames swarmed across the broken walls, eating at the energy in the heart of them. Morgon, his mind still tapping the slow, languageless world beneath his feet, did not feel the dangerous wash of fire around him. A wall crumbled as he passed it; the stones scattered like coals across his shadow. He felt only a distant perturbation in the earth, as if it had shifted slightly in some point deep in its core. Then an odd, gentle touch in his mind brought his thoughts out of the earth to follow it curiously. He broke his own binding, stood blinking in the tumult of sound and fire. The unexpected touch turned imperative, and he realized that the room he had walked into was sliding into itself. He had no time to move; he shaped his mind to the fiery stones thundering toward him, became part of their bulky flow, broke with them and crashed into a fuming stillness. He dragged his shape out of them after a moment, pieced his thoughts back together. He saw Nun, then, elusive in the shimmering air, watching him. She said nothing, vanishing almost as he saw her, the fiery bowl of her pipe lingering a moment alone in the air.

The battle raging in the heart of the school was rocking the ground. He picked his way carefully toward it. From the flare of light through the jagged, beautiful windows, he knew that it was centered where it had begun: in the great circular hall that still echoed the cry of the Founder's name. He sensed suddenly, from the ease with which power was deflected away from the hall, that the battle was one-sided as yet. The Founder was toying with the wizards, using their lives as bait to lure Morgon to him. The next moment gave Morgon proof of that. He felt the Founder's mind sweep across the flames like a black beacon, searching. He touched Morgon's mind briefly: a familiar sense of dangerous, immense power yawned before him. But he did not try to hold Morgon. His mind withdrew, and Morgon heard a scream that made his blood run cold.

Aloil was being wrestled out of air into shape not

far from him. He fought the dark pull over his mind
with a desperate, furious intensity, but he could not
free himself. His shape changed again, slowly. Great
wind-twisted limbs pulled from his shoulders; his
desperate face blurred behind oak bark, a dark hollow splitting the trunk where his mouth had been.
Roots forked into the dead ground; his hair tangled
into leafless twigs. A living oak stood on the grounds
where nothing had grown for seven centuries. A
lightning bolt of power seared toward it, to sunder
it to the roots.

Morgon flung his mind open, encompassed it before
it struck the tree. He threw it back at Ghisteslwchlohm, heard one of the walls explode. Then,
reaching ruthlessly into the Founder's stronghold, he
joined their minds, as they had been joined before in
the blackness of Erlenstar Mountain.

He absorbed the power that battered across his
thoughts, letting it burn away at the bottom of his
mind. Slowly his hold strengthened, until the Founder's mind was familiar to him once more, as if it lay
behind his own eyes. He ignored experiences, impulses, the long mysterious history of the Founder's
life, concentrating only on the source of his power, to
drain it to exhaustion. He sensed the moment when
Ghisteslwchlohm realized what he was doing, in the
raw, frantic pulses of energy that nearly shook him
loose again and again, until he forgot he possessed
anything but a will and a mind at war with itself. The
power-play stopped finally. He drew deeper, ferreting
power and drawing it into himself, until the Founder
yielded something to him unexpectedly: he found
himself absorbing once more the knowledge of the
land-law of Hed.

His hold faltered, broke in a wave of fury and re-
vulsion at the irony. A chaotic flare of rage slapped
him across the ground. He groped dizzily for shelter,
but his mind could shape nothing but fire. The power
broke through him again, sent him sprawling across

burning rock. Someone pulled him off; the wizards, surrounding him, drew Ghisteslwchlohm's attention with a swift, fierce barrage that shook the inner buildings. Talies, beating at his smoldering tunic, said tersely, "Just kill him."

"No."

"You stubborn farmer from Hed, if I survive this battle I am going to study riddlery." His head turned suddenly. "There is fighting in the city. I hear death cries."

"There's an army of shape-changers. They came in the front gate while we were watching the back. I saw . . . I think I saw Yrth. Can he talk to crows?"

The wizard nodded. "Good. He must be fighting with the traders." He helped Morgon to his feet. The earth rocked beneath them, sent him sprawling to the ground on top of Morgon. He shifted to his knees. Morgon rolled wearily to his feet and stood gazing at the shell of the hall. "He's weakening in there."

"He is?"

"I'm going in."

"How?"

"I'll walk. But I have to distract his attention . . ." He thought a moment, rubbing a burn on his wrist. His mind, scanning the grounds carefully, came to rest in the ancient, ruined library, with its hundreds of books of wizardry. The half-charred pages were still charged with power: with bindings woven into their locks, with unspoken names, with the energy of the minds that had scrawled all their experiences of power onto the pages. He woke that dormant power, gathered threads of it into his mind. Its chaos nearly overwhelmed him for a moment. Speaking aloud, he spun a weird fabric of names, words, scraps of students' grotesque spells, a tumult of knowledge and power that formed strange shapes in the flaring lights. Shadows, stones that moved and spoke, eyeless birds with wings the colors of wizards' fire, shambling forms that built themselves out of the scorched earth,

he sent marching toward Ghisteslwchlohm. He woke
the wraiths of animals killed during the destruction:
bats, crows, weasels, ferrets, foxes, shadowy white
wolves; they swarmed through the night around him,
seeking their lives from him until he sent them to the
source of power. He had begun to work the roots of
dead trees out of the earth when the vanguard of his
army struck the Founder's stronghold. The onslaught
of fragments of power, clumsy, nearly harmless, yet
too complex to ignore, drew the Founder's attention.
For a moment there was another lull, during which
the wraith of a wolf whined an eerie death song.
Morgon ran noiselessly toward the hall. He was nearly
there when his own army fled back out of the hall,
running around him and over him, scattering into the
night toward the city.

Morgon flung his thoughts outward, herding the
strange, misshapen creatures he had made back into
oblivion before they terrorized Lungold. The effort of
finding bats' wraiths and shapes made out of clods of
earth drained all his attention. When he finished
finally, his mind spun again with names and words
he had had to take back into himself. He filled his
mind with fire, dissolving the remnants of power in it,
drawing from its strength and clarity. He realized
then, his heart jumping, that he stood in near-
darkness.

An eerie silence lay over the grounds. Piles of
broken wall still blazed red-hot from within, but the
night was undisturbed over the school, and he could
see stars. He stood listening, but the only fighting he
heard came from the streets. He moved again, soundlessly, entered the hall.

It was black and silent as the caves of Erlenstar
Mountain. He made one futile attempt to batter
against the darkness and gave up. On impulse, he
shaped the sword at his side and drew it. He held it
by the blade, turned the eye of the stars to the darkness. He drew fire out of the night behind him, kin-

dled it in the stars. A red light split across the dark, showed him Ghisteslwchlohm.

They looked at one another silently. The Founder seemed gaunt under the strange light, the bones pushing out under his skin. He voice sounded tired, neither threatening nor defeated. He said curiously, "You still can't see in the dark."

"I'll learn."

"You must eat darkness. . . . You are a riddle, Morgon. You track a harpist all the way across the realm to kill him because you hated his harping, but you won't kill me. You could have, while you held my mind, but you didn't. You should try now. But you won't. Why?"

"You don't want me dead. Why?"

The wizard grunted. "A riddle-game . . . I might have known. How did you survive to escape from me that day on Trader's Road? I barely escaped, myself."

Morgon was silent. He lowered the sword, let the tip rest on the ground. "What are they? The shape-changers? You are the High One. You should know."

"They were a legend here and there, a fragment of poetry, a bit of wet kelp and broken shell . . . a strange accusation made by a Ymris prince, until you left your land to find me. Now . . . they are becoming a nightmare. What do you know about them?"

"They're ancient. They can be killed. They have enormous power, but they rarely use it. They're killing traders and warriors in the streets of Lungold. I don't know what in Hel's name they are."

"What do they see in you?"

"Whatever you see, I assume. You will answer that one for me."

"Undoubtedly. The wise man knows his own name."

"Don't taunt me." The light shivered a little between his hands. "You destroyed Lungold to keep my name from me. You hid all knowledge of it, you kept watch over the College at Caithnard—"

"Spare me the history of my life."

"That's what I want from you. Master Ohm. High One. Where did you find the courage to assume the name of the High One?"

"No one else claimed it."

"Why?"

The wizard was silent a moment. "You could force answers from me," he said at length. "I could reach out, bind the minds of the Lungold wizards again, so that you could not touch me. I could escape; you could pursue me. You could escape; I could pursue you. You could kill me, which would be exhausting work, and you would lose your most powerful protector."

"Protector." He dropped the syllables like three dry bones.

"I do want you alive. Do the shape-changers? Listen to me—"

"Don't," he said wearily, "even try. I'll break your power once and for all. Oddly enough I don't care if you live or die. At least you make sense to me, which is more than I can say for the shape-changers, or . . ." He stopped. The wizard took a step toward him.

"Morgon, you have looked at the world out of my eyes and you have my power. The more you touch land-law, the more men will remember that."

"I have no intention of meddling with land-law! What do you think I am?"

"You have already started."

Morgon stared at him. He said softly, "You are wrong. I have not even begun to see out of your eyes. What in Hel's name do you see when you look at me?"

"Morgon, I am the most powerful wizard in this realm. I could fight for you."

"Something frightened you that day on Trader's Road. You need me to fight for you. What happened? Did you see the limits of your power in the reflection of a sea-green eye? They want me, and you don't want to yield me to them. But you are not so sure anymore that you can fight an army of seaweed."

Ghisteslwchlohm was silent, his face hollowed with a scarlet wash of shadows. "Can you?" he asked softly. "Who will help you? The High One?" Then Morgon felt the sudden stirring of his mind, a wave of thought encompassing the hall, the grounds, seeking out the minds of the wizards, to shape itself to them, bind them once again. Morgon raised the sword; the stars kindled a blade of light in Ghisteslwchlohm's eyes. He winced away from it, his concentration broken. Then his hands rose, snarling threads of light between his fingers. The light swept back into the stars as if they had sucked it into themselves. Darkness crouched like a live thing within the hall, barring even the moonlight. The sword grew cold in Morgon's grip. The coldness welled up his hands, into his bones, behind his eyes: a binding numbing his movements, his thoughts. His own awareness of it only strengthened it; struggling to move only bound him still. So he yielded to it, standing motionless in the night, knowing it was illusion, and that the acceptance of it, like the acceptance of the impossible, was the only way beyond it. He became its stillness, its coldness, so that when the vast power that was gathering in some dim world struck him at last, his numb, dark mind blocked it like a lump of iron.

He heard Ghisteslwchlohm's furious, incredulous curse and shook himself free of the spell. He caught the wizard's mind an instant before he vanished. A last rake of power across his mind shook his hold a little, and he realized that he was close to the edge of his own endurance. But the wizard was exhausted; even his illusion of darkness was broken. Light blazed out of the stars once more; the broken walls around them were luminous with power. Ghisteslwchlohm raised a hand, as if to work something out of the burning stones, then dropped it wearily. Morgon bound him lightly, and spoke his name.

The name took root in his heart, his thoughts. He absorbed not power, but memories, looking at the world for a few unbroken moments out of Ghisteslwchlohm's mind.

He saw the great hall around them in all its first beauty, the windows burning as with the fires of wizardry, the newly panelled walls smelling of cedar. A hundred faces gazed at him that day, a thousand years before, as he spoke the nine structures of wizardry. As he spoke, he harvested in secret, even from the mind of the most powerful of them, all knowledge and memory of three stars.

He sat in restless, uneasy power at Erlenstar Mountain. He held the minds of the land-rulers, not to control their actions, but to know them, to study the land-instincts he could never quite master. He watched a land-ruler of Herun riding alone through Isig Pass, coming closer and closer, to ask a riddle of three stars. He twisted the mind of the Morgol's horse; it reared, screaming, and the Morgol Dhairrhuwyth slid down a rocky cliff, catching desperately at boulders that spoke a deep, terrible warning as they thundered after him.

Long before that, he stood in wonder in the vast throne room at Erlenstar Mountain, where legend so old it had no beginning had placed the High One. It was empty. The raw jewels embedded in the stone walls were dim and weathered. Generations of bats clung to the ceiling. Spiders had woven webs frail as illusion around the throne. He had come to ask a question about a dreamer deep in Isig Mountain. But there was no one to ask. He brushed cobweb from the throne and sat down to puzzle over the emptiness. And as the grey light faded between the rotting doors, he began to spin illusions. . . .

He stood in another silent, beautiful place in another mountain, his mind taking the shape of a strange white stone. It was dreaming a child's dream, and he could barely breathe as he watched the fragile images flow through him. A great city stood on a windy plain, a city that sang with winds in the child's memory. The child saw it from a distance. Its mind was touching leaves, light on tree bark, grass blades; it gazed back at itself from the stolid mind of a toad; its blurred face was refracted in a fish's eyes; its wind-blown hair teased the mind of a bird building a nest. A question beat beneath the dreaming, scoring his heart with fire, as the child reached out to absorb the essence of a single leaf. He asked it finally; the child seemed to turn at his voice, its eye dark and pure and vulnerable as a falcon's eye.

"What destroyed you?"

The sky went grey as stone above the plain; the light faded from the child's face. It stood tensely, listening. The winds snarled across the plain, roiling the long grass. A sound built, too vast for hearing, unendurable. A stone ripped loose from one of the shining walls in the city, sank deep into the ground. Another cracked against a street. The sound broke, then, a deep, shuddering bass roar that held at the heart of it something he recognized, though he could no longer see nor hear, and the fish floated like a white scar on the water, and the bird had been swept out of the tree. . . .

"What is it?" he whispered, reaching through Ghisteslwchlohm's mind, through the child's mind, for the end of the dream. But as he reached, it faded into the wild water, into the dark wind, and the child's eye turned white as stone. Its face became Ghisteslwchlohm's, his eyes sunken with weariness, washed with a light pale as foam.

Morgon, struggling, bewildered, to pick up the thread of his probing, saw something flash out of the corner of his eye. His head snapped around. Stars struck his face; reeling, he lost consciousness a moment. He wrestled back into shimmering light and found himself on the rubble, swallowing blood from a cut in his mouth. He raised his head. The blade of his own sword touched his heart.

The shape-changer who stood over him had eyes as white as the child's. He smiled a greeting and a fine-honed edge of fear rippled the surface of Morgon's thoughts. Ghisteslwchlohm was staring beyond him. He turned his head and saw a woman standing among the broken stones. Her face, quiet, beautiful, was illumined briefly by a red-gold sky. Morgon heard the battle that raged behind her: of swords and spears, wizardry and weapons made of human bone scoured clean in the depths of the sea.

The woman's head bowed. "Star-Bearer." There was no mockery in her voice. "You are beginning to see far too much."

"I'm still ignorant." He swallowed again. "What do you want from me? I still need to ask that. My life or my death?"

"Both. Neither." She looked across the room at Ghisteslwchlohm. "Master Ohm. What shall we do with you? You woke the Star-Bearer to power. The wise man does not forge the blade that will kill him."

"Who are you?" the Founder whispered. "I killed the embers of a dream of three stars a thousand years ago. Where were you then?"

"Waiting."

"What are you? You have no true shape, you have no name—"

"We are named." Her voice was still clear, quiet, but Morgon heard a tone in it that was not human: as if stone or fire had spoken in a soft, rational, ageless voice. The fear stirred through him again, a dead-winter wind, spun of silk and ice. He shaped his fear into a riddle, his own voice sounding numb.

"When—when the High One fled from Erlenstar Mountain, who was it he ran from?"

A flare of power turned half her face liquid gold. She did not answer him. Ghisteslwchlohm's lips parted;

the long draw of his breath sounded clear in the turmoil, like the tide's withdrawal.

"No." He took a step back. "No."

Morgon did not realize he had moved until he felt the sudden pain over his heart. His hand reached out toward the wizard. "What is it?" he pleaded. "I can't see!" The cold metal forced him back. His need spat in fire out of the stars in the sword hilt, jolting the shape-changer's hold. The sword clanged to the floor, lay smoldering. He tried to rise. The shape-changer twisted the throat of his tunic, his burned hand poised to strike. Morgon, staring into his expressionless eyes, sent a blaze of power like a cry into his mind. The cry was lost in a cold, heaving sea. The shape-changer's hand dropped. He pulled Morgon to his feet, left him standing free and bewildered by both the power and the restraint. He flung a last, desperate tendril of thought into the wizard's mind and heard only the echo of the sea.

The battle burst through the ruined walls. Shape-changers pushed traders, exhausted warriors, the Morgol's guards into the hall. Their blades of bone and iron from lost ships thrashed mercilessly through the chaos. Morgon saw two of the guards slain before he could even move. He reached for his sword, the breath pushing hard through his chest. The shape-changer's knee slammed into his heart as he bent. He sagged to his hands and knees, whimpering for one scrap of air. The room grew very quiet around him; he saw only the rubble under his fingers. The silence eddied dizzily about him, whirling to a center. As from a dream he heard at its core the clear, fragile sound of a single harp note.

The battle noises rolled over him again. He heard his voice, dragging harshly at the air. He lifted his head, looking for the sword, and saw Lyra dodging between traders in the doorway. Something stung back of his throat. He wanted to call out, stop the battle until she left, but he had no strength. She worked her way closer to him. Her face was worn, drawn; there were half-circles like bruises under her eyes. There was dried blood on her tunic, in her hair. Scanning the battlefield, she saw him suddenly. The spear spun in her hand; she flung it toward him. He watched it come without moving, without breathing. It whistled past him, struck the shape-changer and dragged him away from Morgon's side. He grasped the sword and got to his feet unsteadily. Lyra bent, swept up the spear beneath one of the fallen guards. She balanced it, turning in a single swift, clean movement, and threw it.

It soared above the struggle, arched downward, ripping the air with a silver wake in a path to the Founder's heart. His eyes, the color of mist over the sea, could not even blink as he watched it come. Morgon's thoughts flew faster than its shadow. He saw Lyra's expression change into a stunned, weary horror as she realized the wizard was bound, helpless against her; there was no skill, no honor, not even choice in her death-giving. Morgon wanted to shout, snapping the spear with his voice to rescue a dream of truth hidden behind a child's eye, a wizard's eye. His hands moved instead, pulling the harp at his back out of the air. He played it as he shaped it: the last low string whose reverberations set his own sword belling in anguish and shattered every other weapon inside and out of the hall.

Silence settled like old dust over the room. Ymris warriors were staring in disbelief at the odd bits of metal in their hands. Lyra was still watching the air where the spear had splintered apart, two feet from Ghisteslwchlohm. She turned slowly, making the only movement in the hall. Morgon met her eyes; she seemed suddenly so tired she could barely stand. The handful of guard left alive were looking at Morgon, their faces haunted, desperate. The shape-changers were very still. Their shapes seemed uncertain, suddenly, as if at his next movement they would flow into a tide of nothingness. Even the woman he knew as Eriel was still, watching him, waiting.

He caught a glimpse then of the fearsome power they saw in him, lying in some misty region beyond his awareness. The depths of his ignorance appalled him. He turned the harp aimlessly in his hands, holding the shape-changers trapped and having absolutely no idea what to do with them. At the slight uncertain movement, the expression in Eriel's eyes turned to simple amazement.

She moved forward quickly; to take the harp, to kill him with his own sword, to turn his mind, like Ghisteslwchlohm's, vague as the sea, he could only guess. He picked up the sword and stepped back. A hand touched his shoulder, stopped him.

Raederle stood beside him. Her face was pure white within her fiery hair, as if it had been shaped, like the Earth-Masters' children, out of stone. She held him lightly, but she was not seeing him. She said softly to Eriel, "You will not touch him."

The dark eyes held hers curiously. "Ylon's child. Have you made your choice?" She moved again, and Morgon felt the vast, leashed power in Raederle's mind strain free. For one moment, he saw the shape that Eriel had taken begin to fray away from her, reveal something incredibly ancient, wild, like the dark heart of earth or fire. He stood gripped in wonder, his face ashen, knowing he could not move even if the thing Raederle was forcing into shape was his own death.

Then a shout slapped across his mind, jarred him out of his fascination. He stared dizzily across the room. The ancient wizard he had seen at the gates of the city caught his eyes, held them with his own strange light-seared gaze.

The silent shout snapped through him again: *Run!* He did not move. He would not leave Raederle, but he could not help her; he felt incapable even of thought. Then a power gripped his exhausted mind, wrenched him out of shape. He cried out, a fierce, piercing, hawk's protest. The power held him, flung him like a dark, wild wind out of the burning School of Wizards, out of the embattled city into the vast, pathless wasteland of the night.

9

THE SHAPE-CHANGERS PURSUED HIM ACROSS THE backlands. The first night, he bolted across the sky in hawk-shape, the fiery city behind him growing smaller and smaller in the darkness. He flew northward instinctively, away from the kingdoms, marking his path by the smell of water beneath him. By dawn he felt safe. He dropped downward toward the lake shore. Birds drifting to the gentle morning tide swarmed up at his approach. He felt strands of their minds like a network. He broke through it, arching back up in midair. They drove him across the lake into the trees, where he dropped again suddenly, plummeting through air and light like a dark fist, until he touched the ground and vanished. Miles away to the north, he appeared again, kneeling beside the channel of water between two lakes, retching with exhaustion. He sagged down on the bank beside the water. After a while he moved again, dropped his face in the current and drank.

They found him again at dusk. He had caught fish and eaten for the first time in two days. The changeless afternoon light, the river's monotonous voice had lulled him to sleep. He woke abruptly at a squirrel's chattering, and saw high in the blue-grey air a great flock of wheeling birds. Rolling into the water, he

changed shape. The current flung him from one relentless sluice of water to another, spun him back
downstream into still pools, where hungry water birds
dove at him. He fought his way upstream, seeing
nothing but a constant, darkening blur that shrugged
him from side to side and roared whenever he broke
the surface. Finally he foundered into still water. It
deepened as he swam. He dove toward the bottom to
rest, but the water grew dark and still, so deep he had
to come up to breathe before he found the bottom. He
swam slowly near the surface, watching moths flutter
in the moonlight. He drifted until the lake bottom
angled upward, and he found weeds to hide in. He
did not move until morning.

Then a tiny fish dove into the sunlight near him,
snapped at an insect. Rings of water broke above him.
He rose out of the weeds; the water burned around
him with the morning sun as he changed shape. He
waded out of the lake, stood listening to the silence.

It seemed to roar soundlessly out of lands beyond
the known world. The soft morning wind seemed
alien, speaking a language he had never learned. He
remembered the wild, ancient voices of Wind Plain
that had echoed across Ymris with a thousand names
and memories. But the voices of the backlands seemed
even older, a rootwork of winds that held nothing he
could comprehend except their emptiness. He stood
for a long time, breathing their loneliness until he felt
them begin to hollow him into something as nameless
as themselves.

He whispered Raederle's name then. He turned
blindly, his thoughts tangling into a hard knot of fear.
He wondered if she were still alive, if anyone were
left alive in Lungold. He wondered if he should
return to the city. His fists pounded rhythmically
agaist tree bark as he thought of her. The tree
shivered with his uncertainty; a crow startled out of
it, squawking. He raised his head suddenly, stood still
as an animal, scenting. The placid lake waters began

to stir, boil shapes out of their depths. The blood hammered through him. He opened his mind to the minds of the backland. Several miles away he joined a vast herd of elk moving northward toward the Thul.

He stayed with them as they grazed. He decided to break away at the Thul, follow it eastward until the shape-changers lost him, and then double back to Lungold. Two days later, when the slow herd began gathering at the river, he roamed away from it, eastward along the banks. But part of the herd followed him. He changed shape again, desperately, began flying south in the night. But shapes rose, swirling out of the darkness, beat him northward across the Thul, northward toward White Lady Lake, northward, he began to realize, toward Erlenstar Mountain.

The realization filled him with both fury and terror. On the shores of White Lady Lake, he turned to fight. He waited for them in his own shape, the stars in his sword-hilt flaring a blood-red signal to them across the backlands. But nothing answered his challenge. The hot afternoon was motionless; the waters of the huge lake lay still as beaten silver. Groping, he could not even touch their minds. Finally, as the waning sun drew shadows after it across the lake, he began to breathe a tentative freedom. He sheathed his sword, shrugged himself into wolf-shape. And then he saw them, motionless as air, ranged across his path, shaping themselves out of the blur of light and darkness.

He sparked a flame from the dying sun in his sword hilt, let it burn down the blade. Then he frayed himself into shadow, filled his mind with darkness. He attacked to kill, yet in his exhaustion and hopelessness, he knew he was half-goading them to kill him. He killed two shape-changers before he realized that in some terrible mockery, they had permitted it. They would not fight; they would not let him go south. He changed back into wolf-shape, ran northward along the lake shore into the trees. A great herd of wolves massed behind him. He turned again, flung himself at them. They grappled with him, snarling, snapping until he realized, as he rolled over and over on the bracken with a great wolf whose teeth were locked on his forearm, that it was real. He shook it away from him with a shudder of energy, burned a circle of light around himself. They milled around him restlessly in the dusk, not sure what he was, smelling blood from his torn shoulder. Looking at them, he wanted to laugh suddenly at his mistake. But something far more bitter than laughter spilled into his throat. For a while he could not think. He could only watch a starless night flowing across the wastes and smell the musk of a hundred wolves as they circled him. Then, with a vague idea of attacking the shape-changers, he squatted, holding wolves' eyes, drawing their minds under his control. But something broke his binding. The wolves faded away into the night, leaving him alone. He could not fly; his arm was stiffening, burning. The smell of loneliness from the cold, darkening water overwhelmed him. He let the fire around him go out. Trapped between the shape-changers and the black horror of Erlenstar Mountain, he could not move. He stood shivering in the dark wind, while the night built around him, memory by memory.

The light wing-brush of another mind touched his mind, and then his heart. He found he could move again, as though a spell had been broken. The voice of the wind changed; it filled the black night from every direction with the whisper of Raederle's name.

His awareness of her lasted only a moment. But he felt, reaching down to touch the bracken into flame, that she might be anywhere and everywhere around him, the great tree rising beside him, the fire sparking up from dead leaves to warm his face. He ripped the sleeves off his tunic, washed his arm and bound it. He lay beside the fire, gazing into the heart of it, trying to comprehend the shape-changers and their intentions. He realized suddenly that tears were burning

down his face, because Raederle was alive, because
she was with him. He reached out, buried the fire
under a handful of earth. He hid himself within an
illusion of darkness and began to move again, northward, following the vast shore of White Lady Lake.

He did not meet the shape-changers again until he
reached the raging white waters of the Cwill River, as
it broke away from the northernmost tip of the lake.
From there, he could see the back of Isig Pass, the
distant rolling foothills and bare peaks of Isig Mountain and Erlenstar Mountain. He made another desperate bid for freedom then. He dropped into the
wild current of the Cwill, let it whirl him, now as a
fish, now a dead branch, through deep, churning
waters, down rapids and thundering falls until he lost
all sense of time, direction, light. The current jarred
him over endless rapids before it loosed him finally
in a slow, green pool. He spun awhile, a piece of
water-soaked wood, aware of nothing but a fibrous
darkness. The gentle current edged him toward the
shore into a snarl of dead leaves and branches. He
pulled himself onto the snag finally, a wet, bedraggled
muskrat, and picked his way across the branches onto
the shore.

He changed shape again in the shadows. He had
not gone as far east as he had thought. Erlenstar
Mountain, flanked with evening shadows, stood enormous and still in the distance. But he was closer to
Isig, he knew; if he could reach it safely, he could
hide himself interminably in its maze of underground
passages. He waited until nightfall to move again.
Then, in the shape of a bear, he lumbered off into the
dark toward the pattern of stars above Isig Mountain.

He followed the stars until they faded at dawn; and
then, without realizing it, he began to alter his path.
Trees thickened around him, hiding his view of the
mountain; thick patches of scrub and bramble forced
him to veer again and again. The land sloped downward sharply; he followed a dry stream bed through a

ravine, thinking he was going north, until the stream
bed rose up to level ground and he found himself
facing Erlenstar Mountain. He angled eastward again.
The trees clustered around him, murmuring in the
wind; the underbrush thickened, crossing his path,
imperceptibly changing his direction until, shambling
across a shallow river, he saw Erlenstar Mountain
again in a break between the trees ahead of him.

He stopped in the middle of the river. The sun
hung suspended far to the west, crackling in the sky
like a torch. He felt hot, dusty, and hungry within the
shaggy bear pelt. He heard bees droning and scented
the air for honey. A fish flickered past him in the
shallow water; he slapped at it and missed. Then
something rumbling beneath the bear-brain sharpened
into language. He reared in the water, his head weaving from side to side, his muzzle wrinkled, as if he
could smell the shapes that had been forming around
him, pushing him away from Isig.

He felt something build in him and loosed it: a
deep, grumbling roar that shattered the silence and
bellowed back at him from hills and stone peaks.
Then, in hawk-shape, he burned a golden path upward high into the sky until the backlands stretched
endlessly beneath him, and he shot towards Isig
Mountain.

The shape-changers melted out of the trees, flew
after him. For a while he raced ahead of them in a
blinding surge of speed toward the distant green
mountain. But as the sun set, they began to catch up
with him. They were of a nameless shape. Their
wings gathered gold and red from the sunset; their
eyes and talons were of flame. Their sharp beaks
were bone-white. They surrounded him, dove at him,
snapping and tearing, until his wings grew ragged and
his breast was flecked with blood. He faltered in the
air; they flung themselves at him, blinding him with
their wings, until he gave one piercing, despairing cry
and turned away from Isig.

All night he flew among their burning eyes. At dawn, he saw the face of Erlenstar Mountain rising up before him. He took his own shape then, in midair, and simply fell, the air battering out of him, the forests whirling up to meet him. Something cracked across his mind before he reached the ground. He spun into darkness.

He woke in total darkness. It smelled of wet stone. Far away, he could hear a faint perpetual trickle of water. He recognized it suddenly, and his hands clenched. He lay on his back, on cold, bare stone. Every bone in his body ached, and his skin was scored with claw marks. The mountain's silence sat like a nightmare on his chest. His muscles tensed; he listened, feverish, blind, expecting a voice that did not come, while memories like huge, bulky animals paced back and forth across him.

He began to breathe the darkness into his mind; his body seemed to fray into it. He sat up, panicked, his eyes wide, straining into nothing. From somewhere in the starless night of his thoughts, he pulled a memory of light and fire. He ignited it in his palm, nursed it until he could see the vast hollow of stone rising about him; the prison where he had spent the most unendurable year of his life.

His lips parted. A word stuck like a jewel in his throat. The flame glittered back at him endlessly, off walls of ice and fire, of gold, of sky-blue streaked with wind-swept silver like the night of the backlands rimed with a million stars. The inner mountain was of the stone of the Earth-Masters' cities, and he could see the frozen wrinkles where blocks of stone had been hewn free.

He stood up slowly. His face stared back at him out of wedges and facets of jewellike color. The chamber was enormous; he nursed the flame from its reflection until it shot higher than his head, but still he could see nothing but a vaulting of darkness, flickering vaguely with a network of pure gold.

The water, whose endless, changeless voice he had heard, had wept a diamond-white groove into a sheer wall of stone as it trickled downward into water. He shifted the flame; it billowed across a lake so still it seemed carved of darkness. The shores of the immense lake were of solid stone; the far wall curving around it was pure as hoarfrost.

He knelt, touched the water. Rings melted into rings slowly across its dark face. He thought suddenly of the spiralling circles of Wind Tower. His throat contracted, fiery with thirst, and he bent over the lake, scooping water with his free hand. He swallowed a mouthful and gagged. It was acrid with minerals.

"Morgon."

Every muscle in his body locked. He swung on his haunches, met Ghisteslwchlohm's eyes.

They were haunted, restless with a power not his own. That much Morgon saw before the darkness swallowed the flame in his hand, leaving him blind again.

"So," he whispered, "the Founder himself is bound." He stood up noiselessly, trying, in the same movement, to step into the fragment of dawn beyond the splintered doors in the High One's throne room. He stepped instead over the edge of a chasm. He lost his balance, crying out, and fell into nothingness. He landed on the lake shore, clinging to the stones at Ghisteslwchlohm's feet.

He dropped his face against his forearm, trying to think. He caught at the mind of a bat tucked in its secret corner, but the wizard gripped him before he could change shape.

"There is no escape." The voice had changed; it was slow, soft, as if he were listening beneath it for another voice, or a distant, uneasy rhythm of tides. "Star-Bearer, you will use no power. You will do nothing but wait."

"Wait," he whispered. "For what? For death?" He stopped, the word flickering back and forth between two meanings in his mind. "There is no harping this time to keep me alive." He lifted his head, his eyes straining again at the blackness. "Or are you expecting the High One? You can wait until I turn to stone here like the Earth-Masters' children before the High One shows any interest in me."

"I doubt that."

"You. You hardly exist. You no longer have the ability to doubt. Even the wraiths of An have more will than you do. I can't even tell if you're dead or alive still, deep in you, the way the wizards lived, somehow, beneath your power." His voice dropped a little. "I could fight for you. I would do even that for freedom."

The hand left his arm. He groped into the strange, sea-filled mind, to find the name it held. It eluded him. He struggled through swells and heaving tides, until the wizard's mind heaved him back on the shore of his own awareness. He was gasping, as if he had forgotten to breathe. He heard the wizard's voice finally, withdrawing into the dark.

"For you, there is no word for freedom."

He slept a little, then, trying to regain strength. He dreamed of water. His raging thirst woke him; he felt for the water, tried to drink it again. He spat it out before he swallowed it, knelt racked with coughing. He drifted finally back into a feverish sleep and dreamed again of water. He felt himself falling into it, drawing a cool darkness around himself, moving deeper and deeper into its stillness. He breathed in water and woke himself, panicked, drowning. Hands dragged him out of the lake, left him retching bitter water on the shore.

The water cleared his head a little. He lay quietly, staring into the darkness, wondering, if he let it fill his mind, whether it would drown him like water. He let it seep slowly into his thoughts until the memories of a long year's night overwhelmed him and he panicked again, igniting the air with fire. He saw Ghisteslwchlohm's face briefly; then the wizard's hand slapped at his flame and it broke into pieces like glass.

He whispered, "For every doorless tower there is a riddle to open the door. You taught me that."

"There is one door and one riddle here."

"Death. You don't believe that. Otherwise you would have let me drown. If the High One isn't interested in my life or my death, what will you do then?"

"Wait."

"Wait." He shifted restlessly, his thoughts speeding feverishly towards some answer. "The shape-changers have been waiting for thousands of years. You named them, the instant before they bound you. What did you see? What could be strong enough to overpower an Earth-Master? Someone who takes the power and law of his existence from every living thing, from earth, fire, water, from wind. . . . The High One was driven out of Erlenstar Mountain by the shape-changers. And you came then and found an empty throne where legend had placed the High One. So you became the High One, playing a game of power while you waited for someone the stone children knew only as the Star-Bearer. You kept watch on places of knowledge and power, gathering the wizards at Lungold, teaching at Caithnard. And one day the son of a Prince of Hed came to Caithnard with the smell of cowdung on his boots and a question on his face. But that wasn't enough. You're still waiting. The shape-changers are still waiting. For the High One. You are using me for bait, but he could have found me in here long before this, if he had been interested."

"He will come."

"I doubt that. He allowed you to deceive the realm for centuries. He is not interested in the welfare of men or wizards in the realm. He let you strip me of the land-rule, for which I should have killed you. He is not interested in me . . ." He was silent again, his eyes on the expressionless face of darkness. He said, listening to the silence that gathered and froze in every drop of liquid stone, "What could be powerful enough to destroy the Earth-Masters' cities? To force the High One himself into hiding? What is as powerful as an Earth-Master?" He was silent again. Then an answer like a glint of fire burning itself into ash moved in the depths of his mind.

He sat up. The air seemed suddenly thin, fiery; he found it hard to breathe. "The shape-changers . . ." The blade of dryness was back in his throat. He raised his hands to his eyes, gathering darkness to stare into. Voices whispered out of his memory, out of the stones around him: *The war is not finished, only silenced for the regathering. . . . Those from the sea. Edolen. Sec. They destroyed us so we could not live on earth any more; we could not master it. . . .* The voices of the Earth-Masters' dead, the children. His hands dropped heavily on the stone floor, but still the darkness pushed against his eyes. He saw the child turn from the leaf it touched in its dreaming, look across a plain, its body tense, waiting. "They could touch a leaf, a mountain, a seed, and know it, become it. That's what Raederle saw, the power in them she loved. Yet they killed each other, buried their children beneath a mountain to die. They knew all the languages of the earth, all the laws of its shapes and movement. What happened to them? Did they stumble into the shape of something that had no law but power?" His voice was whispering away from him as if out of a dream. "What shape?"

He fell silent abruptly. He was shivering, yet sweating. The smell of water pulled at him mercilessly. He reached out to it again, his throat tormented with thirst. His hands halted before they broke the surface. Raederle's face, dreamlike in its beauty, looked back at him from the still water between his hands. Her long hair flowed away from her face like the sun's fire. He forgot his thirst. He knelt motionless for a long time, gazing down at it, not knowing if it was real or if he had fashioned it out of longing, and not caring.

Then a hand struck at it, shattering the image, sending rings of movement shivering to the far edges of the lake.

A murderous, uncontrollable fury swept Morgon to his feet. He wanted to kill Ghisteslwchlohm with his hands, but he could not even see the wizard. A power battered him away again and again. He scarcely felt pain; shapes were reeling faster than language in his mind. He discarded them, searching for the one shape powerful enough to contain his rage. He felt his body fray into shapelessness; a sound filled his mind, deep, harsh, wild, the voices out of the farthest reaches of the backlands. But they were no longer empty. Something shuddered through him, flinging off a light snapping through the air. He felt thoughts groping into his mind, but his own thoughts held no language except a sound like a vibrant, untuned harp string. He felt the fury in him expand, shape itself to all the hollows and forms of the stone chamber. He flung the wizard across the cavern, held him like a leaf before the wind, splayed against the stones.

Then he realized what shape he had taken.

He fell back into his own shape, the wild energy in him suddenly gone. He knelt on the stones, trembling, half-sobbing in fear and amazement. He heard the wizard stumble away from the wall, breathing haltingly, as if his ribs were cracked. As he moved across the cavern, Morgon heard voices all around him, speaking various complex languages of the earth.

He heard the whispering of fire, the shiver of leaves, the howl of a wolf in the lonely, moonlit backlands, the dry riddling of corn leaves. Then, far away, he heard a sound, as if the mountain itself had sighed. He felt the stone shift slightly under him. A sea bird cried harshly. Someone with a hand of tree bark and light flung Morgon onto his back.

He whispered bitterly, feeling the starred sword wrenched from his side, "One riddle and one door."

But, though he waited in the eye of darkness for

the sword to fall, nothing touched him. He was caught suddenly, breathless, in their tension of waiting. Then Raederle's voice, raised in a Great Shout, shook stones loose from the ceiling and jarred him out of his waiting. "Morgon!"

The sword hummed wildly with the aftermath of the shout. Morgon heard it bounce against the stones. He shouted Raederle's name involuntarily, in horror, and the floor lurched under him again, shrugging him toward the lake. The sword slid after him. It was still vibrating, a strange high note that stilled as Morgon caught it and sheathed it. There was a sound as if a crystal in one of the walls had cracked.

It sang as it broke: a low, tuned note that shattered its own core. Other crystals began to hum; the ground floor of the mountain rumbled. The great slabs of ceiling stone ground themselves together. Dust and rubble hissed down; half-formed crystals snapped and pounded to pieces on the floor. Languages of bats, dolphins, bees brushed through the chamber. A tension snaked through the air, and Morgon heard Raederle scream. Sobbing a curse, he pulled himself to his feet. The floor grumbled beneath him, then roared. One side of it lifted, fell ponderously onto the other. It flung him into the lake. The whole lake basin, a huge, round bowl carved into solid stone, began to tilt.

He was buried for a few moments in a wave of black water. When he surfaced again, he heard a sound as if the mountain itself, torn apart at its roots, had groaned.

A wind blasted into the stone chamber. It blinded Morgon, drove his own cry back into his throat. It whirled the lake into a black vortex that dragged him down into it. He heard, before he was engulfed, something that was either the ring of blood in his ears or a note like a fine-tuned string at the core of the deep wind's voice.

The water spat him back up. The basin had tilted farther, pouring him out with the water toward the sheer wall at the far side. He snatched a breath, dove under water, trying to swim against the wave. But it hurled him back, heaved him at solid stone. As he sensed the wall blur up before him, it split open. The wave poured through the crack, dragging him with it. Through the thunder of water, he heard the final reverberations of the mountain burying its own heart.

The lake water dragged him through the jagged split, poured over a lip of stone into a roiling stream. He tried to pull himself out, catching at ledges, at walls rough with jewels, but the wind was still with him, pushing him back into the water, driving the water before it. The stream flooded into another; a whirlpool dragged him under a ledge of stone into another river. The river cast him finally out of the mountain, dragged him down foaming rapids, and threw him, half-drowned, his veins full of bitter water, into the Ose.

He pulled himself ashore finally, lay hugging the sunlit ground. The wild winds still pounded at him; the great pines were groaning as they bent. He coughed up the bitter water he had swallowed. When he moved finally to drink the sweet waters of the Ose, the wind nearly flung him back in. He raised his head, looked at the mountain. A portion of its side had been sucked in; trees lay uprooted, splintered in the shift of stone and earth. All down the pass, as far as he could see, the wind raged, bending trees to their breaking point.

He tried to stand, but he had no strength left. The wind seemed to be hounding him out of his own shape. He reached out; his hands closed on huge roots. He felt, as the tree shivered in his hold, the core of its great strength.

Clinging to it, he pulled himself up by its knots and boles. Then he stepped away from it and lifted his arms as if to enclose the wind.

Branches grew from his hands, his hair. His thoughts tangled like roots in the ground. He strained upward. Pitch ran like tears down his bark. His name formed his core; ring upon ring of silence built around it. His face rose high above the forests. Gripped to earth, bending to the wind's fury, he disappeared within himself, behind the hard, wind-scrolled shield of his experiences.

10

E DWINDLED BACK INTO HIS OWN SHAPE ON A rainy, blustery autumn day. He stood in the cold winds, blinking rain out of his eyes, trying to remember a long, wordless passage of time. The Ose, grey as a knife blade, shivered past him; the stone peaks of the pass were half-buried under heavy cloud. The trees around him clung deeply to the earth, engrossed in their own existences. They pulled at him again. His mind slid past their tough wet bark, back into a slow peace around which tree rings formed and hardened. But a wind vibrated through his memories, shook a mountain down around him, throwing him back into water, back into the rain. He moved reluctantly, breaking a binding with the earth, and turned toward Erlenstar Mountain. He saw the scar in its side under a blur of mist and the dark water still swirling out of it to join the Ose.

He gazed at it a long time, piecing together fragments of a dark, troubling dream. The implications of it woke him completely; he began to shiver in the driving rain. He scented through the afternoon with his mind. He found no one—trapper, wizard, shapechanger—in the pass. A windblown crow sailed past him on an updraft; he caught eagerly at its mind. But it did not know his language. He loosed it. The wild, sonorous winds boomed hollowly through the peaks; the trees roared around him, smelling of winter. He turned finally, hunched in the wind, to follow the flow of the Ose back into the world.

But he stood still after a step, watching the water rush away from him toward Isig and Osterland and the northern trade-ports of the realm. His own power held him motionless. There was no place anywhere in the realm for a man who unbound land-law and shaped wind. The river echoed the voices he had heard, speaking languages not even the wizards could understand. He thought of the dark, blank face of wind that was the High One, who would give him nothing except his life.

"For what?" he whispered. He wanted to shout the words suddenly at the battered, expressionless face of Erlenstar Mountain. The wind would simply swallow his cry. He took another step down the river toward Harte, where he would find shelter, warmth, comfort from Danan Isig. But the king could give him no answers. He was trapped by the past, the pawn of an ancient war he was finally beginning to understand. The vague longing in him to explore his own strange, unpredictable power frightened him. He stood at the river's edge for a long time, until the mists along the peaks began to darken and a shadow formed across the face of Erlenstar Mountain. Finally, he turned away from it, wandered through the rain and icy mists toward the mountains bordering the northern wastes.

He kept his own shape as he crossed them, though the rains in the high peaks turned to sleet sometimes and the rocks under his hands as he climbed were like ice. His life hung in a precarious balance the first few days, though he hardly realized it. He found himself eating without remembering how he had killed, or awake at dawn in a dry cave without remembering how he had found it. Gradually, as he realized his disinclination to use power, he gave some thought to

survival. He killed wild mountain sheep, dragged them
into a cave and skinned them, living on the meat while
the pelts dried and weathered. He sharpened a rib,
prodded holes in the pelts and laced them together
with strips of cloth from his tunic. He made a great
shaggy hooded cloak and lined his boots with fur.
When they were finished, he put them on and moved
again, down the north face of the pass into the wastes.

There was little rain in the wasteland, only the driving, biting winds, and frost that turned the flat, monotonous land into fire at sunrise. He moved like a
wraith, killing when he was hungry, sleeping in the
open, for he rarely felt the cold, as if his body frayed
without his knowledge into the winds. One day he
realized he was no longer moving across the arc of the
sun; he had turned east, wandering toward the morning. In the distance, he could see a cluster of foothills,
with Grim Mountain jutting out of them, a harsh,
blue-gray peak. But it was so far away that he scarcely
put a name to it. He walked into mid-autumn, hearing nothing but the winds. One night as he sat before
his fire, vaguely feeling the winds urge against his
shape, he looked down and saw the starred harp in his
hands.

He could not remember reaching back for it. He
gazed at it, watching the silent run of fire down the
strings. He shifted after a while and positioned it.
His fingers moved patternlessly, almost inaudibly over
the strings, following the rough, wild singing of the
winds.

He felt no more compulsion to move. He stayed at
that isolated point in the wastes, which was no more
than a few stones, a twisted shrub, a crack in the hard
earth where a stream surfaced for a few feet, then
vanished again underground. He left the place only to
hunt; he always found his way back to it, as if to the
echo of his own harping. He harped with the winds
that blew from dawn until night, sometimes with only
one high string, as he heard the lean, tense, wailing

east wind; sometimes with all strings, the low note thrumming back at the boom of the north wind. Sometimes, looking up, he would see a snow hare listening or catch the startled glance of a white falcon's eyes. But as the autumn deepened, animals grew rare, seeking the mountains for food and shelter. So he harped alone, a strange, furred, nameless animal with no voice but one strung between his hands. His body was honed to the wind's harshness; his mind lay dormant like the wastes. How long he would have stayed there, he never knew, for glancing up one night at a shift of wind across his fire, he found Raederle.

She was cloaked in rich silvery furs; her hair, blown out of her hood, streaked the dark like fire. He sat still, his hands stopped on the harp strings. She knelt down beside his fire, and he saw her face more clearly, weary, winter-pale, sculpted to a fine, changeless beauty. He wondered if she were a dream, like the face he had seen between his hands in the dark lake water. Then he saw that she was shivering badly. She took her gloves off, drew his windblown fire to a still bright blaze with her hands. Slowly he realized how long it had been since they had spoken.

"Lungold," he whispered. The word seemed meaningless in the tumult of the wastes. But she had journeyed out of the world to find him here. He reached through the fire, laid his hand against her face. She gazed at him mutely as he sat back again. She drew her knees up, huddled in her furs against the wind.

"I heard your harping," she said. He touched the strings soundlessly, remembering.

"I promised you I would harp." His voice was husky with disuse. He added curiously, "Where have you been? You followed me across the backlands; you were with me in Erlenstar Mountain. Then you vanished."

She stared at him again; he wondered if she were going to answer. "I didn't vanish. You did." Her voice

was suddenly tremulous. "Off the face of the realm.
The wizards have been searching everywhere for you.
So have the shape—the shape-changers. So have I. I
thought maybe you were dead. But here you are,
harping in this wind that could kill and you aren't even
cold."

He was silent. The harp that had sung with the
winds felt suddenly chilled under his hands. He set it
on the ground beside him. "How did you find me?"

"I searched. In every shape I could think of. I
thought maybe you were with the vesta. So I went to
Har and asked him to teach me the vesta-shape. He
started to, but when he touched my mind, he stopped
and told me he did not think he had to teach me. So,
I had to explain that to him. Then he made me tell
him everything that had happened in Erlenstar Mountain. He said nothing, except that you must be found.
Finally, he took me across Grim Mountain to the vesta
herds. And while I travelled with them, I began to
hear your harping on the edge of my mind, on the
edge of the winds. . . . Morgon, if I can find you, so
can others. Did you come out here to learn to harp?
Or did you just run?"

"I just ran."

"Well, are you—are you planning to come back?"

"For what?"

She was silent. The fire flickered wildly in front of
her, weaving itself into the wind. She stilled it again,
her eyes never leaving his face. She moved abruptly to
his side and held him tightly, her face against the
shaggy fur at his shoulder.

"I could learn to live in the wastes, I guess," she
whispered. "It's so cold here, and nothing grows . . .
but the winds and your harping are beautiful."

His head bowed. He put his arm around her, drawing her hood back so that he could feel her cheek
against his. Something touched his heart, an ache of
cold that he finally felt, or a painful stirring of
warmth.

"You heard the voices of the shape-changers in Erlenstar Mountain," he said haltingly. "You know what they are. They know all languages. They are Earth-Masters, still at war, after thousands of years, with the High One. And I am bait for their traps. That's why they never kill me. They want him. If they destroy him, they will destroy the realm. If they cannot find me, perhaps they will not find him." She started to speak, but he went on, his voice thawing, harsher, "You know what I did in that mountain. I was angry enough to murder, and I shaped myself into wind to do it. There is no place in the realm for anyone of such power. What will I do with it? I'm the Star-Bearer. A promise made by the dead to fight a war older than the names of the kingdoms. I was born with power that leaves me nameless in my own world ... and with all the terrible longing to use it."

"So you came here to the wastes, where you would have no reason to use it."

"Yes."

She slid a hand beneath his hood, her fingers brushing his brow and his scarred cheekbone. "Morgon," she said softly, "I think if you wanted to use it, you would. If you found a reason. You gave me a reason to use my own power, at Lungold and across the backlands. I love you, and I will fight for you. Or sit here with you in the wastes until you drift into snow. If the need of the land-rulers, all those who love you, can't stir you from this place, what can? What hurt you in the dark at Erlenstar Mountain?"

He was silent. The winds roared out of the night, a vast chaos converging upon a single point of light. They had no faces, no language he could understand. He whispered, gazing at them, "The High One cannot speak my name, any more than a slab of granite can. We are bound in some way, I know. He values my life, but he does not even know what it is. I am the Star-Bearer. He will give me my life. But nothing else. No hope, no justice, no compassion. Those words belong to men. Here in the wastes, I am threatening no one. I am keeping myself safe, the High One safe, and the realm untroubled by a power too dangerous to use."

"The realm is troubled. The land-rulers put more hope in you than they do in the High One. You they can talk to."

"If I made myself into a weapon for Earth-Masters to battle with, not even you would recognize me."

"Maybe. You told me a riddle once, when I was afraid of my own power. About the Herun woman Arya, who brought a dark, frightening animal she could not name into her house. You never told me how it ended."

He stirred a little. "She died of fear."

"And the animal? What was it?"

"No one knew. It wailed for seven days and seven nights at her grave, in a voice so full of love and grief that no one who heard it could sleep or eat. And then it died, too."

She lifted her head, her lips parted, and he remembered a moment out of a dead past: he sat in a small stone chamber at Caithnard, studying riddles and feeling his heart twist with joy and terror and sorrow to their unexpected turnings. He added, "It has nothing to do with me."

"I suppose not. You would know."

He was silent again. He shifted so that her head lay in the crook of his shoulder, and his arms circled her. He laid his cheek against his hair. "I'm tired," he said simply. "I have answered too many riddles. The Earth-Masters began a war before history, a war that killed their own children. If I could fight them, I would, for the sake of the realm; but I think I would only kill myself and the High One. So I'm doing the only thing that makes any sense to me. Nothing."

She did not answer for a long time. He held her quietly, watching the fire spark a silvery wash across her cloak. She said slowly, "Morgon, there is one more riddle maybe you should answer. You stripped all illusions from Ghisteslwchholm; you named the shape-changers; you woke the High One out of his silence. But there is one more thing you have not named, and it will not die . . ." Her voice shook into silence. He felt suddenly, through all the bulky fur between them, the beat of her heart.

"What?" The word was a whisper she could not have heard, but she answered him.

"In Lungold, I talked to Yrth in crow-shape. So I did not know then that he is blind. I went to Isig, searching for you, and I found him there. His eyes are the color of water burned by light. He told me that Ghisteslwchlohm had blinded him during the destruction of Lungold. And I didn't question that. He is a big, gentle, ancient man, and Danan's grandchildren followed him all over the mountain while he was searching for you among the stones and trees. One evening Bere brought a harp he had made to the hall and asked Yrth to play it. He laughed a little and said that though he had been known once as the Harpist of Lungold, he hadn't touched a harp for seven centuries. But he played a little. . . . And, Morgon, I knew that harping. It was the same awkward, tentative harping that haunted you down Trader's Road and drew you into Ghisteslwchlohm's power."

He lifted her face between his hands. He was feeling the wind suddenly, scoring all his bones with rime. "What are you telling me?"

"I don't know. But how many blind harpists who cannot harp can there be in the world?"

He took a breath of wind; it burned through him like cold fire. "He's dead."

"Then he's challenging you out of his grave. Yrth harped to me that night so that I would carry the riddle of his harping to you, wherever in the realm you were."

"Are you sure?"

"No. But I know that he wants to find you. And that

if he was a harpist named Deth who travelled with
you, as Yrth did, down Trader's Road, then he spun
riddles so secretly, so skillfully, that he blinded even
Ghisteslwchlohm. And even you—the Riddle-Master
of Hed. I think maybe you should name him. Because
he is playing his own silent, deadly game, and he may
be the only one in this realm who knows exactly what
he is doing."

"Who in Hel's name is he?" He was shivering suddenly, uncontrollably. "Deth took the Black of Mastery at Caithnard. He was a riddler. He knew my
name before I did. I suspected once that he might be
a Lungold wizard. I asked him."

"What did he say?"

"He said he was the High One's harpist. So I asked
him what he was doing in Isig while Yrth made my
harp, a hundred years before he was born. He told me
to trust him. Beyond logic, beyond reason, beyond
hope. And then he betrayed me." He drew her against
him, but the wind ran between them like a knife. "It's
cold. It was never this cold before."

"What are you going to do?"

"What does he want? Is he an Earth-Master, playing his own solitary game for power? Does he want me
alive or dead? Does he want the High One alive or
dead?"

"I don't know. You're the riddler. He's challenging
you. Ask him."

He was silent, remembering the harpist on Trader's
Road who had drawn him without a word, with only
a halting, crippled harping out of the night into Ghisteslwchlohm's hands. He whispered, "He knows me
too well. I think whatever he wants, he will get." A
gust struck them, smelling like snow, gnawing icily at
his face and hands. It drove him to his feet, breathless,
blinded, full of a sudden, helpless longing for hope.
When he could see again, he found that Raederle had
already changed shape. A vesta shod and crowned
with gold gazed at him out of deep purple eyes. He

caressed it; its warm breath nuzzled at his hands. He rested his brow against the bone between its eyes. "All right," he said with very little irony, "I will play a riddle-game with Deth. Which way is Isig?"

She led him there by sunlight and starlight, south across the wastes, and then eastward down the mountains of the pass until at the second dawn he saw the green face of Isig Mountain rising beyond the Ose. They reached the king's house at dusk, on a wild, grey autumn day. The high peaks were already capped with snow; the great pines around Harte sang in the north wind. The travellers changed out of vesta-shape when they reached Kyrth and walked the winding mountain road to Harte. The gates were barred and guarded, but the miners, armed with great broadswords tempered in Danan's forge fires, recognized them and let them in.

Danan and Vert and half a dozen children left their supper to meet them as they entered the house. Danan, robed in fur against the cold, gave them a bear's bulky embrace and sent children and servants alike scurrying to see their comfort. But, gauging their weariness, he asked only one question.

"I was in the wastes," Morgon said. "Harping. Raederle found me." The strangeness of the answer did not occur to him then. He added, remembering, "Before that, I was a tree beside the Ose." He watched a smile break into the king's eyes.

"What did I tell you?" Danan murmured. "I told you no one would find you in that shape." He drew them toward the stairs leading up into the east tower. "I have a thousand questions, but I am a patient old tree, and they can wait until morning. Yrth is in this tower; you'll be safe near him."

A question nagged at Morgon as they wound up the stairs, until he realized what it was. "Danan, I have never seen your house guarded. Did the shapechangers come here looking for me?"

The king's hands knotted. "They came," he said

grimly. "I lost a quarter of my miners. I would have lost more if Yrth had not been here to fight with us." Morgon had stopped. The king opened a hand, drew him forward. "We grieved enough for them. If we only knew what they are, what they want . . ." He sensed something in Morgon. His troubled eyes drew relentlessly at the truth. "You know."

Morgon did not answer. Danan did not press him, but the lines in his face ran suddenly deep.

He left them in a tower room whose walls and floor and furniture were draped with fur. The air was chilly, but Raederle lit a fire and servants came soon, bringing food, wine, more firewood, warm, rich clothes. Bere followed with a cauldron of steaming water. As he hoisted it onto a hook above the firebed, he smiled at Morgon, his eyes full of questions, but he swallowed them all with an effort. Morgon ridded himself of a well-worn tunic, matted sheepskin, and what dirt the harsh winds had not scoured from his body. Clean, fed, dressed in soft fur and velvet, he sat beside the fire and thought back with amazement on what he had done.

"I left you," he said to Raederle. "I can understand almost everything but that. I wandered out of the world and left you . . ."

"You were tired," she said drowsily. "You said so. Maybe you just needed to think." She was stretched out beside him on the ankle-deep skins; she sounded warmed by fire and wine, and almost asleep. "Or maybe you needed a place to begin to harp . . ."

Her voice trailed away into a dream; she left him behind. He drew blankets over her, sat for a while without moving, watching light and shadows pursue one another across her weary face. The winds boomed and broke against the tower like sea waves. They held the echo of a note that haunted his memories. He reached automatically for his harp, then remembered he could not play that note in the king's house without disrupting its fragile peace.

He played others softly, fragments of ballads wandering into patternless echoes of the winds. His fingers stopped after a while. He sat plucking one note over and over, soundlessly, while a face formed and vanished constantly in the flames. He stood up finally, listening. The house seemed still around him, with only a distant murmuring of voices here and there within its walls. He moved quietly past Raederle, past the guards outside the door, whom he made oblivious to his leaving. He went up the stairs to a doorway hung with white furs that yielded beneath them a strip of light. He parted them gently, walked into semidarkness and stopped.

The wizard was napping, an old man nodding in a chair beside a fire, his scarred hands lying open on his knees. He looked taller than Morgon remembered, broad-shouldered yet lean beneath the long, dark robe he wore. As Morgon watched him, he woke, opening light, unstartled eyes. He bent down, sighing, groped for wood and positioned it carefully, feeling with his fingers through the lagging flames. They sprang up, lighting a rock-hard face, weathered like a tree stump with age. He seemed to realize suddenly that he was not alone; for an instant his body went motionless as stone. Morgon felt an almost imperceptible touch in his mind. The wizard stirred again, blinking.

"Morgon?" His voice was deep, resonant, yet husky, full of hidden things, like the voice of a deep well. "Come in. Or are you in?"

Morgon moved after a moment. "I didn't mean to disturb you," he said softly. Yrth shook his head.

"I heard your harping a while ago. But I didn't expect to talk to you until morning. Danan told me that Raederle found you in the northern wastes. Were you pursued? Is that why you hid there?"

"No. I simply went there, and stayed because I could think of no reason to come back. Then Raederle came and gave me a reason . . ."

The wizard contemplated the direction of his voice

silently. "You are an amazing man," he said. "Will you sit down?"

"How do you know I'm not sitting?" Morgon asked curiously.

"I can see the chair in front of you. Can you feel the mind-link? I am seeing out of your eyes."

"I hardly notice it . . ."

"That's because I am not linked to your thoughts, only to your vision. I travelled Trader's Road through men's eyes. That night you were attacked by horse thieves, I knew one of them was a shape-changer because I saw through his eyes the stars you kept hidden from men. I searched for him, to kill him, but he eluded me."

"And the night I followed Deth's harping? Did you see beneath that illusion, also?"

The wizard was silent again. His head bowed, away from Morgon; the hard lines of his face shifted with such shame and bitterness that Morgon stepped toward him, appalled at his own question.

"Morgon, I am sorry. I am no match for Ghisteslwchlohm."

"You couldn't have done anything to help." His hands gripped the chair back. "Not without endangering Raederle."

"I did what little I could, reinforcing your illusion when you vanished, but . . . that was very little."

"You saved our lives." He had a sudden, jarring memory of the harpist's face, eyes seared pale with fire, staring at nothing until Morgon wavered out of existence in front of him. His hands loosed the wood, slid up over his eyes. He heard Yrth stir.

"I can't see."

His hands dropped. He sat down, in utter weariness. The winds wailed around the tower in a confusion of voices. Yrth was still, listening to his silence. He said gently, when Morgon did not break it, "Raederle told me what she could of the events in Erlenstar Mountain. I did not go into her mind. Will you let me see into your memories. Or do you prefer to tell me? Either way, I must know."

"Take it from my mind."

"Are you too tired now?"

He shook his head a little. "It doesn't matter. Take what you want."

The fire grew small in front of him, broke into bright fragments of memory. He endured once more his wild, lonely flight across the backlands, falling out of the sky into the depths of Erlenstar Mountain. The tower flooded with night; he swallowed bitterness like lake water. The fire beyond his vision whispered in languages he did not understand. A wind smashed through the voices, whirling them out of his mind. The tower stones shook around him, shattered by the deep, precise tuning of a wind. Then there was a long silence, during which he drowsed, warmed by a summer light. Then he woke again, a strange, wild figure in a sheepskin coat that hung open to the wind. He drifted deeper and deeper into the pure, deadly voices of winter.

He sat beside a fire, listening to the winds. But they were beyond a circle of stone; they touched neither him nor the fire. He stirred a little, blinking, puzzling night and fire and the wizard's face back into perspective. His thoughts centered once more in the tower. He slumped forward, murmuring, so tired he wanted to melt into the dying fire. The wizard rose, paced a moment, soundlessly, until a clothes chest stopped him.

"What did you do in the wastes?"

"I harped. I could play that low note there, the one that shatters stone . . ." He heard his voice from a distance, amazed that it was vaguely rational.

"How did you survive?"

"I don't know. Maybe I was part wind, for a while . . . I was afraid to come back. What will I do with such power?"

"Use it."

"I don't dare. I have power over land-law. I want it. I want to use it. But I have no right. Land-law is the heritage of kings, bound into them by the High One. I would destroy all law . . ."

"Perhaps. But land-law is also the greatest source of power in the realm. Who can help the High One but you?"

"He hasn't asked for help. Does a mountain ask for help? Or a river? They simply exist. If I touch his power, he may pay enough attention to me to destroy me, but—"

"Morgon, have you no hope whatsoever in those stars I made for you?"

"No." His eyes closed; he dragged them open again, wanting to weep with the effort. He whispered, "I don't speak the language of stone. To him, I simply exist. He sees nothing but three stars rising out of countless centuries of darkness, during which power-less shapes called men touched the earth a little, hardly enough to disturb him."

"He gave them land-law."

"I was a shape possessing land-law. Now, I am simply a shape with no destiny but in the past. I will not touch the power of another land-ruler again."

The wizard was silent, gazing down at a fire that kept blurring under Morgon's eyes. "Are you so angry with the High One?"

"How can I be angry with a stone?"

"The Earth-Masters have taken all shapes. What makes you so certain the High One has shaped him-self to everything but the shape and language of men?"

"Why—" He stopped, staring down at the flames until they burned the shadows of sleep out of his mind and he could think again. "You want me to loose my own powers into the realm."

Yrth did not answer. Morgon looked up at him, giving him back the image of his own face, hard, an-cient, powerful. The fire washed over his thoughts again. He saw suddenly, for the first time, not the slab of wind speaking the language of stone that he thought was the High One, but something pursued, vulnerable, in danger, whose silence was the single weapon he possessed. The thought held him still, wondering. Slowly he became aware of the silence that built moment by moment between his question and the answer to it.

He stopped breathing, listening to the silence that haunted him oddly, like a memory of something he had once cherished. The wizard's hands turned a little toward the light and then closed, hiding their scars. He said, "There are powers loosed all over the realm to find the High One. Yours will not be the worst. You are, after all, bound by a peculiar system of restraints. The best, and the least comprehensible of them, seems to be love. You could ask permission from the land-rulers. They trust you. And they were in great despair when neither you nor the High One seemed to be anywhere on the face of the realm."

Morgon's head bowed. "I didn't think of them." He did not hear Yrth move until the wizard's dark robe brushed the wood of his chair. The wizard's hand touched his shoulder, very gently, as he might have touched a wild thing that had moved fearfully, tentatively, toward him into his stillness.

Something drained out of Morgon at the touch: confusion, anger, arguments, even the strength and will to wrestle with all the wizard's subtlety. Only the silence was left, and a helpless, incomprehensible longing.

"I'll find the High One," he said. He added, in warning or in promise, "Nothing will destroy him. I swear it. Nothing."

11

E SLEPT FOR TWO DAYS IN THE KING'S HOUSE, waking only once to eat, and another time to see Raederle sitting beside him, waiting patiently for him to wake up. He linked his fingers into hers, smiling a little, then rolled over and went back to sleep. He woke finally, clear-headed, at evening. He was alone. From the faint chaos of voices and crockery that seeped into his listening, he knew that the household was at supper, and Raederle was probably with Danan. He washed and drank some wine, still listening. Beneath the noises of the house, he heard the vast, dark, ageless silence forming the hollows and mazes within Isig Mountain.

He stood linked to the silence until it formed channels in his mind. Then, impulsively, he left the tower, went unobtrusively to the hall, where only Raederle and Bere noticed him, falling quiet amid the noise to watch his passage. He followed the path of a dream then, through the empty upper shafts. He took a torch from the wall at the mouth of a dark tunnel; as he entered it, the walls blazed around him with fiery, uncut jewels. He moved unhesitantly through his memory, down a honeycomb of passageways, along the sides of shallow streams and deep crevices, through unmined caves shimmering with gold, moving deeper and deeper into the immensity of darkness and stone until he seemed to breathe its stillness and age into his bones. At last he sensed something older, even, than the great mountain. The path he followed dwindled into crumbled stone. The torch fire washed over a deep green slab of a door that had opened once before to the sound of his name. There he stopped incredulously.

The ground floor was littered with the shards of broken rock. The door to the Earth-Masters' dead was split open; half of it had fallen ponderously back into the cave. The tomb itself was choked with great chunks of jewelled ceiling stone; the walls had shrugged themselves together, hiding whatever was left of the strange pale stones within.

He picked his way to the door, but he could not enter. He crooked one arm on the door, leaned his face against it. He let his thoughts flow into the stone, seep through marble, amethyst, and gold until he touched something like the remnant of a half-forgotten dream. He explored farther; he found no names, only a sense of something that had once lived.

He stood for a long time, leaning against the door without moving. After a while, he knew why he had come down into the mountain, and he felt the blood beat through him, quick, cold, as it had the first time he had brought himself to that threshold of his destiny. He became aware, as he had never been before, of the mountain settled over his head, and of the king within it, his ancient mind shaped to its mazes, holding all its peace and all its power. His thoughts moved once again, slowly, into the door, until he touched at the core of the stone, the sense of Danan's mind, shaped to that tiny fragment of mountain, bound to it. He let his brain become stone, rich, worn, ponderous. He drew all knowledge of it into himself, of its great strength, its inmost colors, its most fragile point where he might have shattered it with a thought. The knowledge became a binding, a part of himself, deep in his own mind. Then, searching within the stone, he found once more the wordless awareness, the law that bound king to stone, land-ruler to every portion of his kingdom. He encompassed that awareness, broke it, and the stone held no name but his own.

He let his own awareness of the binding dwindle into some dark cave deep in his mind. He straightened slowly, sweating in the cool air. His torch was out; he touched it, lit it again. Turning, he found Danan in front of him, massive and still as Isig, his face expressionless as a rock.

Morgon's muscles tensed involuntarily. He wondered for a second if there was any language in him to explain what he was doing to a rock, before the slow, ponderous weight of Danan's anger roused stones from their sleep to bury him beside the children's tomb. Then he saw the king's broad fist unclench.

"Morgon." His voice was breathless with astonishment. "It was you who drew me down here. What are you doing?" He touched Morgon when he could not answer. "You're frightened. What are you doing that you need to fear me?"

Morgon moved after a moment. His body felt drained, cumbersome as stone. "Learning your landlaw." He leaned back against the damp wall behind him, his face uplifted, vulnerable to Danan's searching.

"Where did you get such power? From Ghisteslwchlohm?"

"No." He repeated the word suddenly, passionately, "No. I would die before I did that to you. I will never go into your mind—"

"You are in it. Isig is my brain, my heart—"

"I won't break your bindings again. I swear it. I will simply form my own."

"But why? What do you want with such a knowledge of trees and stones?"

"Power. Danan, the shape-changers are Earth-Masters. I can't hope to fight them unless—"

The king's fingers wound like a tree root around his wrist. "No," he said, as Ghisteslwchlohm had said, faced with the same knowledge. "Morgon, that's not possible."

"Danan," he whispered, "I have heard their voices. The languages they spoke. I have seen the power locked behind their eyes. It is possible."

Danan's hand slipped away from him. The king sat down slowly, heavily, on a pile of rock shard. Morgon, looking down at him, wondered suddenly how old he was. His hands, calloused with centuries of work among stones, made a futile gesture. "What do they want?"

"The High One."

Danan stared at him. "They'll destroy us." He reached out to Morgon again. "And you. What do they want with you?"

"I'm their link to the High One. I don't know how I am bound to him, or why—I only know that because of him I have been driven out of my own land, harried, tormented into power, until now I am driving myself into power. The Earth-Masters' power seems bound, restrained by something . . . perhaps the High One, which is why they are so desperate to find him. When they do, whatever power they unleash against him may destroy us all. He may stay bound forever in his silence; it's hard for me to risk my life and all your trust for someone who never speaks. But at least if I fight for him, I fight for you." He paused, his eyes on the flecks of fire catching in the rough, rich walls around him. "I can't ask you to trust me," he said softly. "Not when I don't even trust myself. All I know is where both logic and hunger lead me."

He heard the king's weary sigh in the shadows. "The ending of an age. . . . That's what you told me the last time you came to this place. Ymris is nearly destroyed. It seems only a matter of time before that war spills into An, into Herun, then north across the realm. I have an army of miners, the Morgol has her guard, the wolf-king . . . has his wolves. But what is that against an army of Earth-Masters coming back into their power? And how can one Prince of Hed, even with whatever knowledge of land-law you have the strength to acquire, fight that?"

"I'll find a way."

"How?"

"Danan, I'll find a way. It's either that or die, and I am too stubborn to die." He sat down beside the king, gazing at the rubble around them. "What happened to this place? I wanted to go into the minds of the dead children, to see into their memories, but there is nothing left of them."

Danan shook his head. "I felt it, near the end of summer: a turmoil somewhere in the center of my world. It happened shortly before the shape—the Earth-Masters came here looking for you. I don't know how this place was destroyed, or by whom . . ."

"I know," he whispered. "Wind. The deep wind that shatters stone. . . . The High One destroyed this place."

"But why? It was their one final place of peace."

"I don't know. Unless . . . unless he found another place for them, fearing for their peace even here. I don't know. Maybe somehow I will find him, hold him to some shape that I can understand, and ask him why."

"If you can do even that much—only that—you will repay the land-rulers for whatever power you take from the realm. At least we will die knowing why." He pushed himself up and dropped a hand on Morgon's shoulder. "I understand what you are doing. You need an Earth-Master's power to fight Earth-Masters. If you want to take a mountain onto your shoulders, I'll give you Isig. The High One gives us silence; you give us impossible hope."

The king left him alone. Morgon dropped the torch

to the ground, watched it burn away into darkness. He stood up, not fighting his blindness, but breathing the mountain-blackness into himself until it seeped into his mind and hollowed all his bones. His thoughts groped into the stone around him, slid through stone passages, channels of air, sluices of slow, black water. He carved the mountain out of its endless night, shaped it to his thoughts. His mind pushed into solid rock, expanded outward through stone, hollows of silence, deep lakes, until earth crusted over the rock and he felt the slow, downward groping of tree roots. His awareness filled the base of the mountain, flowed slowly, relentlessly upward. He touched the minds of blind fish, strange insects living in a changeless world. He became the topaz locked in a stone that a miner was chiseling loose; he hung upside down, staring at nothing in the brain of a bat. His own shape was lost; his bones curved around an ancient silence, rose endlessly upward, heavy with metal and jewels. He could not find his heart. When he probed for it within masses of stone, he sensed another name, another's heart.

He did not disturb that name bound into every fragment of the mountain. Slowly, as hours he never measured passed, he touched every level of the mountain, groping steadily upward through mineshafts, through granite, through caves, like Danan's secret thoughts, luminous with their own beauty. The hours turned into days he did not count. His mind, rooted to the ground floor of Isig, shaped to all its rifts and channels, broke through finally to peaks buried under the first winter snows.

He felt ponderous with mountain. His awareness spanned the length and bulk of it. In some minute corner of the darkness far beneath him, his body lay like a fragment of rock on the floor of the mountain. He seemed to gaze down at it, not knowing how to draw the immensity of his thoughts back into it. Finally, wearily, something in him like an inner eye simply closed, and his mind melted into darkness.

He woke once more as hands came out of darkness, turned him over. He said, before he even opened his eyes, "All right. I learned the land-law of Isig. With one twist of thought I could hold the land-rule. Is that what you'll ask of me next?"

"Morgon."

He opened his eyes. At first he thought dawn had come into the mountain, for the walls around him and Yrth's worn, blind face seemed darkly luminous. Then he whispered, "I can see."

"You swallowed a mountain. Can you stand?" The big hands hauled him to his feet without waiting for his answer. "You might try trusting me a little. You've tried everything else. Take one step."

He started to speak, but the wizard's mind filled his with an image of a small firelit chamber in a tower. He stepped into it and saw Raederle rise, trail fire with her as she came to meet him. He reached out to her; she seemed to come endlessly toward him, dissolving into fire when he finally touched her.

He woke to hear her playing softly on a flute one of the craftsmen had given her. She stopped, smiling as he looked at her, but she looked weary and pale. He sat up, waited for a mountain to shift into place in his head. Then he kissed her.

"You must be tired of waiting for me to wake up."

"It would be nice to talk to you," she said wistfully. "Either you're asleep or you vanish. Yrth was here most of the day. I read to him out of old spell books."

"That was kind of you."

"Morgon, he asked me to. I wanted so badly to question him, but I couldn't. There seemed suddenly nothing to question . . . until he left. I think I'll study wizardry. They knew more odd, petty spells than even witches. Do you know what you're doing? Other than half-killing yourself?"

"I'm doing what you told me to do. I'm playing a

riddle-game." He got to his feet, suddenly ravenously hungry, but found only wine. He gulped a cup, while she went to the door, spoke to one of the miners guarding them. He poured more wine and said when she came back, "I told you I would do whatever he wanted me to do. I always have." She looked at him silently. He added simply, "I don't know. Maybe I have already lost. I'll go to Osterland and request that same thing from Har. Knowledge of his land-law. And then to Herun, if I am still alive. And then to Ymris. . . ."

"There are Earth-Masters all over Ymris."

"By that time, I will begin to think like an Earth-Master. And maybe by then the High One will reach out of his silence and either doom me for touching his power, or explain to me what in Hel's name I'm doing." He finished the second cup of wine, then said to her suddenly, intensely, "There is nothing I can trust but the strictures of riddlery. The wise man knows his own name. My name is one of power. So I reach out to it. Does that seem wrong to you? It frightens me. But still I reach. . . ."

She seemed as uncertain as he felt, but she only said calmly, "If it ever seems wrong, I'll be there to tell you."

He spoke with Yrth and Danan in the king's hall late that night. Everyone had gone to bed. They sat close to the hearth; Morgon, watching the old, rugged faces of king and wizard as the fire washed over them, sensed the love of the great mountain in them both. He had shaped the harp at Yrth's request. The wizard's hands moved from string to string, listening to their tones. But he did not play it.

"I must leave for Osterland soon," Morgon said to Danan, "to ask of Har what I asked of you."

Danan looked at Yrth. "Are you going with him?"

The wizard nodded. His light eyes touched Morgon's as if by accident. "How are you planning to get there?" he asked.

"We'll fly, probably. You know the crow-shape."

"Three crows above the dead fields of Oster-land . . ." He plucked a string softly. "Nun is in Yrye, with the wolf-king. She came here while you were sleeping, bringing news. She had been in the Three Portions, helping Talies search for you. Mathom of An is gathering a great army of the living and dead to help the Ymris forces. He says he is not going to sit waiting for the inevitable."

Danan straightened. "He is." He leaned forward, his blunt hands joined. "I'm thinking of arming the miners with sword, ax, pick—every weapon we possess—and taking them south. I have shiploads of arms and armor in Kyrth and Kraal bound for Ymris. I could bring an army with them."

"You . . ." Morgon said. His voice caught. "You can't leave Isig."

"I've never done it," the king admitted. "But I am not going to let you battle alone. And if Ymris falls, so will Isig, eventually. Ymris is the stronghold of the realm."

"But, Danan, you aren't a fighter."

"Neither are you," Danan said inarguably.

"How are you going to battle Earth-Masters with picks?"

"We did it here. We'll do it in Ymris. You have only one thing to do, it seems. Find the High One before they can."

"I'm trying. I touched every binding of land-law in Isig, and he didn't seem to care. It's as though I might be doing exactly what he wants." His words echoed oddly through his mind. But Yrth interrupted his thoughts, reaching a little randomly for his wine. Morgon handed it to him before he spilled it. "You aren't using our eyes."

"No. Sometimes I see more clearly in the dark. My mind reaches out to shape the world around me, but judging small distances is not so easy . . ." He gave the starred harp back to Morgon. "Even after all these years, I can still remember what mountain stream, what murmur of fire, what bird cry I pitched each note to . . ."

"I would like to hear you play it," Morgon said. The wizard shook his head imperturbably.

"No, you wouldn't. I play very badly these days, as Danan could tell you." He turned toward Danan. "If you leave at all for Ymris, you should leave soon. You'll be warring on the threshold of winter, and there may be no time when you will be needed more. Ymris warriors dislike battling in snow, but the Earth-Masters would not even notice it. They and the weather will be merciless adversaries."

"Well," Danan said after a silence, "either I fight them in the Ymris winter, or I fight them in my own house. I'll begin gathering men and ships tomorrow. I'll leave Ash here. He won't like it, but he is my land-heir, and it would be senseless to risk both our lives in Ymris."

"He'll want to go in your place," Yrth said.

"I know." His voice was calm, but Morgon sensed the strength in him, the obdurate power of stone that would thunder into movement perhaps once during its existence. "He'll stay. I'm old, and if I die . . . the great, weathered, ancient trees are the ones that do the most damage as they fall."

Morgon's hands closed tightly on the arms of his chair. "Danan," he pleaded, "don't go. There is no need for you to risk your life. You are rooted in our minds to the first years of the realm. If you die, something of hope in us all will die."

"There is need. I am fighting for all things precious to me. Isig. All the lives within it, bound to this mountain's life. You."

"All right," he whispered. "All right. I will find the High One if I have to shake power from his mind until he reaches out of his secret place to stop me."

He talked to Raederle for a long time that night after he left the king's hall. He lay at her side on the

soft furs beside the fire. She listened silently while he
told her of his intentions and Danan's war plans and
the news that Nun had brought to Isig about her
father. She said, twisting tufts of sheep pelt into knots,
"I wonder if the roof of Anuin fell in with all the
shouting there must have been over that decision."

"He wouldn't have made it unless he thought war
was inevitable."

"No. He saw that war coming long ago, out of his
crow's eyes . . ." She sighed, wrenching at the wool. "I
suppose Rood will be at one side and Duac at the
other, arguing all the way to Ymris." She stopped, her
eyes on the fire, and he saw the sudden longing in her
face. He touched her cheek.

"Raederle. Do you want to go home for a while
and see them? You could be there in a few days,
flying, and then meet me somewhere—Herun, perhaps."

"No."

"I dragged you down Trader's Road in the dust and
heat; I harried you until you changed shape; I put
you into Ghisteslwchlohm's hands; and then I left you
facing Earth-Masters by yourself while I ran—"

"Morgon."

"And then, after you came into your own power
and followed me all the way across the backlands into
Erlenstar Mountain, I walked off into the wastes and
left you without a word, so you had to search for me
through half the northlands. Then you lead me home,
and I hardly even talk to you. How in Hel's name
can you stand me by this time?"

She smiled. "I don't know. I wonder sometimes,
too. Then you touch my face with your scarred hand
and read my mind. Your eyes know me. That's why I
keep following you all over the realm, barefoot or
half-frozen, cursing the sun or the wind, or myself
because I have no more sense than to love a man
who does not even possess a bed I can crawl into at
night. And sometimes I curse you because you have

spoken my name in a way that no other man in the realm will speak it, and I will listen for that until I die. So," she added, as he gazed down at her mutely, "how can I leave you?"

He dropped his face against hers, so that their brows and cheekbones touched, and he looked deeply into a single, amber eye. He watched it smile. She put her arms around him, kissed the hollow of his throat, and then his heart. Then she slid her hand between their mouths. He murmured a protest into her palm. She said, "I want to talk."

He sat up, breathing deeply, and tossed another log on the fire. "All right."

"Morgon, what will you do if that wizard with his harpist's hands betrays you again? If you find the High One for him, and then realize too late that he has a mind more devious than Ghisteslwchlohm's?"

"I already know he has." He was silent, brooding, his arms around his knees. "I've thought of that again and again. Did you see him use power in Lungold?"

"Yes. He was protecting the traders as they fought."

"Then he is not an Earth-Master; their power is bound."

"He is a wizard."

"Or something else we have no name for . . . that's what I'm afraid of." He stirred a little. "He didn't even try to dissuade Danan from bringing the miners to Ymris. They aren't warriors; they'll be slaughtered. And Danan has no business dying on the battlefield. He said once he wanted to become a tree, under the sun and stars, when it was time for him to die. Still, he and Yrth have known each other for many centuries. Maybe Yrth knew it was futile to argue with a stone."

"If it is Yrth. Are you even sure of that?"

"Yes. He made certain I knew that. He played my harp."

She was silent, her fingers trailing up and down his

backbone. "Well," she said softly, "then maybe you can trust him."

"I have tried," he whispered. Her hand stilled. He lay back down beside her, listening to the pine keen as it burned. He put his wrist over his eyes. "I'm going to fail. I could never win an argument with him. I couldn't even kill him. All I can do is wait until he names himself, and by then it may be too late . . ."

She said something after a moment. What it was he did not hear, for something without definition in the dark of his mind had stirred. It felt at first like a mind-touch he could not stop. So he explored it, and it became a sound. His lips parted; the breath came quick, dry out of him. The sound heaved into a bellow, like the bellow of the sea smashing docks and beached boats and fishermen's houses, then riding high, piling up and over a cliff to tear at fields, topple trees, roar darkly through the night, drowning screams of men and animals. He was on his feet without knowing it, echoing the cry he heard in the mind of the land-ruler of Hed.

"No!"

He heard a tangle of voices. He could not see in the whirling black flood. His body seemed veined with land-law. He felt the terrible wave whirled back, sucking with it broken sacks of grain, sheep and pigs, beer barrels, the broken walls of barns and houses, fenceposts, soup cauldrons, harrows, children screaming in the dark. Someone gripped him, crying his name over and over. Fear, despair, helpless anger washed through him, his own and Eliard's. A mind caught at his mind, but he was bound to Hed, a thousand miles away. Then a hand snapped painfully across his face, rocking him back, out of his vision.

He found himself staring into Yrth's blind eyes. A hot, furious sense of the wizard's incomprehensible injustice swept through him so strongly he could not even speak. He doubled his fist and swung. Yrth was far heavier than he expected: the blow wrenched his bones from wrist to shoulder, and split his knuckles, as if he had struck stone or wood. Yrth, looking vaguely surprised, wavered in the air before he might have fallen and then vanished. He reappeared a moment later and sat down on the rim of the firebed, cupping a bleeding cheekbone.

The two guards in the doorway and Raederle all had the same expression on their faces. They seemed also to be bound motionless. Morgon, catching his breath, the sudden fury dissipated, said, "Hed is under attack. I'm going there."

"No."

"The sea came up over the cliffs. I heard—I heard their voices, Eliard's voice. If he's dead—I swear, if he is dead—if you hadn't hit me, I would know! I was in his mind. Tol—Tol was destroyed. Everything. Everyone." He looked at Raederle. "I'll be back as soon as I can."

"I'm coming," she whispered.

"No."

"Yes."

"Morgon," Yrth said. "You will be killed."

"Tristan." His hands clenched; he swallowed a painful, burning knot. "I don't know if she's alive or dead!" He closed his eyes, flinging his mind across the dark, rain-drenched night, across the vast forests, as far as he could reach. He stepped toward the edge of his awareness. But an image formed in his mind, drew him back as he moved, and he opened his eyes to the firelit walls of the tower.

"It's a trap," Yrth said. His voice sounded hollow with pain, but very patient. Morgon did not bother to answer. He drew the image of a falcon out of his mind, but swiftly, even before he had begun to change shape, the image changed to light, burned eyes that saw into his mind. They pulled him back into himself.

"Morgon, I'll go. They are expecting you; they hardly know me. I can travel swiftly; I'll be back very soon . . ." He stood up abruptly as Morgon filled his mind with illusions of fire and shadow and disappeared within them. He had nearly walked out of the room when the wizard's eyes pierced into his thoughts, breaking his concentration.

The anger flared in him again. He kept walking and brought himself up against an illusion of solid stone in the doorway. "Morgon," the wizard said, and Morgon whirled. He flung a shout into Yrth's mind that should have jarred the wizard's attention away from his illusion. But the shout echoed harmlessly into a mind like a vast chasm of darkness.

He stood still, then, his hands flat on the illusion, a fine sweat of fear and exhaustion forming on his face. The darkness was like a warning. But he let his mind touch it again, form around it, try to move through its illusion to the core of the wizard's thoughts. He only blundered deeper into darkness, with the sense of some vast power constantly retreating before his searching. He followed it until he could no longer find his way back. . . .

He came out of the darkness slowly, to find himself sitting motionless beside the fire. Raederle was beside him, her fingers locked to his limp hand. Yrth stood in front of them. His face looked almost grey with weariness; his eyes were bloodshot. His boots and the hem of his long robe were stained with dry mud and crusted salt. The cut on his cheek had closed.

Morgon started. Danan, on his other side, stooped to lay a hand on his shoulder. "Morgon," he said softly, "Yrth has just come back from Hed. It's midmorning. He has been gone two nights and a day."

"What did you—" He stood up, too abruptly. Danan caught him, held him while the blood behind his eyes receded. "How did you do that to me?" he whispered.

"Morgon, forgive me." The strained, weary voice seemed haunted with overtones of another voice. "The Earth-Masters were waiting for you in Hed. If you had gone, you would have died there, and more lives

would have been lost battling for you. They couldn't
find you anywhere; they were trying to drive you out
of your hiding."

"Eliard—"

"He's safe. I found him standing among the ruins of
Akren. The wave destroyed Tol, Akren, most of the
farms along the western coast. I spoke to the farmers;
they saw some fighting between strange, armed men,
they said, who did not belong in Hed. I questioned
one of the wraiths; he said there was little to be done
against the shape of water. I told Eliard who I am,
where you are . . . he was stunned with the sudden-
ness of it. He said that he knew you had sensed the
destruction, but he was glad you had had sense
enough not to come."

Morgon drew breath; it seemed to burn through
him. "Tristan?"

"As far as Eliard knows, she's safe. Some feeble-
minded trader told her you had disappeared. So she
left Hed to look for you, but a sailor recognized her in
Caithnard and stopped her. She is on her way home."
Morgon put his hand over his eyes. The wizard's
hand rose, went out to him, but he drew back.
"Morgon." The wizard was dredging words from
somewhere out of his exhaustion. "It was not a complex binding. You were not thinking clearly enough
to break it."

"I was thinking clearly," he whispered. "I did not
have the power to break it." He stopped, aware of
Danan behind him, puzzled, yet trusting them both.
The dark riddle of the wizard's power loomed again
over his thoughts, over the whole of the realm, from
Isig to Hed. There seemed no escape from it. He
began to sob harshly, hopelessly, possessing no other
answer. The wizard, his shoulders slumping as if the
weight of the realm dragged at his back, gave him
nothing but silence.

12

THEY LEFT ISIG THE NEXT DAY: THREE CROWS
flying among the billowing smoke from Danan's
forges. They crossed the Ose, flew over the
docks at Kyrth; every ship moored there was being
overhauled for a long journey down the river to the
heavy autumn seas. The grey rains beat against them
over the forests of Osterland; the miles of ancient pine
were hunched and weary. Grim Mountain rose in the
distance out of a ring of mist. The east and north
winds swarmed around them; the crows dipped from
current to current, their feathers alternately sleeked and
billowed by the erratic winds. They stopped to rest
frequently. By nightfall they were barely halfway to
Yrye.

They stopped for the night under the broad eaves
of an old tree whose thick branches sighed resignedly
in the rain. They found niches in it to protect themselves from the weather. Two crows huddled together
on a branch; the third landed below them, a big, dark,
windblown bird who had not spoken since they left
Isig. For hours they slept, shielded by the weave of
branches, lulled by the wind.

The winds died at midnight. The rains slowed to a
whisper, then faded. The clouds parted, loosing the

stars cluster by cluster against a dazzling blackness. The unexpected silence found its way into Morgon's crow-dreams. His eyes opened.

Raederle was motionless beside him, a little cloud of soft black plumage. The crow beneath him was still. His own shape pulled at him dimly, wanting to breathe the spices of the night, wanting to become moonlight. He spread his wings after a moment, dropped soundlessly to the ground, and changed shape.

He stood quietly, enfolded in the Osterland night. His mind opened to all its sounds and smells and shapes. He laid his hand against the wet, rough flank of the tree and felt it drowsing. He heard the pad of some night hunter across the soft, damp ground. He smelled the rich, tangled odors of wet pine, of dead bark and loam crumbled under his feet. His thoughts yearned to become part of the land, under the light, silvery touch of the moon. He let his mind drift finally into the vast, tideless night.

He shaped his mind to the roots of trees, to buried stones, to the brains of animals moving obliviously across the path of his awareness. He sensed in all things the ancient sleeping fire of Har's law, the faint, perpetual fire behind his eyes. He touched fragments of the dead within the earth, the bones and memories of men and animals. Unlike the wraiths of An, they were quiescent, at rest in the heart of the wild land. Quietly, unable to resist his own longings, he began weaving his bindings of awareness and knowledge into the law of Osterland.

Slowly he began to understand the roots of the land-law. The bindings of snow and sun had touched all life. The wild winds set the vesta's speed; the fierceness of seasons shaped the wolf's brain; the winter night seeped into the raven's eye. The more he understood, the deeper he drew himself into it: gazing at the moon out of a horned owl's eyes, melting with a wild cat through the bracken, twisting his thoughts even into the fragile angles of a spider's web, and into the endless, sinuous wind of ivy spiralling a tree trunk. He was so engrossed that he touched a vesta's mind without questioning it. A little later, he touched another. And then, suddenly, his mind could not move without finding vesta, as if they had shaped themselves out of the moonlight around him. They were running: a soundless white wind coming from all directions. Curiously, he explored their impulse. Some danger had sent them flowing across the night, he sensed, and wondered what would dare trouble the vesta in Har's domain. He probed deeper. Then he shook himself free of them; the swift, startled breath he drew of the icy air cleared his head.

It was nearly dawn. What he thought was moonlight was the first silver-grey haze of morning. The vesta were very close, a great herd wakened by Har, their minds drawn with a fine instinct towards whatever had brought the king out of his sleep and disturbed the ancient workings of his mind. Morgon stood still, considering various impulses: to take the crow-shape and escape into the tree; to take the vesta-shape; to try to reach Har's mind, and hope he was not too angry to listen. Before he could act, he found Yrth standing next to him.

"Be still," he said, and Morgon, furious at his own acquiescence, followed the unlikely advice.

He began to see the vesta all around them, through the trees. Their speed was incredible; the unwavering drive toward one isolated point in the forests was eerie. They were massed around him in a matter of moments, surrounding the tree. They did not threaten him; they simply stood in a tight, motionless circle, gazing at him out of alien purple eyes, their horns sketching gold circles against the trees and the pallid morning sky as far as he could see.

Raederle woke. She gave one faint, surprised squawk. Her mind reached into Morgon's; she said his name on a questioning note. He did not dare answer, and she was silent after that. The sun whitened a wall of cloud in the east, then disappeared. The rain began again, heavy, sullen drops that plummeted straight down from a windless sky.

An hour later, something began to ripple through the herd. Morgon, drenched from head to foot and cursing Yrth's advice, watched the movement with relief. One set of gold horns was moving through the herd; he watched the bright circles constantly fall apart before it and rejoin in its wake. He knew it must be Har. He wiped rain out of his eyes with a sodden sleeve and sneezed suddenly. Instantly, the vesta nearest him, standing so placidly until then, belled like a stag and reared. One gold hoof slashed the air apart inches from Morgon's face. His muscles turned to stone. The vesta subsided, dropping back to gaze at him again, peacefully.

Morgon stared back at it, his heartbeat sounding uncomfortably loud. The front circle broke again, shifting to admit the great vesta. It changed shape. The wolf-king stood before Morgon, the smile in his eyes boding no good to whoever had interrupted his sleep.

The smile died as he recognized Morgon. He turned his head, spoke one word sharply; the vesta faded like a dream. Morgon waited silently, tensely, for judgment. It did not come. The king reached out, pushed the wet hair back from the stars on his face, as if answering a doubt. Then he looked at Yrth.

"You should have warned him."

"I was asleep," Yrth said. Har grunted.

"I thought you never slept." He glanced up into the tree and his face gentled. He held up his hand. The crow dropped down onto his fingers, and he set it on his shoulder. Morgon stirred, then. Har looked at him, his eyes glinting, ice-blue, the color of wind across the sky above the wastes.

"You," he said, "stealing fire from my mind. Couldn't you have waited until morning?"

"Har . . ." Morgon whispered. He shook his head, not knowing where to begin. Then he stepped forward, his head bowed, into the wolf-king's embrace. "How can you trust me like this?" he demanded.

"Occasionally," Har admitted, "I am not rational." He loosed Morgon, held him back to look at him. "Where did Raederle find you?"

"In the wastes."

"You look like a man who has been listening to those deadly winds . . . Come to Yrye. A vesta can travel faster than a crow, and this deep into Osterland, vesta running together will not be noticed." He dropped his hand lightly onto the wizard's shoulder. "Ride on my back. Or on Morgon's."

"No," Morgon said abruptly, without thinking. Har's eyes went back to him.

Yrth said, before the king could speak, "I'll ride in crow-shape." His voice was tired. "There was a time when I would have chanced running blind for the sheer love of running, but no more . . . I must be getting old." He changed shape, fluttered from the ground to Har's other shoulder.

The wolf-king, frowning a little, his lined face shadowed by crows, seemed to hear something behind Morgon's silence. But he only said, "Let's get out of the rain."

They ran through the day until twilight: three vesta running north toward winter, one with a crow riding in the circle of its horns. They reached Yrye by nightfall. As they slowed and came to a halt in the yard, their sides heaving, the heavy doors of weathered oak and gold were thrown open. Aia appeared with wolves at her knees and Nun behind her, smiling out of her smoke.

Nun hugged Raederle in vesta-shape and again in her own shape. Aia, her smooth ivory hair unbraided, stared at Morgon a little, then kissed his cheek very gently. She patted Har's shoulder, and Yrth's, and said in her placid voice, "I sent everyone home. Nun told me who was coming."

"I told her," Yrth said, before Har had to ask. The king smiled a little. They went into the empty hall. The fire roared down the long bed; platters of hot meat, hot bread, hissing brass pots of spiced wine, steaming stews and vegetables lay on a table beside the hearth. They were eating almost before they sat down, quickly, hungrily. Then, as the edge wore off, they settled in front of the fire with wine and began to talk a little.

Har said to Morgon, who was half-drowsing on a bench with his arm around Raederle, "So. You came to Osterland to learn my land-law. I'll make a bargain with you."

That woke him. He eyed the king a moment, then said simply, "No. Whatever you want, I'll give you."

"That," Har said softly, "sounds like a fair exchange for land-law. You may wander freely through my mind, if I may wander freely through yours." He seemed to sense something in a vague turn of Yrth's head. "You have some objection?"

"Only that we have very little time," Yrth said. Morgon looked at him.

"Are you advising me to take the knowledge from the earth itself? That would take weeks."

"No."

"Then, are you advising me not to take it at all?" The wizard sighed. "No."

"Then what do you advise me to do?" Raederle stirred in his hold, at the faint, challenging edge to his voice. Har was still in his great carved chair; the wolf at his knee opened its eyes suddenly to gaze at Morgon.

"Are you," Har said amazedly, "picking a quarrel with Yrth in my hall?"

The wizard shook his head. "It's my fault," he explained. "There is a mind-hold Morgon was not aware of. I used it to keep him in Isig a few days ago when

Hed was attacked. It seemed better than to let him walk into a trap."

Morgon, his hands locking around the rim of his cup, checked a furious retort. Nun said, puzzled, "What hold?" Yrth looked toward her silently. Her face grew quiet for a moment, remote as if she were dreaming. Yrth loosed her, and her brows rose. "Where in Hel's name did you learn that?"

"I saw the possibility of it long ago, and I explored it into existence." He sounded apologetic. "I would never have used it except under extreme circumstances."

"Well, I would be upset, too. But I can certainly understand why you did it. If the Earth-Masters are searching for Morgon at the other end of the realm, there's no reason to distract them by giving them what they want."

Morgon's head bowed. He felt the touch of Har's gaze, like something physical, forcing his face up. He met the curious, ungentle eyes helplessly. The king loosed him abruptly.

"You need some sleep."

Morgon stared down into his wine. "I know." He felt Raederle's hand slide from his ribs to touch his cheek, and the weight of despair in him eased a little. He said haltingly, breaking the silence that had fallen over the hall, "But first, tell me how the vesta are bound like that into the defense of land-law. I was never aware of it as a vesta."

"I was hardly aware of it myself," the king admitted. "It's an ancient binding, I think; the vesta are extremely powerful, and I believe they rouse to the defense of the land, as well as land-law. But they have not fought anything but wolves for centuries, and the binding lay dormant at the bottom of my mind . . . I'll show you the binding, of course. Tomorrow." He looked across the fire at the wizard, who was refilling his cup slowly with hot spiced wine. "Yrth, did you go to Hed?"

"Yes." The pitch of liquid pouring into the cup changed as it neared the rim, and Yrth set the pot down.

"How did you cross Ymris?"

"Very carefully. I took no more time than necessary on my way to Hed, but returning, I stopped a few minutes to speak to Aloil. Our minds are linked; I was able to find him without using power. He was with Astrin Ymris, and what is left of the king's forces around Caerweddin."

There was another silence. A branch snapped in the fire and a shower of sparks fled towards the smoke hole in the roof. "What is left of the king's forces?" Har asked.

"Astrin was unsure. Half the men were pushed into Ruhn when Wind Plain was lost; the rest fled northward. The rebels—whatever they are: living men, dead men, Earth-Masters—have not attacked Caerweddin or any of the major cities in Ymris." He gazed thoughtfully through someone else's eyes at the fire. "They keep taking the ancient, ruined cities. There are many across Ruhn, one or two in east Umber, and King's Mouth Plain, near Caerweddin. Astrin and his generals are in dispute about what to do. The war lords contend that the rebels will not take King's Mouth Plain without attacking Caerweddin. Astrin does not want to waste lives warring over a dead city. He is beginning to think that the king's army and the rebel army are not fighting the same war . . ."

Har grunted. He rose, the wolf's head sliding from his knee. "A one-eyed man who can see. . . . Does he see an end to the war?"

"No. But he told me he is haunted by dreams of Wind Plain, as if some answer lies there. The tower on the plain is still bound by a living force of illusion."

"Wind Tower." The words came out of Morgon unexpectedly, some shard of a riddle the wizard's words unburied. "I had forgotten. . . ."

"I tried to climb it once," Nun said reminiscently.

Har took his cup to the table for more wine. "So did I." He asked, as Morgon glanced at him, "Have you?"

"No."

"Why not? It's a riddle. You're a riddler."

He thought back. "The first time I was on Wind Plain with Astrin I had lost my memory. There was only one riddle I was interested in answering. The second time . . ." He shifted a little. "I passed through very quickly, at night. I was pursuing a harpist. Nothing could have stopped me."

"Then perhaps," Har said softly, "you should try."

"You're not thinking," Nun protested. "The plain must be full of Earth-Masters."

"I am always thinking," Har said. A thought startled through Morgon; he moved again without realizing it, and Raederle lifted her face, blinking.

"It's bound by illusion . . . no one can reach the top of it. No one works an illusion unless there is something to be hidden, unseen. . . . But what would be hidden for so long at the top of the tower?"

"The High One," Raederle suggested sleepily. They gazed at her, Nun with her pipe smoldering in her fingers, Har with his cup halfway to his mouth. "Well," she added, "that's the one thing everyone is looking for. And the one place maybe that no one has looked."

Har's eyes went to Morgon. He ran his hand through his hair, his face clearing, easing into wonder. "Maybe. Har, you know I will try. But I always thought the binding of that illusion was some forgotten work of dead Earth-Masters, not . . . not of a living Earth-Master. Wait." He sat straight, staring ahead of him. "Wind Tower. The name of it . . . the name . . . wind." They roused suddenly through his memories: the deep wind in Erlenstar Mountain, the tumultuous winds of the wastes, singing to all the notes of his harp. "Wind Tower."

"What do you see?"

"I don't know . . . a harp strung with wind." As the winds died in his mind, he realized that he did not know who had asked the question. The vision receded, leaving him with only words and the certainty that they somehow fit together. "The tower. The starred harp. Wind."

Har brushed a white weasel off his chair and sat down slowly. "Can you bind the winds as well as land-law?" he asked incredulously.

"I don't know."

"I see. You haven't tried, yet."

"I wouldn't know how to begin." He added, "Once I shaped wind. To kill. That's all I know I can do."

"When—" He checked, shaking his head. The hall was very still; animals' eyes glowed among the rushes. Yrth set his cup down with a small, distracting clink as it hit the edge of a tray. Nun guided it for him.

"Small distances," he murmured ruefully.

"I think," the wolf-king said, "that if I start questioning you, it will be the longest riddle I have ever asked."

"You already asked the longest riddle," Morgon said. "Two years ago, when you saved my life in that blizzard and brought me into your house. I'm still trying to answer it for you."

"Two years ago, I gave you the knowledge of the vesta shape. Now you have come back for knowledge of my land-law. What will you ask of me next?"

"I don't know." He drained his cup and slid his hands around the mouth of it. "Maybe trust." He set the cup down abruptly, traced the flawless rim with his fingertips. He was exhausted suddenly; he wanted to lay his head on the table among the plates and sleep. He heard the wolf-king rise.

"Ask me tomorrow."

Har touched him. As he dragged his eyes open and stood up to follow the king out of the hall, he found nothing strange in the answer.

He slept dreamlessly until dawn beside Raederle

in the warm, rich chamber Aia had prepared for them. Then, as the sky lightened, vesta slowly crowded into his mind, forming a tight, perfect circle about him so that he could not move, and all their eyes were light, secret, blind. He woke abruptly, murmuring. Raederle groped for him, said something incoherent. He waited until she was quiet again. Then he got up soundlessly and dressed. He could smell one last sweet pine log burning into embers from the silent hall, and he knew, somehow, that Har was still there.

The king watched him as he came into the hall. He stepped quietly past small animals curled asleep beside the hearth and sat down beside Har. The king dropped a hand on his shoulder, held him a moment in a gentle, comfortable silence.

Then he said, "We'll need privacy or traders will spread rumors from here to Anuin. They have been flocking to my house lately, asking me questions, asking Nun . . ."

"There's the shed in the back," Morgon suggested, "where you taught me the vesta-shape."

"It seems appropriate . . . I'll wake Hugin; he can tend to our needs." He smiled a little. "For a while, I thought Hugin might return to the vesta; he became so shy among men. But since Nun came and told him everything she knew about Suth, I think he might turn into a wizard . . ." He was silent, sending a thought, Morgon suspected, through the quiet house. Hugin wandered in a few moments later, blinking sleepily and combing his white hair with his fingers. He stopped short when he saw Morgon. He was big-boned and graceful like the vesta, his deep eyes still shy. He stirred the rushes a little, flushing, looking like a vesta might if it were on the verge of smiling.

"We need your help," Har said. Hugin's head ducked an acquiescence. Then, gazing at Morgon, he found his tongue.

"Nun said you ·battled the wizard who killed Suth.

That you saved the lives of the Lungold wizards. Did
you kill the Founder?"

"No."

"Why not?"

"Hugin," Har murmured. Then he checked himself
and looked at Morgon curiously. "Why not? Did you
spend all your passion for revenge on that harpist?"

"Har . . ." His muscles had tensed under Har's
hand. The king frowned suddenly.

"What is it? Are you wraith-driven? Yrth told me
last night how the harpist died."

Morgon shook his head wordlessly. "You're a riddler," he said abruptly. "You tell me. I need help."

Har's mouth tightened. He rose, telling Hugin,
"Bring food, wine, firewood to the shed. And pallets.
When Raederle of An wakes, let her know where we
are. Bring her." He added a little impatiently as the
boy flushed scarlet, "You've talked to her before."

"I know." He was smiling suddenly. Under Har's
quizzical eye, he sobered and began to move. "I'll
bring her. And everything else."

They spent that day and the next nine nights together in the smokey, circular shed behind the king's
house. Morgon slept by day. Har, seemingly inex-
haustible, kept his court by day. Morgon, pulling out
of Har's mind each dawn, found Raederle beside him,
and Hugin, and sometimes Nun, knocking her ashes
into the fire. He rarely spoke to them; waking or sleeping, his mind seemed linked to Har's, forming trees,
ravens, snow-covered peaks, all the shapes deep in
the wolf-king's mind that were bound to his awareness. Har gave him everything and demanded nothing during those days. Morgon explored Osterland
through him, forming his own binding of awareness
with every root, stone, wolf pup, white falcon, and
vesta in the land. The king was full of odd wizardry,
Morgon discovered. He could speak to owls and
wolves; he could speak to an iron knife or arrowtip
and tell it where to strike. He knew the men and ani-

mals of his land as he knew his own family. His land-law extended even into the edges of the northern wastes, where he had raced vesta for miles across a desert of snow. He was shaped by his own law; the power in him tempered Morgon's heart with ice, and then with fire, until he seemed one more shape of Har's brain, or Har a reflection of his own power.

He broke loose from Har then, rolled onto a pallet, and fell asleep. Like a land-heir, he dreamed Har's memories. With a restless, furious intensity, his dreams spanned centuries of history, of rare battles, of riddle-games that lasted for days and years. He built Yrye, heard the wizard Suth give him five strange riddles for his keeping, lived among wolves, among the vesta, fathered heirs, dispensed judgment and grew so old he became ageless. Finally, the rich, feverish dreams came to an end; he drew deeply into himself, into a dreamless night. He slept without moving until a name drifted into his mind. Clinging to it, he brought himself back into the world. He blinked awake, found Raederle kneeling beside him.

She smiled down at him. "I wanted to find out if you were alive or dead." She touched his hand; his fingers closed around hers. "You can move."

He sat up slowly. The shed was empty; he could hear the winds outside trying to pick apart the roof. He tried to speak; his voice would not come for a moment. "How long—how long did I sleep?"

"Har said over two thousand years."

"Is he that old?" He stared at nothing a little, then leaned over to kiss her. "Is it day or night?"

"It's noon. You've slept nearly two days. I missed you. I only had Hugin to talk to most of the time."

"Who?"

Her smile deepened. "Do you remember my name?"

He nodded. "You are a two-thousand-year-old woman named Raederle." He sat quietly, holding her hand, putting the world into shape around him. He

stood up finally; she slid an arm around him to steady
him. The wind snatched the door out of his hand as
he opened it. The first flakes of winter snow swirled
and vanished in the winds. They shattered the silence
in his mind, whipped over him, persistent, icy, shaping him back out of his dreams. He ran across the
yard with Raederle, into the warmth of the king's dark
house.

Har came to him that evening as he lay beside the
fire in his chamber. He was remembering and slowly
absorbing the knowledge he had taken. Raederle had
left him alone, deep in his thoughts. Har, entering,
brought him out of himself. Their eyes met across the
fire in a peaceful, wordless recognition. Then Har sat
down, and Morgon straightened, shifting logs with his
hands until the drowsing fire woke.

"I have come," Har said softly, "for what you owe
me."

"I owe you everything." He waited. The fire slowly
blurred in front of him; he was lost to himself again,
this time among his own memories.

The king worked through them a little randomly, not
sure what he would find. Very early in his exploring,
he loosed Morgon in utter astonishment.

"You struck an old, blind wizard?"

"Yes. I couldn't kill him."

The king's eyes blazed with a glacial light. He
seemed about to speak; instead he caught the thread
of Morgon's memories again. He wove backwards and
forwards, from Trader's Road to Lungold and Erlenstar Mountain, and the weeks Morgon had spent in
the wastes, harping to the winds. He watched the
harpist die; he listened to Yrth speaking to Morgon
and to Danan in Isig; he listened to Raederle giving
Morgon a riddle that drew him back out of the dead
land, once again among the living. Then, he loosed
Morgon abruptly and prowled the chamber like a wolf.

"Deth."

The name chilled Morgon unexpectedly, as though Har had turned the impossible into truth with a word. The king paced to his side and stopped moving finally. He stared down into the fire. Morgon dropped his face against his forearms wearily.

"I don't know what to do. He holds more power than anyone else in this realm. You felt that mind-hold—"

"He has always held your mind."

"I know. And I can't fight him. I can't. You saw how he drew me on Trader's Road . . . with nothing. With a harp he could barely play. I went to him. . . . At Anuin I couldn't kill him. I didn't even want to. More than anything, I wanted a reason not to. He gave me one. I thought he had walked out of my life forever, since I left him no place in the realm to harp. I left him one place. He harped to me. He betrayed me again, and I saw him die. But he didn't die. He only replaced one mask with another. He made the sword I nearly killed him with. He threw me to Ghisteslwchlohm like a bone, and he rescued me from Earth-Masters on the same day. I don't understand him. I can't challenge him. I have no proof, and he would twist his way out of any accusation. His power frightens me. I don't know what he is. He gives me silence like the silence out of trees . . ." His voice trailed away. He found himself listening to Har's silence.

He raised his head. The king was still gazing into the fire, but it seemed to Morgon that he was watching it from the distance of many centuries. He was very still; he did not seem to be breathing. His face looked harsher than Morgon had ever seen it, as if the lines had been riven into it by the icy, merciless winds that scarred his land.

"Morgon," he whispered, "be careful." It was, Morgon realized slowly, not a warning but a plea. The king dropped to his haunches, held Morgon's shoulders very gently, as if he were grasping something elusive, intangible, that was beginning to shape itself under his hands.

"Har."

The king shook away his question. He held Morgon's eyes with an odd intensity, gazing through him into the heart of his confusion. "Let the harpist name himself . . ."

13

THE WOLF-KING GAVE HIM NO MORE ANSWERS than that. Something else lay hidden behind Har's eyes that he would not speak of. Morgon sensed it in him and so did Yrth, who asked, the evening before they left Yrye, "Har, what are you thinking? I can hear something beneath all your words."

They were sitting beside the fire. The winds were whistling across the roof, dragging shreds of smoke up through the opening. Har looked at the wizard across the flames. His face was still honed hard, ancient, by whatever he had seen. But his voice, when he spoke to the wizard, held only its familiar, dry affection.

"It's nothing for you to concern yourself about."

"Why can't I believe that?" Yrth murmured. "Here in this hall, where you have riddled your way through centuries to truth?"

"Trust me," Har said. The wizard's eyes sought toward him through their private darkness.

"You're going to Ymris."

"No," Morgon said abruptly. He had stopped fighting Yrth; he trod warily in the wizard's presence, as in the presence of some powerful, unpredictable animal. But the wizard's words, which seemed to lie somewhere between a statement and a command, startled a protest out of him. "Har, what can you do in Ymris besides get yourself killed?"

"I have no intention," Har said, "of dying in Ymris." He opened a palm to the fire, revealing withered crescents of power; the wordless gesture haunted Morgon.

"Then what do you intend?"

"I'll give you one answer for another."

"Har, this is no game!"

"Isn't it? What lies at the top of a tower of winds?"

"I don't know. When I know, I'll come back here and tell you. If you'll be patient."

"I have no more patience," Har said. He got up, pacing restlessly; his steps brought him to the side of the wizard's chair. He picked up a couple of small logs and knelt to position them on the fire. "If you die," he said, "it will hardly matter where I am. Will it?"

Morgon was silent. Yrth leaned forward, resting one hand on Har's shoulder for balance, and caught a bit of flaming kindling as it rolled toward them. He tossed it back onto the fire. "It will be difficult to get through to Wind Tower. But I think Astrin's army will make it possible." He loosed Har, brushed ash from his hands, and the king rose. Morgon, watching his grim face, swallowed arguments until there was nothing left in his mind but a fierce, private resolve.

He bade Har farewell at dawn the next day; and three crows began the long journey south to Herun. The flight was dreary with rain. The wizard led them with astonishing accuracy across the level rangelands of Osterland and the forests bordering the Ose. They did not change shape again until they had crossed the Winter and the vast no-man's-land between Osterland and Ymris stretched before them. The rains stilled finally near dusk on the third day of their journey, and with a mutual, almost wordless consent, they dropped to the ground to rest in their own shapes.

"How," Morgon asked Yrth almost before the wiz-

ard had coaxed a tangle of soaked wood into flame, "in
Hel's name are you guiding us? You led us straight to
the Winter. And how did you get from Isig to Hed
and back in two days?"

Yrth glanced toward his voice. The flame caught
between his hands, engulfing the wood, and he drew
back. "Instinct," he said. "You think too much while
you fly."

"Maybe." He subsided beside the fire. Raederle,
breathing deeply of the moist, pine-scented air, was
eying the river wistfully.

"Morgon, would you catch a fish? I am so hungry,
and I don't want to change back into a crow-shape
to eat—whatever crows eat. If you do that, I'll look for
mushrooms."

"I smell apples," Yrth said. He rose, wandering toward a scent. Morgon watched him a little incredulously.

"I don't smell apples," he murmured. "And I
hardly think at all when I fly." He rose, then stooped
again to kiss Raederle. "Do you smell apples?"

"I smell fish. And more rain. Morgon . . ." She put
her arm on his shoulders suddenly, keeping him down.
He watched her grope for words.

"What?"

"I don't know." She ran her free hand through her
hair. Her eyes were perplexed. "He moves across the
earth like a master . . ."

"I know."

"I keep wanting—I keep wanting to trust him. Until I remember how he hurt you. Then I became afraid
of him, of where he is leading us, and how skillfully. . . . But I forget my fear again so easily." Her
fingers tugged a little absently at his lank hair. "Morgon."

"What?"

"I don't know." She rose abruptly, impatient with
herself. "I don't know what I'm thinking."

She crossed the clearing to explore a pallid cluster

of mushrooms. Morgon went to the broad river, waded into the shallows, and stood silently as an old tree stump, watching for fish and trying not to think. He splashed himself twice, while trout skidded through his fingers. Finally, he made his mind a mirror of greyness to match the water and the sky and began to think like a fish.

He caught three trout and gutted them awkwardly, for lack of anything else, with his sword. He turned at last to bring them back to the fire and found Yrth and Raederle watching him. Raederle was smiling. The wizard's expression was unfathomable. Morgon joined them. He set the fish on a flat stone and cleaned his blade on the grass. He sheathed it once more within an illusion and squatted down by the fire.

"All right," he said. "Instinct." He took Raederle's mushrooms and began stuffing the fish. "But that doesn't explain your journey to Hed."

"How far can you travel in a day?"

"Maybe across Ymris. I don't know. I don't like moving from moment to moment across distances. It's exhausting, and I never know whose mind I might accidently touch."

"Well," the wizard said softly, "I was desperate. I didn't want you to fight your way out of that mindhold before I returned."

"I couldn't have—"

"You have the power. You can see in the dark."

Morgon stared at him wordlessly. Something shivered across his skin. "Is that what it was?" he whispered. "A memory?"

"The darkness of Isig."

"Or of Erlenstar Mountain."

"Yes. It was that simple."

"Simple." He remembered Har's plea and breathed soundlessly until the ache and snarl of words in his chest loosened. He wrapped the fish in wet leaves, pushed the stone into the fire. "Nothing is simple."

The wizard's fingers traced the curve of a blade

of grass to its tip. "Some things are. Night. Fire. A
blade of grass. If you place your hand in a flame and
think of your pain, you will burn yourself. But if you
think only of the flame, or the night, accepting it,
without remembering . . . it becomes very simple."

"I cannot forget."

The wizard was silent. By the time the fish began to
spatter, the rains had started again. They ate hur-
riedly and changed shape, flew through the drenching
rains to shelter among the trees.

They crossed the Ose a couple of days later and
changed shape again on the bank of the swift, wild
river. It was late afternoon. Light and shadow daz-
zled across their faces from the wet, bright sky. They
gazed at one another a little bewilderedly, as if surprised by their shapes.

Raederle dropped with a sigh on a fallen log. "I
can't move," she whispered. "I am so tired of being
a crow. I am beginning to forget how to talk."

"I'll hunt," Morgon said. He stood still, intending to
move, while weariness ran over him like water.

Yrth said, "I'll hunt." He changed shape again, before either of them could answer. A falcon mounted
the air, higher and higher, in a fierce, blazing flight
into the rain and sunlight, then he levelled finally,
began circling.

"How?" Morgon whispered. "How can he hunt
blind?" He quelled a sudden impulse to burn a path
through the light to the falcon's side. As he watched,
the falcon plummeted down, swift, deadly, into the
shadows.

"He is like an Earth-Master," Raederle said, and an
odd chill ran through Morgon. Her words sounded as
if they hurt. "They all have that terrible beauty."
They watched the bird lift from the ground, dark in
the sudden fading of the light. Something dragged
from its talons. She stood up slowly, began gathering
wood. "He'll want a spit."

Morgon stripped a sapling bough and peeled it as

the bird flew back. It left a dead hare beside Raederle's
fire. Yrth stood before them again. For a moment, his
eyes seemed unfamiliar, full of the clear, wild air, and
the fierce precision of the falcon's kill. Then they
became familiar again. Morgon asked his question in
a voice that sounded timbreless, subdued.

"I scented its fear," the wizard said. He slid a knife
from his boot before he sat down. "Will you skin it?
That would be a problem for me."

Morgon set to work wordlessly. Raederle picked
up the spit, finished peeling it. She said abruptly, almost shyly, "Can you speak a falcon's language?"

The blind, powerful face turned toward her. Its
sudden gentleness at the sound of her voice stilled
Morgon's knife. "A little of it."

"Can you teach me? Do we have to fly all the way to
Herun as crows?"

"If you wish . . . I thought, being of An, you might
be most comfortable as a crow."

"No," she said softly. "I am comfortable now as
many things. But it was a kind thought."

"What have you shaped?"

"Oh . . . birds, a tree, a salmon, a badger, a deer, a
bat, a vesta—I lost count long ago, searching for Morgon."

"You always found him."

"So did you."

Yrth sifted the ground around him absently, for
twigs to hold the spit. "Yes . . ."

"I have shaped a hare, too."

"Hare is a hawk's prey. You shape yourself to the
laws of earth."

Morgon tossed skin and offal into the bracken and
reached for the spit. "And the laws of the realm?" he
asked abruptly. "Are they meaningless to an Earth-
Master?"

The wizard was very still. Something of the falcon's
merciless power seemed to stir behind his gaze, until
Morgon sensed the recklessness of his challenge. He

looked away. Yrth said equivocally, "Not all of them." Morgon balanced the spit above the fire, turned the hare a couple of times to test it. Then the ambiguity of the wizard's words struck him. He slid back on his haunches, gazing at Yrth. But Raederle was speaking to him, and the clear note of pain in her voice held him silent.

"Then why, do you think, are my kinsmen on Wind Plain warring against the High One? If the power is a simple matter of the knowledge of rain and fire, and the laws they shape themselves to are the laws of the earth?"

Yrth was silent again. The sun had vanished, this time into deep clouds across the west. A haze of dusk and mist was beginning to close in upon them. He reached out, felt for the spit and turned it slowly. "I would think," he said, "that Morgon is correct in assuming the High One restrains the Earth-Masters' full power. Which is reason enough in itself for them to want to fight him . . . But many riddles seem to lie beneath that one. The stone children in Isig drew me down into their tomb centuries ago with the sense I felt of their sorrow. Their power had been stripped from them. Children are heirs to power; perhaps that was why they were destroyed."

"Wait," Morgon's voice shook on the word. "Are you saying—are you suggesting the High One's heir was buried in that tomb?"

"It seems possible, doesn't it?" Fat spattered in the blaze, and he turned the hare again. "Perhaps it was the young boy who told me of the stars I must put on a harp and a sword for someone who would come out of remote centuries to claim them . . ."

"But why?" Raederle whispered, still intent on her question. "Why?"

"You saw the falcon's flight . . . its beauty and its deadliness. If such power were bound to no law, that power and the lust for it would become so terrible—"

"I wanted it. That power."

The hard, ancient face melted again to its surprising gentleness. Yrth touched her, as he had touched the grass blade. "Then take it."

He let his hand fall. Raederle's head bent; Morgon could not see her face. He reached out to move her hair. She rose abruptly, turning away from him. He watched her walk through the trees, her hands gripping her arms as if she were chilled. His throat burned suddenly, for no coherent reason, except that the wizard had touched her, and she had left him.

"You left me nothing . . ." he whispered.

"Morgon—"

He stood up, followed Raederle into the gathering mists, leaving the falcon to its kill.

They flew through the next few days sometimes as crows, sometimes as falcons when the skies cleared. Two of the falcons cried to one another, in their piercing voices; the third, hearing them, was silent. They hunted in falcon-shape; slept and woke glaring at the pallid sun out of clear, wild eyes. When it rained, they flew as crows, plodding steadily through the drenched air. The trees flowed endlessly beneath them; they might have been flying again and again over the same point in space. But as the rains battered at them and vanished and the sun peered like a wraith through the clouds, a blur across the horizon ahead of them slowly hardened into a distant ring of hills breaking out of the forest.

The sun came out abruptly for a few moments before it drifted into night. Light glanced across the land, out of silver veins of rivers, and lakes dropped like small coin on the green earth. The falcons were flying wearily, in a staggered line that stretched over half a mile. The second one, bewitched, seemingly, by the light, shot suddenly ahead, in and out of sun and shadow, in a straight, exuberant flight towards their destination. Its excitement shook Morgon out of his monotonous rhythm. He picked up speed, soared past the lead falcon to catch up with the dark bolt hurtling

through the sky. He had not realized Raederle could
fly so fast. He streamed down currents of the north
wind, but still the falcon kept its distance. He pushed
toward it until he felt he had left his shape behind and
was nothing more than a love of speed swept forward
on the crest of light. He gained on the falcon slowly,
until he saw its wingspan and the darkness of its un-
derside and realized it was Yrth.

He kept his speed, wanting then, with all the energy
in him, to overtake the falcon in the pride of its power
and pass it. He sprinted toward it with all his strength,
until the wind seemed to burn past him and through
him. The forest heaved like a sea beneath him. Inch
by inch, he closed the distance between them, until he
was the falcon's shadow in the blazing sky. And then
he was beside it, matching its speed, his wings moving
to its rhythm. He could not pass it. He tore through air
and light until he had to loose even his furious desire, like ballast, to keep his speed. It would not let
him pass, but it lured him even faster, until all his
thoughts and a shadow over his heart were ripped
away and he felt if he went one heartbeat faster, he
would burn into wind.

He gave a cry as he fell away from the falcon's side,
down toward the gentle hills below. He could hardly
move his wings; he let the air currents toss him from
one to another until he touched the ground. He
changed shape. The long grass spun up to meet him.
He burrowed against the earth, his arms outstretched,
clinging to it, until the terrible pounding of his heart
eased and he began breathing air again instead of fire.
He rolled slowly onto his back and stood up. The falcon was hovering above him. He watched it motionlessly, until the wild glimpse into his own power broke
over him again. His hand rose in longing toward the
falcon. It fell toward him like a stone. He let it come.
It landed on his shoulder, clung there, its blind eyes
hooded. He was still in its fierce grip, caught in its
power and its pride.

Three falcons slept that night on the Herun hills. Three crows flew through the wet mists at dawn, above villages and rocky grazing land, where swirling winds revealed here and there a gnarled tree, or the sudden thrust of a monolith. The mists melted into rain that drizzled over them all the way to the City of Circles.

For once, the Morgol had not seen them coming. But the wizard Iff was waiting for them patiently in the courtyard, and the Morgol joined him there, looking curious, as the three black, wet birds lighted in front of her house. She stared at them, amazed, after they had changed shape.

"Morgon . . ." As she took his thin, worn face gently between her hands, he realized who it was that he had brought with him into her house.

Yrth was standing quietly; he seemed preoccupied, as though he had linked himself to all their eyes and had to sort through a confusion of images. The Morgol pushed Raederle's wet hair back from her face.

"You have become the great riddle of An," she said, and Raederle looked away from her quickly, down at the ground. But the Morgol lifted her face and kissed her, smiling. Then she turned to the wizards.

Iff put his hand on Yrth's shoulder, said in his tranquil voice, "El, this is Yrth; I don't think you have met."

"No." She bent her head. "You honor my house, Star-Maker. Come in, out of the rain. Usually I can see who is crossing my hills and prepare for my guests; but I did not pay any attention to three tired crows." She put her hand lightly on Yrth's arm to guide him. "Where have you come from?"

"Isig and Osterland," the wizard said. His voice sounded huskier than usual. Guards in the rich maze of corridors gazed without a change of stance at the visitors, but their eyes were startled, conjecturing. Morgon, watching Yrth's back as he walked beside the Morgol, his head angled toward her voice, realized slowly that Iff had dropped back and was speaking to him.

"The news of the attack on Hed reached us only a few days after it happened—word of it passed that swiftly through the realm. It caused great fear. Most of the people have left Caithnard, but where can they go? Ymris? An, which Mathom will leave nearly defenseless when he brings his army north? Lungold? That city is still recovering from its own terror. There is no place for anyone to go."

"Have the Masters left Caithnard?" Raederle asked.

The wizard shook his head. "No. They refuse to leave." He sounded mildly exasperated. "The Morgol asked me to go to them, see if they needed help, ships to move themselves and their books. They said that perhaps the strictures of wizardry held the secret of eluding death, but the strictures of riddlery hold that it is unwise to turn your back on death, since turning, you will only find it once more in front of you. I asked them to be practical. They suggested that answers, rather than ships, might help them most. I told them they might die there. They asked me if death is the most terrible thing. And at that point, I began to understand riddlery a little. But I had no skill to riddle with them."

"The wise man," Morgon said, "pursues a riddle inflexibly as a miser pursues a coin rolling towards a crack in a floorboard."

"Apparently. Can you do anything? They seemed to me something very fragile and very precious to the realm . . ."

The faint smile in his eyes died. "Only one thing. Give them what they want."

The Morgol stopped in front of a large, light room, with rugs and hangings of gold, ivory, and rich brown. She said to Morgon and Raederle, "My servants will bring what you need to make you comfortable. There will be guards stationed throughout the house.

Join us when you're ready, in Iff's study. We can talk there."

"El," Morgon said softly. "I cannot stay. I did not come to talk."

She was silent, riddling, he suspected, though her expression changed very little. She put her hand on his arm. "I have taken all the guards out of the cities and borders; Goh is training them here, to go south, if that is what you need."

"No," he said passionately. "I saw enough of your guards die in Lungold."

"Morgon, we must use what strength we have."

"There is far more power in Herun than that." He saw her face change then. He was aware of the wizard behind her, still as a shadow, and he wondered then without hope of an answer whether he gathered power by choice or at the falcon's luring. "That is what I have come for. I need that."

Her fingers closed very tightly on his forearm. "The power of land-law?" she whispered incredulously. He nodded mutely, knowing that the first sign of mistrust in her would scar his heart forever. "You have that power? To take it?"

"Yes. I need the knowledge of it. I will not touch your mind. I swear it. I went into Har's mind, with his permission, but you—there are places in your mind where I do not belong."

Some thought was growing behind her eyes. Standing so quietly, still gripping him, she could not speak. He felt as if he were changing shape in front of her into something ancient as the world, around which riddles and legends and the colors of night and dawn clung like priceless, forgotten treasures. He wanted to go into her mind then, to find whatever lay in his harsh, confused past to make her see him like that. But she loosed him and said, "Take from my land, and from me, what you need."

He stood still, watching her move down the hall, her hand beneath Yrth's elbow. Servants came, breaking into his thoughts. While they roused the fire and set water and wine to heat, he spoke softly to Raederle.

"I'll leave you here. I don't know how long I'll be gone. Neither one of us will be very safe, but at least Yrth and Iff are here, and Yrth—he does want me alive. I know that much."

She slid her hand onto his shoulder. Her face was troubled. "Morgon, you bound yourself to him as you flew. I felt it."

"I know." He lifted her hand, held the back of it against his chest. "I know," he repeated. He could not meet her eyes. "He lures me with myself. I told you that if I played with him, I would lose."

"Maybe."

"Watch over the Morgol. I don't know what I have brought into her house."

"He would never hurt her."

"He lied to her and betrayed her once already. Once is enough. If you need me, ask the Morgol where I am. She'll know."

"All right. Morgon . . ."

"What?"

"I don't know . . ." she answered, as she had several times in the past days. "Only I remember, sometimes, what Yrth said about fire and night being such simple things when you see them clearly. I keep thinking that you don't know what Yrth is because you never see him, you see only dark memories . . ."

"What in Hel's name do you expect me to see? He's more than a harpist, more than a wizard. Raederle, I'm trying to see. I'm—"

She put her hand over his mouth as servants glanced at them. "I know." She held him suddenly, tightly, and he felt himself trembling. "I didn't mean to upset you. But—be quiet and listen. I'm trying to think. You don't understand fire until you forget yourself and become fire. You learned to see in the dark when you became a great mountain whose heart was of darkness. You understood Ghisteslwchlohm by assuming his power. So, maybe the only way you will ever understand the harpist is to let him draw you into his power until you are part of his heart and you begin to see the world out of his eyes . . ."

"I may destroy the realm that way."

"Maybe. But if he is dangerous, how can you fight him without understanding him? And if he is not dangerous?"

"If he's not—" He stopped. The world seemed to shift slightly around him, all of Herun, the mountain kingdoms, the southern lands, the entire realm, adjusting into place under the falcon's eye. He saw the falcon's shadow spanning the realm in its powerful, silent flight, felt it fall across his back. The vision lasted a fraction of a moment. Then the shadow became a memory of night and his hands clenched. "He is dangerous," he whispered. "He always has been. Why am I so bound to him?"

He left the City of Circles that evening and spent days and nights he did not count, hidden from the world and almost from himself, within the land-law of Herun. He drifted shapelessly in the mists, seeped down into the still, dangerous marshlands, and felt the morning frost silver his face as it hardened over mud and reeds and tough marsh grasses. He cried a marsh bird's lonely cry and stared at the stars out of an expressionless slab of stone. He roamed through the low hills, linking his mind to rocks, trees, rivulets, searching into the rich mines of iron and copper and precious stones the hills kept enclosed within themselves. He spun tendrils of thought into a vast web across the dormant fields and lush, misty pastureland, linking himself to the stubble of dead roots, frozen furrows, and tangled grasses the sheep fed on. The gentleness of the land reminded him of Hed, but there was a dark, restless force in it that had reared up in the shapes of tors and monoliths. He drifted very close to the Morgol's mind, as he explored it; he sensed that

her watchfulness and intelligence had been born out
of need, the heritage of a land whose marshes and
sudden mists made it very dangerous to those who had
settled it. There was mystery in its strange stones, and
richness within its hills; the minds of the Morgols had
shaped themselves also to those things. As Morgon
drew deep into its law, he felt his own mind grow almost peaceful, bound by necessity to a fine clarity of
awareness and vision. Finally, when he began to see
as the Morgol saw, into things and beyond them, he
returned to the City of Circles.

He came back as he had left: as quietly as a piece
of ground mist wandering in from the still, cold Herun
night. He followed the sound of the Morgol's voice as
he took his own shape once again. He found himself
standing in firelight and shadow in her small, elegant
hall. The Morgol was speaking to Yrth as he appeared; he felt still linked to the calmness of her mind.
He made no effort to break the link, at rest in her
peacefulness. Lyra was sitting beside her; Raederle
had shifted closer to the fire. They had been at supper, but only their cups and flagons of wine remained
of it.

Raederle turned her head and saw Morgon; she
smiled at something in his eyes and left him undisturbed. Lyra caught his attention, then. She was
dressed for supper in a light, flowing, fiery robe; her
hair was braided and coiled under a net of gold
thread. Her face had lost its familiar proud assurance;
her eyes seemed older, vulnerable, haunted with
the memory of watching guards under her command
die at Lungold. She said something to the Morgol
that Morgon did not hear. The Morgol answered her
simply.

"No."

"I am going to Ymris." Her dark eyes held the
Morgol's stubbornly, but her argument was quiet. "If
not with the guard, then at your side."

"No."

"Mother, I am no longer in your guard. I resigned when I returned home from Lungold, so you can't expect me to obey you without thinking. Ymris is a terrible battlefield—more terrible than Lungold. I am going—"

"You are my land-heir," the Morgol said. Her face was still calm, but Morgon sensed the fear, relentless and chill as the Herun mists, deep in her mind. "I am taking the entire guard out of Herun down to Wind Plain. Goh will command it. You said that you never wanted to pick up another spear, and I was grateful you had made that decision. There is no need for you to fight in Ymris, and every need for you to stay here."

"In case you are killed," Lyra said flatly. "I don't understand why you are even going, but I will ride at your side—"

"Lyra—"

"Mother, this is my decision. Obeying you is no longer a matter of honor. I will do as I choose, and I choose to ride with you."

The Morgol's fingers edged slightly around her cup. She seemed surprised at her own movement. "Well," she said calmly, "if there is no honor in your actions in this matter, there will be none in mine. You will stay here. One way or another."

Lyra's eyes flickered a little. "Mother," she protested uncertainly, and the Morgol said:

"Yes. I am also the Morgol. Herun is in grave danger. If Ymris falls, I want you here to protect it in whatever way you can. If we both died in Ymris, it would be disastrous for Herun."

"But why are you going?"

"Because Har is going," the Morgol said softly, "and Danan, and Mathom—the land-rulers of the realm—impelled to Ymris to fight for the survival of the realm . . . or for some even more imperative reason. There is a tangle of riddles at the heart of the realm; I want to see its unravelling. Even at the risk of my life. I want answers."

Lyra was silent. Their faces in the soft light were almost indistinguishable in their fine, clean-lined beauty. But the Morgol's gold eyes hid her thoughts, while Lyra's were open to every flare of fire and pain.

"The harpist is dead," she whispered. "If that is what you are trying to answer."

The Morgol's eyes fell. She stirred after a moment, reached out swiftly to touch Lyra's cheek. "There are more unsolved questions than that in the realm," she said, "and nearly all, I think, more important." But her brows were constricted, as at a sudden, inexplicable pain. "Riddles without answers can be terrible," she added after a moment. "But some are possible to live with. Others. . . . What the Star-Bearer does at Wind Plain will be vital, Yrth thinks."

"Does he think you need to be there also? And if Wind Plain is so vital, where is the High One? Why is he ignoring the Star-Bearer and the entire realm?"

"I don't know. Perhaps Morgon can answer some of—" She lifted her head abruptly and saw him standing quietly in the shadows, his own thoughts waking again in his mind.

She smiled, holding out her hand in welcome. Yrth shifted a little, seeing, perhaps from her eyes, as Morgon came slowly to the table. Morgon saw him strangely for an instant, as something akin to the mists and monoliths of Herun that his mind could explore and comprehend. Then, as he sat down, the wizard's face seemed to avert itself from his eyes. He bent his head to the Morgol wordlessly. She said, "Did you find what you came for?"

"Yes. All I could bear. How long have I been gone?"

"Nearly two weeks."

"Two . . ." He shaped the word without sound. "So long? Has there been news?"

"Very little. Traders came from Hlurle for all the

arms we could spare, to take them to Caerweddin. I have been watching a mist moving south from Osterland, and finally, today, I realized what it is."

"A mist?" He remembered Har's scarred palm, opening to the red wash of firelight. "Vesta? Is Har bringing the vesta to Ymris?"

"There are hundreds of them, moving across the forests."

"They are great fighters," Yrth said. He sounded weary, disinclined to face an argument, but his voice was patient. "And they will not fear the Ymris winter."

"You knew." His thoughts were jarred out of their calm. "You could have stopped him. The miners, the vesta, the Morgol's guard—why are you drawing such a vulnerable, unskilled army across the realm? You may be blind, but the rest of us will have to watch the slaughter of men and animals on that battlefield—"

"Morgon," the Morgol interrupted gently, "Yrth does not make my decisions for me."

"Yrth—" He stopped, sliding his hands over his face, trying to check a futile argument. Yrth rose, drawing Morgon's eyes again. The wizard moved a little awkwardly through the cushions to the fire. He stood in front of it, his head bowed. Morgon saw his scarred hands close suddenly, knotted with words he could not speak, and he thought of Deth's hands, twisted with pain in the firelight. He heard an echo, then, out of the still Herun night, of the strange brief peace he had found beside the harpist's fire, within his silence. All that bound him to the harpist, to the falcon, his longing and his incomprehensible love, overwhelmed him suddenly. As he watched light and shadow search the hard, blind face into shape, he realized he would yield anything: the vesta, the Morgol's guard, the land-rulers, the entire realm, into the scarred, tormented hands in return for a place in the falcon's shadow.

The knowledge brought him to a strange, uneasy calm. His head bowed; he stared down at his dark reflection in the polished stone until Lyra, looking at him, said suddenly, "You must be hungry." She poured him wine. "I'll bring you some hot food." The Morgol watched her cross the room with her lithe, graceful step. She looked tired, more tired than Morgon had ever seen her.

She said to Morgon, "Miners and vesta and my guard may seem useless in Ymris, but Morgon, the land-rulers are giving of all the strength they possess. There is nothing else we can do."

"I know." His eyes moved to her; he knew her own confused love for a memory. He said abruptly, wanting to give her something of peace in return for all she had given him, "Ghisteslwchlohm said that you had been waiting for Deth near Lungold. Is that true?"

She looked a little startled at his brusqueness, but she nodded. "I thought he might come to Lungold. It was the only place left for him to go, and I could ask him. . . . Morgon, you and I are both tired, and the harpist is dead. Perhaps we should—"

"He died—he died for you."

She stared at him across the table. "Morgon," she whispered, warning him, but he shook his head.

"It is true. Raederle could have told you. Or Yrth —he was there." The wizard turned light, burned eyes toward him, then, and his voice shook. But he went on, returning the riddle of the harpist's life to him unanswered, in exchange for nothing. "Ghisteslwchlohm gave Deth a choice between holding either Raederle or you as hostage while he forced me to Erlenstar Mountain. He chose to die instead. He forced Ghisteslwchlohm to kill him. He had no compassion for me . . . maybe because I could endure without it. But you and Raederle, he simply loved." He stopped, breathing a little painfully as she dropped her face into her hands. "Did I hurt you? I didn't mean to—"

"No." But she was crying, he could tell, and he cursed himself. Yrth was still watching him; he wondered how the wizard was seeing, since Raederle's face had disappeared behind her hair. The wizard made a strange gesture, throwing up one open hand to the light, as if he were yielding something to Morgon. He reached out, touched the air at Morgon's back, and the starred harp leaped out of nothingness into his hands.

The Morgol's eyes went to Morgon as the first, sweet notes sounded, but his hands were empty. He was gazing at Yrth, words lumped like ice in his throat. The wizard's big hands moved with a flawless precision over the strings he had tuned; tones of wind and water answered him. It was the harping out of a long, black night in Erlenstar Mountain, with all its deadly beauty; the harping kings across the realm had heard for centuries. It was the harping of a great wizard who had once been called the Harpist of Lungold, and the Morgol, listening silently, seemed only awed and a little surprised. Then the harpist's song changed, and the blood ran completely out of her face.

It was a deep, lovely, wordless song that pulled out of the back of Morgon's memories a dark, misty evening above the Herun marshes, a fire ringed with faces of the Morgol's guard, Lyra appearing soundlessly out of the night, saying something. . . . He strained to hear her words. Then, looking at the Morgol's white, numb face as she stared at Yrth, he remembered the song Deth had composed only for her.

A shudder ran through Morgon. He wondered, as the beautiful harping drew to a close, how the harpist could possibly justify himself to her. His hands slowed, picked a final, gentle chord from the harp, then flattened on the strings to still them. He sat with his head bowed slightly over the harp, his hands resting above the stars. Firelight shivered over him, weaving patterns of light and shadow in the air. Morgon waited for him to speak. He said nothing; he did not move. Moments wore away; still he sat with the silence of trees or earth or the hard, battered face of granite; and Morgon, listening to it, realized that his silence was not the evasion of an answer, but the answer itself.

He closed his eyes. His heart beat suddenly, painfully, in his throat. He wanted to speak, but he could not. The harpist's silence circled him with the peace he had found deep in living things all over the realm. It eased through his thoughts, into his heart, so that he could not even think. He only knew that something he had searched for so long and so hopelessly had never, even in his most desperate moments, been far from his side.

The harpist rose then, his weary, ancient face the wind-swept face of a mountain, the scarred face of the realm. His eyes held the Morgol's for a long moment, until her face, so white it seemed translucent, shook, and she stared blindly down at the table. Then he moved to Morgon, slipped the harp back onto his shoulder. Morgon felt as from a dream the light, quick movements. He seemed to linger for a moment; his hand touched Morgon's face very gently. Then, walking toward the fire, he melted into its weave.

14

ORGON MOVED THEN, UNBOUND FROM THE
silence. He cast with his mind into the night,
but everywhere he searched he found only its
stillness. He rose. Words seemed gripped in his chest
and in his clenched hands, as if he dared not let them
go. The Morgol seemed as reluctant to speak. She
stirred a little, stiffly, then stilled again, gazing down at
a star of candlelight reflected on the table. The blood
came back into her face slowly. Watching her expression change, Morgon found his voice.

"Where did he go?" he whispered. "He spoke to
you."

"He said—he said that he had just done the only
foolish thing in his very long life." Her hands moved,
linked themselves; she frowned down at them, concentrating with an effort. "That he had not intended for
you to know him until you had gathered enough power
to fight for yourself. He left because he is a danger to
you now. He said—other things." She shook her head
slightly, then spoke again. "He said that he had not
realized there was a limit to his own endurance."

"Wind Plain. He'll be in Ymris."

She raised her eyes then, but she did not argue.

"Find him, Morgon. No matter how dangerous it is for both of you. He has been alone long enough."

"I will." He turned, knelt beside Raederle. She was staring into the fire; he brushed at the reflection of a flame on her face. She looked at him. There was something ancient, fierce, only half-human in her eyes, as if she had seen into the High One's memories. He took her hand. "Come with me."

She stood up. He linked their minds, cast far into the Herun night until he touched a stone he remembered on the far side of the marshes. As Lyra entered the hall, bringing his supper, he took one step toward her and vanished.

They stood together in the mists, seeing nothing but a shadowy whiteness, like a gathering of wraiths. Morgon sent his awareness spiralling outward, out of the mists, through the low hills, far across them, farther than he had ever loosed his mind before. His thoughts anchored in the gnarled heart of a pine. He pulled himself toward it.

Standing beside it, in the wind-whipped forests between Herun and Ymris, he felt his overtaxed powers suddenly falter. He could barely concentrate; his thoughts seemed shredded by wind. His body, to which he had been paying only sporadic attention, was making imperative demands. He was shivering; he kept remembering the smell of hot meat Lyra had brought him. Pieces of the harpist's life kept flashing into his mind. He heard the fine, detached voice speaking to kings, to traders, to Ghisteslwchlohm, riddling always, not with his words, but with all he did not say. Then one memory seared through all Morgon's thoughts, shaking a sound from him. He felt the north wind whittle at his bones.

"I nearly killed him." He was almost awed at his own blundering. "I tracked the High One all the way across the realm to kill him." Then a sharp, familiar pain bore into his heart. "He left me in Ghisteslwchlohm's hands. He could have killed the Founder with half a word. Instead, he harped. No wonder I never recognized him."

"Morgon, it's cold." Raederle put her arm around him; even her hair felt chill against his face. He tried to clear his mind, but the winds wept into it, and he saw the harpist's face again, staring blindly at the sky.

"He was a Master . . ."

"Morgon." He felt her mind grope into his. He let it come, surprised. The sense of her quieted him; her own thoughts were very clear. He drew apart from her, looked through the darkness into her face.

"You were never that angry for my sake."

"Oh, Morgon." She held him again. "You said it yourself: you endure, like the hard things of the realm. He needed you that way, so he left you to Ghisteslwchlohm. I'm saying it badly . . ." she protested, as his muscles tensed. "You learned to survive. Do you think it was easy for him? Harping for centuries in Ghisteslwchlohm's service, waiting for the Star-Bearer?"

"No," he said after a moment, thinking of the harpist's broken hands. "He used himself as mercilessly as he used me. But for what?"

"Find him. Ask him."

"I can't even move," he whispered. Her mind touched his again; he let his thoughts rest finally in her tentative hold. He waited patiently while she worked, exploring across distance. She touched him finally. He moved without knowing where he was going, and he began to understand the patience and trust he had demanded of her. They did not go very far, he sensed, but he waited wearily, gratefully, while she found her way step by step across the forests. By dawn, they had reached the north border of Ymris. And there, as the red sun of storms and ill winds rose in the east, they rested.

They flew over Marcher as carrion crows. The rough, hilly borderland seemed quiet; but in the late afternoon, the crows spied a band of armed men guarding a line of trade-carts lumbering toward Caerweddin. Morgon veered down toward them. He caught one of the warrior's mind as he landed on the road, to avoid being attacked when he changed shape. He drew the sword out of its sheath of air, held the stars up as the man stared at him. They flared uneasily in the grey light.

"Morgon of Hed," the warrior breathed. He was a grizzled, scarred veteran; his eyes, shadowed and bloodshot, had gazed across the dawn and deadly twilight of many fields. He halted the train of cars behind him and dismounted. The men behind were silent.

"I need to find Yrth," Morgon said. "Or Aloil. Or Astrin Ymris."

The man touched the stars on his upraised sword with a curious gesture, almost a ritual of fealty. Then he blinked as a gor-crow landed on Morgon's shoulder. He said, "I am Lien Marcher, cousin of the High Lord of Marcher. I don't know Yrth. Astrin Ymris is in Caerweddin; he could tell you where Aloil is. I'm taking arms and supplies to Caerweddin, for whatever good they'll do there. If I were you, Star-Lord, I would not show an eyelash in this doomed land. Let alone three stars."

"I've come to fight," Morgon said. The land whispered to him, then, of law, legends, the ancient dead beneath his feet, and his own body seemed to yearn toward the shape of it. The man's eyes ran over his lean face, the rich, worn tunic that seemed mildly absurd in those dangerous, wintry hills.

"Hed," he said. A sudden, amazed smile broke through the despair in his eyes. "Well. We've tried everything else. I would offer to take you with me, Lord, but I think you're safer on your own. There is only one man Astrin might want to see more than you, but I wouldn't want to lay any bets on that."

"Heureu. He's still missing."

The man nodded wearily. "Somewhere in the realm between the dead and the living. Not even the wizard can find him. I think—"

"I can find him," Morgon said abruptly. The man was silent, the smile in his eyes wiped away by a naked, unbearable hope.

"Can you? Not even Astrin can, and his dreams are full of Heureu's thoughts. Lord, what—what are you, that you can stand there shivering in the cold and have me believing in your power? I survived the carnage on Wind Plain. Some nights when I wake from my own dreams, I wish I had died there." He shook his head; his hand moved to Morgon again, then dropped without touching him. "Go, now. Take your stars out of eyesight. Find your way safely to Caerweddin. Lord, hurry."

The crows flew eastward. They passed other long convoys of supply-carts and strings of horses; they rested in the eaves of great houses, whose yards were choked with smoke and the din of forges. The brilliant colors of battle livery and the dark, sweating flanks of plow horses flickered through the smoke, as men gathered to march to Caerweddin. There were young boys among them, and the rough, weathered faces of shepherds, farmers, smiths, even traders, receiving a crude, desperate introduction to arms before they joined the forces at Caerweddin. The sight spurred the crows onward. They followed the Thul as it ran toward the sea, cutting a dark path through the dying fields.

They reached Caerweddin at sunset; the sky was shredded like a brilliant banner by the harsh winds. The whole of the city was ringed by a thousand fires, as if it were besieged by its own forces. But the harbor was clear; trade-ships from Isig and Anuin were homing toward it on the evening tide. The beautiful house of the Ymris kings, built of the shards of an Earth-Masters' city, burned like a jewel in the last light. The crows dropped down into the shadows just outside its closed gates.They changed shape in the empty street.

They did not speak as they looked at one another.
Morgon drew Raederle against him, wondering if his
own eyes were as stunned with weariness. He touched
her mind; then, searching into the heart of the king's
house, he found Astrin's mind.

He appeared in front of the Ymris land-heir as he
sat alone in a small council chamber. He had been
working; maps, messages, supply lists were strewn all
over his desk. But the room was nearly in darkness,
and he had not bothered to light candles. He was staring ahead of him into the fire, his face harrowed,
colorless. Morgon and Raederle, stepping out of the
street into the blur of light and shadow, did not even
startle him. He gazed at them a moment as if they had
no more substance than his hope. Then his expression
changed; he stood up, his chair falling behind him
with a crash. "Where have you been?"

There was a realm of relief, compassion, and exas-
peration in the question. Morgon, casting a glance at
his past with an eye as probing as the single, wintry
eye of the Ymris prince, said simply, "Answering riddles."

Astrin rounded his desk and eased Raederle into a
chair. He gave her wine and the numbness began to
wear out of her face. Astrin, half-kneeling beside her,
looked up at Morgon incredulously.

"Where did you come from? I have been thinking
about you and Heureu—you and Heureu. You're
thin as an awl, but in one piece. You look—if ever
I've seen a man who looks like a weapon, you do.
There is a quiet thunder of power all over this room.
Where did you get it?"

"All over the realm." He poured himself wine and
sat.

"Can you save Ymris?"

"I don't know. Maybe. I don't know. I need to find
Yrth."

"Yrth. I thought he was with you."

He shook his head. "He left me. I need to find him. I need him . . ." His voice had sunk to a whisper; he stared into the fire, the cup a hollow of gold in his hands. Astrin's voice startled through him, and he realized he was nearly asleep.

"I haven't seen him, Morgon."

"Is Aloil here? His mind is linked to Yrth's."

"No; he is with Mathom's army. It's massed in the forests near Trader's Road. Morgon." He leaned forward to grip Morgon, bringing him out of the sudden despair overwhelming him.

"He was there beside me, if only I had had enough sense to turn and face him, instead of pursuing his shadow all over the realm. I harped with him, I fought with him, I tried to kill him, and I loved him, and the moment I name him he vanishes, leaving me still pursuing . . ." Astrin's grip was suddenly painful.

"What are you saying?"

Morgon, realizing his own words, gazed back at him mutely. He saw once again the strange, colorless face that had been over him when he had wakened, voiceless, nameless, in a strange land. The warrior before him, with a dark, tight tunic buttoned haphazardly over a shift of mail, became the half-wizard once more in his hut by the sea, riddling over the bones of the city on Wind Plain.

"Wind Plain . . ." he whispered. "No. He can't have gone there without me. And I'm not ready."

Astrin's hand slackened. His face was expressionless, skull-white. "Exactly who is it you're looking for?" He spoke very carefully, fitting the words together like shards. The harpist's name shocked through Morgon then: the first dark riddle the harpist had given him long ago on a sunlit autumn day at the docks at Tol. He swallowed dryly, wondering suddenly what he was pursuing.

Raederle shifted in her chair, pillowing her face against a fur cloak drapped over it. Her eyes were closed. "You've answered so many riddles," she murmured. "Where is there one last, unanswered riddle but on Wind Plain?"

She burrowed deeper into the fur as Morgon eyed her doubtfully. She did not move again; Astrin took her cup before it dropped from her fingers. Morgon rose abruptly, crossed the room. He leaned over Astrin's desk; the map of Ymris lay between his hands.

"Wind Plain . . ." The shaded areas of the map focussed under his gaze. He touched an island of darkness in west Ruhn. "What is this?"

Astrin, still hunched beside the fire, got to his feet. "An ancient city," he said. "They have taken nearly all the Earth-Masters' cities in Meremont and Tor, parts of Ruhn."

"Can you get through the Wind Plain?"

"Morgon, I would march there with no other army but my shadow if you want it. But can you give me a reason I can give to my war lords for taking the entire army away from Caerweddin and leaving the city unguarded to fight over a few broken stones?"

Morgon looked at him. "Can you get through?"

"Here." He drew a line down from Caerweddin, between Tor and the dark area in east Umber. "With some risk." He traced the southern border of Meremont. "Mathom's army will be here. If it were only men we were fighting, I would call them doomed, caught between two great armies. But Morgon, I can't calculate their strength, none of us can. They take what they want in their own time. They aren't pretending to fight us anymore; they simply overrun us whenever we happen to get in their way. The realm is their chessboard, and we are their pawns . . . and the game they are playing seems incomprehensible. Give me a reason to move the men south, to pick a fight in the bitter cold over land that no one has lived on for centuries."

Morgon touched a point on Wind Plain where a lonely tower might have stood. "Danan is coming south with his miners. And Har with the vesta. And the

Morgol with her guard. Yrth wanted them there at Wind Plain. Astrin, is that enough reason? To protect the land-rulers of the realm?"

"Why?" His fist slammed down on the plain, but Raederle did not even stir. "Why?"

"I don't know."

"I'll stop them in Marcher."

"You won't stop them. They are drawn to Wind Plain, as I am, and if you want to see any of us alive next spring, then take your army south. I didn't choose the season. Or the army that is following me across the realm. Or the war itself. I am—" He stopped, as Astrin's hands closed on his shoulders. "Astrin. I have no time left to give you. I have seen too much. I have no choices left. No other seasons."

The single eye would have searched into his thoughts, if he had let it. "Then who is making your choices?"

"Come to Wind Plain."

The prince loosed him. "I'll be there," he whispered.

Morgon turned away from him after a moment, sat down again. "I have to leave," he said tiredly.

"Tonight?"

"Yes. I'll sleep a little and then leave. I need answers . . ." He gazed across at Raederle's face, hidden in the fur; only the line of her cheek and chin, brushed by light, showed beneath her hair. He said very softly, "I'll let her sleep. She might follow me when she wakes; tell her to be careful flying across Wind Plain."

"Where are you going?"

Raederle's hair blurred into fire; his eyes closed. "To find Aloil. . . . To find a wind."

He slept without dreaming and woke a few hours later. Astrin had covered Raederle; she was barely visible, huddled under fur-lined blankets. Astrin, lying between them on skins beside the fire, was guarding them. His sword was unsheathed; one hand rested on the bare blade. Morgon thought he had fallen asleep, but his good eye opened as Morgon stood. He said nothing. Morgon leaned down to touch his shoulder in a silent farewell. Then he caught at the night beyond the stones.

The night winds snarled in furious contention around him as he flew. He did not dare use power in the stretch between Caerweddin and Wind Plain. Dawn broke in sheets of cold, grey rain over hunched trees and lifeless fields. He flew through the day, fighting the winds. By twilight, he reached Wind Plain.

He flew low over it, a huge black carrion crow casting a bitter eye over the remains of the unburied warriors of Heureu's army. Nothing else moved on the plain; not even birds or small animals had come to scavenge in the fierce rain. A treasure of arms gleamed in the twilight all over the plain. The rain was hammering jewelled sword hilts, pieces of armor, horse's skulls and the bones of men alike down into the wet earth. The crow's eye saw nothing else as it winged slowly toward the ruined city; but beyond the shield of its instincts, Morgon sensed the silent, deadly warning ringing the entire plain.

The great tower rose above the city, spiralling into night as he winged past it. He kept his mind empty of all thought, aware only of the smells of the wet earth, and the slow, weary rhythm of his flight. He did not stop until he had crossed the plain and the south border of Ymris and finally saw the midnight fires of Mathom's army sprawled along the river near Trader's Road. He descended then and found shelter among the thick, leafless oak. He did not move until morning.

Dawn crusted the earth with frost and a chill like the bite of a blade. He felt it as he changed shape; his breath froze in a quick, startled flash in front of him. Shivering, he followed the smell of wood smoke and hot wine to the fires beside the river. Dead warriors of An were posted as sentries. They seemed to recognize something of An in him, for they gave him

white, eyeless grins and let him pass among them un-
challenged.

He found Aloil talking to Talies beside the fire outside the king's pavilion. He joined the wizards quietly, stood warming himself. Through the bare trees,
he saw other fires, men rousing out of tents, stamping
the blood awake in their bodies. Horses snorted the
chill out of their lungs, pulling restively at their ropes.
Tents, horse trappings, men's arms, and tunics all bore
the battle colors of Anuin: blue and purple edged
with the black of sorrow. The wraiths bore their own
ancient colors when they bothered to clothe themselves with the memories of their bodies. They moved
vividly and at will among the living, but the living,
inured to many things at that point, took more interest in their breakfast than in the dead.

Morgon, finally warm, caught Aloil's attention as he
began listening to their conversation. The big wizard
broke off mid-sentence and turned his blue, burning
gaze across the fire. The preoccupied frown in his eyes
turned to amazement.

"Morgon . . ."

"I'm looking for Yrth," Morgon said. "Astrin told
me he was with you." Talies, both thin brows raised,
started to comment. Then he stepped to the king's pavilion and flung the flap open. He said something;
Mathom followed him back out.

"He was here a moment ago," Talies said, and
Morgon sighed. "He can't be far. How in Hel's name
did you cross Wind Plain?"

"At night. I was a carrion crow." He met the black,
searching eyes of the King of An. Mathom, pulling his
cloak off, said crustily, "It's cold enough to freeze the
bare bones of the dead." He threw it around Morgon's shoulders. "Where did you leave my daughter?"

"Asleep at Caerweddin. She'll follow me when she
wakes."

"Across Wind Plain? Alone? You aren't easy on one

another." He prodded the fire until it groped for the low boughs of the oak.

Morgon asked, pulling the cloak tight, "Was Yrth with you? Where did he go?"

"I don't know. I thought he came out for a cup of hot wine. This is no season for old men. Why? There are two great wizards here, both at your service." He did not wait for an answer; he cast a quizzical eye at Aloil. "You are linked to him. Where is he?"

Aloil, staring down at the fuming oak logs, shook his head. "Napping, perhaps. His mind is silent. He made a swift journey across Ymris."

"So did Morgon, by the look of it," Talies commented. "Why didn't Yrth travel with you?"

Morgon, caught without an answer, ran one hand through his hair vaguely. He saw a sudden glitter in the crow's eyes. "No doubt," Mathom said, "Yrth had his reasons. A man with no eyes sees marvels. You stopped at Caerweddin? Are Astrin and his war lords still at odds?"

"Possibly. But Astrin is bringing the entire army to Wind Plain."

"When?" Aloil demanded. "He said nothing of that to me, and I was with him three nights ago."

"Now." He added, "I asked him to."

There was a silence, during which one of the sentries, wearing nothing more than his bones under gold armor, rode soundlessly past the fire. Mathom's eyes followed the wraith's passage. "So. What does a man with one eye see?" He answered himself, with a blank shock of recognition in his voice, "Death."

"This is hardly a time," Aloil said restlessly, "for riddles. If the way is clear between Umber and Thor, it will take him four days to reach the plain. If it is not . . . you had better be prepared to march north to aid him. He could lose the entire strength of Ymris. Do you know what you're doing?" he asked Morgon. "You have gained awesome powers. But are you ready to use them alone?"

Talies dropped a hand on his shoulder. "You have the brain of an Ymris warrior," he said, "full of muscle and poetry. I'm no riddler, either, but living for centuries in the Three Portions taught me a little subtlety. Can you listen to what the Star-Bearer is saying? He is drawing the force of the realm to Wind Plain, and he is not intending to battle alone. Wind Plain. Astrin saw it. Yrth saw it. The final battleground . . ."

Aloil gazed silently at him. Something like a frail, reluctant hope struggled into his face. "The High One." He swung his gaze again to Morgon. "You think he is on Wind Plain?"

"I think," Morgon said softly, "that wherever he is, if I don't find him very soon, we are all dead. I have answered one riddle too many." He shook his head as both wizards began to speak. "Come to Wind Plain. I'll give you whatever answers I have there. That's where I should have gone in the first place, but I thought perhaps—" He broke off. Mathom finished his sentence.

"You thought Yrth was here. The Harpist of Lungold." He made a harsh, dry sound, like a crow's laugh. But he was staring into the fire as if he were watching it weave a dream to its ending. He turned away from it abruptly, but not before Morgon saw his eyes, black and expressionless as the eyes of his dead, who had been eaten to the bone by truth.

MORGON STOOD IN THE TREES AT THE EDGE OF WIND Plain at twilight, waiting as the night slowly drew the empty city and the long, whispering grasses into itself once again. He had been there for hours, motionless, waiting, so still he might have rooted himself to earth like a bare, twisted oak without realizing it. The sky spilled a starless black over the world, until even with his night-vision, the jewellike colors of the tower stones seemed permeated with the dark. He moved then, aware of his body again. As he took one final step toward the tower, clouds parted unexpectedly. A single star drifted through the unfathomable blackness above it.

He stood at the foot of the stairs, looking up at them as he had when he first saw them one wet autumn day two years before. Then, he remembered, he had turned away, uncurious, uncompelled. The stairs were gold, and according to all legend they wound away from the earth forever.

He bowed his head as if he were walking into a hard wind and began to climb. The walls around him were of the lustrous burning black between stars. The gold stairs ringed around the core of the tower, slanting gently upward. As he rounded it once and began the second spiral, the black gave way to a rich crimson. The winds, he realized, were no longer the thin, angry winds of the day; their voices were forceful, sinewy. The stairs beneath his feet seemed carved of ivory.

He heard the voices of the winds change again at the third spiral. They held tones he had harped to in the northern wastes, and his hands yearned to match their singing. But harping would be deadly, so he kept his hands still. At the fourth level the walls seemed of solid gold and the stairs carved out of star fire. They wound endlessly upward; the plain, the broken city grew farther and farther away from him. The winds grew colder as he climbed. At the ninth level he wondered if he were climbing a mountain. The winds, the stairs, and the walls around him were clear as melted snow. The spirals were getting smaller, and he thought he must be near the top. But the next level plunged him into an eerie darkness, as if the stairs were carved out of night wind. It seemed interminable, but when he came out of it again, the moon was exactly where he had seen it last. He continued upward. The walls turned a beautiful dawn-grey; the stairs were pale rose. The winds had a cutting edge, merciless and deadly. They were prodding him out of his own shape. He kept walking, half-man, half-wind, and the colors around him changed again and again, until he realized, as others had realized before him, that he could spiral through their changing forever.

He stopped. The city was so far beneath him he could no longer see it in the dark. Looking up, he could see the elusive top of the tower very near him. But it had been that near him, it seemed, for hours. He wondered if he were walking through a piece of a dream that had stood among the abandoned stones for thousands of years. Then he realized it was not a dream, but an illusion, an ancient riddle bound to someone's mind, and he had carried the answer to it with him all the way.

He said softly, "Death."

15

THE WALLS ROSE AROUND HIM, CIRCLED HIM.
Twelve windows opened through midnight blue
stone to the restless, murmuring winds. He felt
a touch and turned, startled back into his body.

The High One stood before him. He had the wizard's scarred hands, and the harpist's fine, worn face.
But his eyes were neither the harpist's nor the wizard's. They were the falcon's eyes, fierce, vulnerable,
frighteningly powerful. They held Morgon motionless,
half-regretting that he had spoken the name that had
turned in his mind after all that time to show its dark
side. For the first time in his life he had no courage
for questions; his mouth was too dry for speaking.

He whispered into the void of the High One's silence, "I had to find you . . . I have to understand."

"You still don't." His voice sounded shadowy with
winds. Then he bound the awesomeness of his power
somewhere within him and became the harpist, quiet,
familiar, whom Morgon could question. The moment's
transition bound Morgon's voice again, for it loosed a
conflict of emotion. He tried to control them. But as
the High One touched the stars at his side and his
back, bringing them irrevocably into shape, his own
hands rose, caught the harpist's arms and stilled him.

"Why?"

The falcon's eyes held him again; he could not look away. He saw, as if he were reading memories within the dark eyes, the silent, age-old game the High One had played, now with Earth-Masters, now with Ghisteslwchlohm, now with Morgon himself, a ceaseless tapestry of riddles with some threads as old as time and others spun at a step across the threshold into a wizard's chamber, at a change of expression on the Star-Bearer's face. His fingers tightened, feeling bone. An Earth-Master moved alone out of the shadows of some great, unfinished war . . . hid for thousands of years, now a leaf on a rich, matted forest floor of dead leaves, now the brush of sunlight down the flank of a pine. Then, for a thousand years, he took a wizard's face, and for another thousand, a harpist's still, secret face, gazing back at the twisted shape of power out of its own expressionless eyes. "Why?" he whispered again, and saw himself in Hed, sitting at the dock end, picking at a harp he could not play, with the shadow of the High One's harpist flung across him. The sea wind or the High One's hand bared the stars at his hairline. The harpist saw them, a promise out of a past so old it had buried his name. He could not speak; he spun his silence into riddles . . .

"But why?" Tears or sweat were burning in his eyes. He brushed at them; his hands locked once more on the High One's arms, as if to keep his shape. "You could have killed Ghisteslwchlohm with a thought. Instead you served him. You. You gave me to him. Were you his harpist so long you had forgotten your own name?"

The High One moved; Morgon's own arms were caught in an inflexible grip. "Think. You're the riddler."

"I played the game you challenged me to. But I don't know why—"

"Think. I found you in Hed, innocent, ignorant, oblivious of your own destiny. You couldn't even harp.

Who in this realm was there to wake you to power?"

"The wizards," he said between his teeth. "You could have stopped the destruction of Lungold. You were there. The wizards could have survived in freedom, trained me for whatever protection you need—"

"No. If I had used power to stop that battle, I would have battled Earth-Masters long before I was ready. They would have destroyed me. Think of their faces. Remember them. The faces of the Earth-Masters you saw in Erlenstar Mountain. I am of them. The children they once loved were buried beneath Isig Mountain. How could you, with all your innocence, have understood them? Their longing and their lawlessness? In all the realm, who was there to teach you that? You wanted a choice. I gave it to you. You could have taken the shape of power you learned from Ghisteslwchlohm: lawless, destructive, loveless. Or you could have swallowed darkness until you shaped it, understood it, and still cried out for something more. When you broke free of Ghisteslwchlohm's power, why was it me you hunted, instead of him? He took the power of land-law from you. I took your trust, your love. You pursued what you valued most . . ."

Morgon's hands opened, closed again. His breath was beginning to rack through him. He caught it, stilled it long enough to shape one final question. "What is it you want of me?"

"Morgon, think." The even, familiar voice was suddenly gentle, almost inaudible. "You can shape the wild heart of Osterland, you can shape wind. You saw my son, dead and buried in Isig Mountain. You took the stars of your own destiny from him. And in all your power and anger, you found your way here, to name me. You are my land-heir."

Morgon was silent. He was gripping the High One as if the tower floor had suddenly vanished under him. He heard his own voice, oddly toneless, from a distance. "Your heir,"

"You are the Star-Bearer, the heir foreseen by the dead of Isig, for whom I have been waiting for centuries beyond hope. Where did you think the power you have over land-law sprang from?"

"I didn't—I wasn't thinking." His voice had dropped to a whisper. He thought of Hed, then. "You are giving me—you are giving Hed back to me."

"I am giving you the entire realm when I die. You seem to love it, even all its wraiths and thick-skulled farmers and deadly winds—" He stopped, as a sound broke out of Morgon. His face was scored with tears, as riddles wove their pattern strand by gleaming strand around the heart of the tower. His hands loosened; he slid to the High One's feet and crouched there, his head bowed, his scarred hands closed, held against his heart. He could not speak; he did not know what language of light and darkness the falcon who had so ruthlessly fashioned his life would hear. He thought numbly of Hed; it seemed to lay where his heart lay, under his hands. Then the High One knelt in front of him, lifted Morgon's face between his hands. His eyes were the harpist's, night-dark, and no longer silent but full of pain.

"Morgon," he whispered, "I wish you had not been someone I loved so."

He put his arms around Morgon, held him as fiercely as the falcon had held him. He circled Morgon with his silence, until Morgon felt that his heart and the tower walls and the starred night sky beyond were built not of blood and stone and air, but of the harpist's stillness. He was still crying noiselessly, afraid to touch the harpist, as if he might somehow change shape again. Something hard and angled, like grief, was pushing into his chest, into his throat, but it was not grief. He said, above its pain, feeling the High One's pain as one thing he could comprehend, "What happened to your son?"

"He was destroyed in the war. The power was

stripped from him. He could no longer live. . . . He gave you the starred sword."

"And you . . . you have been alone since then. Without an heir. With only a promise."

"Yes. I have lived in secret for thousands of years with nothing to hope in but a promise. A dead child's dream. And then you came. Morgon, I did anything I had to do to keep you alive. Anything. You were all my hope."

"You are giving me even the wastelands. I loved them. I loved them. And the mists of Herun, the vesta, the backlands . . . I was afraid, when I realized how much I loved them. I was drawn to every shape, and I couldn't stop myself from wanting—" The pain broke through his chest like a blade. He drew a harsh, terrible breath. "All I wanted from you was truth. I didn't know . . . I didn't know you would give me everything I have ever loved."

He could not speak any more. Sobbing wrenched him until he did not know if he could endure his own shape. But the High One held him to it, soothing him with his hands and his voice until Morgon quieted. He still could not speak; he listened to the winds whispering through the tower, to the occasional patter of rain on the stones. His face was bowed against the High One's shoulder. He was silent, resting in the High One's silence, until his voice came again, hoarse, weary, calmer.

"I never guessed. You never let me see that far beyond my anger."

"I didn't dare let you see too much. Your life was in such danger, and you were so precious to me. I kept you alive any way I could, using myself, using your ignorance, even your hatred. I did not know if you would ever forgive me, but all the hope of the realm lay in you, and I needed you powerful, confused, always searching for me, yet never finding me, though I was always near you . . ."

"I told . . . I told Raederle if I came back out of

the wastes to play a riddle-game with you that I would lose."

"No. You startled the truth out of me in Herun. I lost to you, there. I could endure everything from you but your gentleness." His hand smoothed Morgon's hair, then dropped to hold him tightly again. "You and the Morgol kept my heart from turning into stone. I was forced to turn everything I had ever said to her into a lie. And you turned it back into truth. You were that generous with someone you hated."

"All I wanted, even when I hated you most, was some poor, barren, parched excuse to love you. But you only gave me riddles. . . . When I thought Ghisteslwchlohm had killed you, I grieved without knowing why. When I was in the northern wastes, harping to the winds, too tired even to think, it was you who drew me out. . . . You gave me a reason for living." His hands had opened slowly. He raised one, almost tentatively, to the High One's shoulder and shifted back a little. Something of his own weariness showed in his eyes, and the endless, terrible patience that had kept him alive so long, alone and unnamed, hunted by his own kind in the world of men. Morgon's head bowed again after a moment.

"Even I tried to kill you."

The harpist's fingers touched his cheekbone, drew the hair back from his eyes. "You kept my enemies from suspecting me very effectively, but Morgon, if you had not stopped yourself that day in Anuin, I don't know what I would have done. If I had used power to stop you, neither of us would have lived too long afterward. If I had let you kill me, out of despair, because we had brought one another to such an impasse, the power passing into you would have destroyed you. So I gave you a riddle, hoping you would consider that instead."

"You knew me that well," he whispered.

"No. You constantly surprised me . . . from the very first. I am as old as the stones on this plain. The great cities the Earth-Masters built were shattered by a war that no man could have survived. It was born out of a kind of innocence. We held so much power, and yet we did not understand the implications of power. That's why, even if you hated me for it, I wanted you to understand Ghisteslwchlohm and how he destroyed himself. We lived so peacefully once, in these great cities. They were open to every change of wind. Our faces changed with every season; we took knowledge from all things: from the silence of the backlands to the burning ice sweeping across the northern wastes. We did not realize, until it was too late, that the power inherent in every stone, every movement of water, holds both existence and destruction." He paused, no longer seeing Morgon, tasting a bitter word. "The woman you know as Eriel was the first of us to begin to gather power. And I was the first to see the implications of power . . . that paradox that tempers wizardry and compelled the study of riddlery. So, I made a choice, and began binding all earth-shapes to me by their own laws, permitting nothing to disturb that law. But I had to fight to keep the land-law, and we learned what war is then. The realm as you know it would not have lasted two days in the force of those battles. We razed our own cities. We destroyed one another. We destroyed our children, drew the power even out of them. I had already learned to master the winds, which was the only thing that saved me. I was able to bind the power of the last of the Earth-Masters so they could use little beyond the power they were born to. I swept them into the sea while the earth slowly healed itself. I buried our children, then. The Earth-Masters broke out of the sea eventually, but they could not break free of my hold over them. And they could never find me, because the winds hid me, always . . .

"But I am very old, and I cannot hold them much longer. They know that. I was old even when I became a wizard named Yrth so that I could fashion the harp and the sword that my heir would need. Ghis-teslwchlohm learned of the Star-Bearer from the dead of Isig, and he became one more enemy lured by the promise of enormous power. He thought that if he controlled the Star-Bearer, he could assimilate the power the Star-Bearer would inherit and become the High One in more than name. It would have killed him, but I did not bother explaining that to him. When I realized he was waiting for you, I watched him—in Lungold, and later in Erlenstar Mountain. I took the shape of a harpist who had died during the destruction and entered his service. I wanted no harm to come to you without my consent. When I found you at last, sitting on the dock at Tol, oblivious of your own destiny, content to rule Hed, with a harp in your hands you could barely play and the crown of the Kings of Aum under your bed, I realized that the last thing I had been expecting after all those endless, lonely centuries was someone I might love . . ." He paused again, his face blurred into pale, silvery lines by Morgon's tears. "Hed. No wonder that land shaped the Star-Bearer out of itself, a loving Prince of Hed, ruler of ignorant, stubborn farmers who believed in nothing but the High One . . ."

"I am hardly more than that now . . . ignorant and thick-skulled. Have I destroyed us both by coming here to find you?"

"No. This is the one place no one would expect us to be. But we have little time left. You crossed Ymris without touching the land-law."

Morgon dropped his hands. "I didn't dare," he said. "And all I could think of was you. I had to find you before the Earth-Masters found me."

"I know. I left you in a perilous situation. But you found me, and I hold the land-law of Ymris. You'll need it. Ymris is a seat of great power. I want you to take the knowledge from my mind. Don't worry," he added, at Morgon's expression. "I will only give

you that knowledge, nothing that you cannot bear,
yet. Sit down."

Morgon slid back slowly onto the stones. The rain
had begun again, blown on the wind through the open-
ings in the chamber, but he was not cold. The harpist's face was changing; his worn, troubled expression
had eased into an ageless peace as he contemplated
his realm. Morgon looked at him, drawing hungrily
from his peace until he was enveloped in stillness and
the High One's touch seemed to lay upon his heart.
He heard the deep, shadowy voice again, the falcon's
voice.

"Ymris . . . I was born here on Wind Plain. Listen
to its power beneath the rain, beneath the cries of the
dead. It is like you, a fierce and loving land. Be still
and listen to it . . ."

He grew still, so still he could hear the grass bending beneath the weight of the rain and the ancient
names from early centuries that had been spoken
there. And then he became the grass.

HE DREW HIMSELF OUT OF YMRIS SLOWLY, HIS HEART
thundering to its long and bloody history, his body
shaped to its green fields, wild shores, strange, brooding forests. He felt old as the earliest stone hewn out
of Erlenstar Mountain to rest on the earth, and he
knew far more than he had ever cared to know of the
devastation the recent war had loosed across Ruhn.
He sensed great untapped power in Ymris that he had
winced away from, as if a sea or a mountain had
loomed before him that his mind simply could not
encompass. But it held odd moments of quiet; a still,
secret lake mirroring many things; strange stones that
had once been made to speak; forests haunted with
pure black animals so shy they died if men looked
upon them; acres of oak woods on the western borders whose trees remembered the first vague passage
of men into Ymris. These, he treasured. The High
One had given him no more of his mind than the

awareness of Ymris; the power he had feared in the falcon's eyes was still leashed when he looked into them again.

It was dawn, of some day, and Raederle was beside him. He made a surprised noise. "How did you get up here?"

"I flew."

The answer was so simple it seemed meaningless for a moment. "So did I."

"You climbed the stairs. I flew to the top."

His face looked so blank with surprise that she smiled. "Morgon, the High One let me come in. Otherwise I would have flown around the tower squawking all night."

He grunted and linked his fingers into hers. She was very tired, he sensed, and her smile faded quickly, leaving something disturbing in her eyes. The High One was standing beside one of the windows. The blue-black stone was rimed with the first light; against the sky the harpist's face looked weary, the skin drawn taut, colorless against the bones. But the eyes were Yrth's, light-filled, secret. Morgon looked at him for a long time without moving, still enmeshed in his peace, until the changeless, familiar face seemed to meld with the pale silver of the morning. The High One turned then to meet his eyes.

He drew Morgon to his side without a gesture, only his simple wordless desire. Morgon loosed Raederle's hand and rose stiffly. He crossed the room. The High One put a hand on his shoulder.

Morgon said, "I couldn't take it all."

"Morgon, the power you sensed is in the Earth-Masters' dead: those who died fighting at my side on this plain. The power will be there when you need it."

Something in Morgon, deep beneath his peace, lifted its muzzle like a blind hound in the dark, scenting at the High One's words. "And the harp, and the sword?" He kept his voice tranquil. "I barely understand the power in them."

"They will find uses for themselves. Look."

There was a white mist of vesta along the plain, beneath the low, lumbering cloud. Morgon gazed down at them incredulously, then leaned his face against the cool stone. "When did they get here?"

"Last night."

"Where is Astrin's army?"

"Half of it was trapped between Tor and Umber, but the vanguard made it through, clearing a path for the vesta and the Morgol's guard and Danan's miners. They are behind the vesta." He read Morgon's thoughts; his hand tightened slightly. "I did not bring them here to fight."

"Then why?" he whispered.

"You will need them. You and I must end this war quickly. That is what you were born to do."

"How?"

The High One was silent. Behind his tranquil, indrawn gaze, Morgon sensed a weariness beyond belief, and a more familiar patience: the harpist's waiting for Morgon's understanding, perhaps, or for something beyond his understanding. He said finally, very gently, "The Prince of Hed and his farmers have gathered on the south border with Mathom's army. If you need to keep them alive, you'll find a way."

Morgon whirled. He crossed the chamber, hung out a south window, as if he could see among the leafless oaks a grim battery of farmers with rakes and hoes and scythes. His heart swelled with sudden pain and fear that sent tears to his eyes. "He left Hed. Eliard turned his farmers into warriors and left Hed. What is it? The end of the world?"

"He came to fight for you. And for his own land."

"No." He turned again, his hands clenched, but not in anger. "He came because you wanted him. That's why the Morgol came, and Har—you drew them, the way you draw me, with a touch of wind at the heart, a mystery. What is it? What is it that you aren't telling me?"

"I have given you my name."

Morgon was silent. It began to snow lightly, big, random flakes scattered on the wind. They caught on his hands, burned before they vanished. He shuddered suddenly and found that he had no inclination left for questions. Raederle had turned away from them both. She looked oddly isolated in the center of the small chamber. Morgon went to her side; her head lifted as he joined her, but her face turned away from him to the High One.

He came to her, as if she had drawn him, the way he drew Morgon. He smoothed a strand of her windblown hair away from her face. "Raederle, it is time for you to leave."

She shook her head. "No." Her voice was very quiet. "I am half Earth-Master. You will have at least one of your kind fighting for you after all these centuries. I will not leave either of you."

"You are in the eye of danger."

"I chose to come. To be with those I love."

He was silent; for a moment he was only the harpist, ageless, indrawn, lonely. "You," he said softly, "I never expected. So powerful, so beautiful, and so loving. You are like one of our children, growing into power before our war." He lifted her hand and kissed it, then opened it to the small angular scar on her palm. "There are twelve winds," he said to Morgon. "Bound, controlled, they are more precise and terrible than any weapon or wizard's power in the realm. Unbound, they could destroy the realm. They are also my eyes and ears, for they shape all things, hear all words and movements, and they are everywhere. . . . That jewel that Raederle held was cut and faceted by winds. I did that one day when I was playing with them, long before I ever used them in our war. The memory of that was mirrored in the stone."

"Why are you telling me?" His voice jerked a little.
"I can't hold the winds."

"No. Not yet. Don't be concerned, yet." He put his
arm around Morgon's shoulders, held him easily again
within his stillness. "Listen. You can hear the voices
of all the winds of the realm in this chamber. Listen
to my mind."

Morgon opened his mind to the High One's silence.
The vague, incoherent murmurings outside the walls
were refracted through the High One's mind into all
the pure, beautiful tones on the starred harp. The
harping filled Morgon's heart with soft, light summer
winds, and the deep, wild winds that he loved; the
slow, rich measures matched the beat of his blood. He
wanted suddenly to hold the harping and the harpist
within that moment until the white winter sky broke
apart once more to light.

The harping stilled. He could not speak; he did not
want the High One to move. But the arm around his
shoulders shifted; the High One gripped him gently,
facing him.

"Now," he said, "we have a battle on our hands. I
want you to find Heureu Ymris. This time, I'll warn
you: when you touch his mind, you will spring a trap
set for you. The Earth-Masters will know where you
are and that the High One is with you. You will ignite
war again on Wind Plain. They have little mind-
power of their own—I keep that bound; but they hold
Ghisteslwchlohm's mind, and they may use his powers
of wizardry to try to hurt you. I'll break any bindings
he forges."

Morgon turned his head, looked at Raederle. Her
eyes told him what he already knew: that nothing he
could say or do could make her leave them. He bent
his head again, in silent acquiescence to her and to
the High One. Then he let his awareness venture beyond the silence into the damp earth around the
tower. He touched a single blade of grass, let his mind
shape it from hair roots to tip. Rooted also within the

structure of land-law in Heureu's mind, it became his link with the King of Ymris.

He sensed a constant, nagging pain, a turmoil of helpless anger and despair, and heard a distant, hollow drag and ebb of the sea. He had learned every shape of cliff and stone boring out of the shores, and he recognized the strip of Meremont coast. He smelled wet wood and ashes; the king lay in a half-burned fisher's hut on the beach, no more than a mile or two from Wind Plain.

He started to glance up, to speak. Then the sea flooded over him, spilled through all his thoughts. He seemed to stare down a long, dark passageway into Ghisteslwchlohm's alien, gold-flecked eyes.

He felt the startled recognition in the bound mind. Then a mind-hold raked at him, and the wizard's eyes burned into him, searching for him. The mind-hold was broken; he reeled back away from it. The High One gripped his shoulder, holding him still. He started to speak again, but the falcon's eyes stopped him.

He waited, shaken suddenly by the pounding of his heart. Raederle, bound to the same waiting, seemed remote again, belonging to another portion of the world. He wanted desperately to speak, to break the silence that held them all motionless as if they were carved of stone. But he seemed spellbound, choiceless, an extension of the High One's will. A movement streaked the air, and then another. The dark, delicately beautiful Earth-Master, whom Morgon knew as Eriel, stood before them, and beside her, Ghisteslwchlohm.

For a moment, the High One checked the power gathered against him. There was astonishment and awe in the woman's eyes as she recognized the harpist. The wizard, face to face with the High One, whom he had been searching for so long, nearly broke the hold over his mind. A faint smile touched the falcon's eyes, icy as the heart of the northern wastes.

"Even death, Master Ohm," he said, "is a riddle."

A rage blackened Ghisteslwchlohm's eyes. Something spun Morgon across the chamber. He struck the dark wall; it gave under him, and he fell into a luminous, blue-black mist of illusion. He heard Raederle's cry, and then a crow streaked across his vision. He caught at it, but it fluttered away between his hands. A mind gripped his mind. The binding was instantly broken. A power he did not feel flashed at him and was swallowed. He saw Ghisteslwchlohm's face again, blurred in the strange light. He felt a wrench at his side, and he cried out, though he did not know what had been taken from him. Then he turned on his back and saw the starred sword in Ghisteslwchlohm's hands, rising endlessly upward, gathering shadow and light, until the stars burst with fire and darkness above Morgon. He could not move; the stars drew his eyes, his thoughts. He watched them reach their apex and halt, then blur into their descent toward him. Then he saw the harpist again, standing beneath their fall, as quietly as he had stood in the king's hall at Anuin.

A cry tore through Morgon. The sword fell with a terrible speed, struck the High One. It drove into his heart, then snapped in Ghisteslwchlohm's hands. Morgon, freed to move at last, caught him as he fell. He could not breathe; a blade of grief was thrusting into his own heart. The High One gripped his arms; his hands were the harpist's crippled hands, the wizard's scarred hands. He struggled to speak; his face blurred from one shape to another under Morgon's tears. Morgon pulled him closer, feeling something build in him, like a shout of fury and agony, but the High One was already beginning to vanish. He reached up with a hand shaped of red stone or fire, touched the stars on Morgon's face.

He whispered Morgon's name. His hand slid down over Morgon's heart. "Free the winds."

16

SHOUT THAT WAS NOT A SHOUT BUT A WIND-voice came out of Morgon. The High One turned to flame in his hands, and then into a memory. The sound he had made reverberated through the tower: a low bass note that built and built until the stones around him began to shake. Winds were battering at the tower; he felt struck and struck again, like a harp string, by his grief. He did not know, out of all the wild, chaotic, beautiful voices around him, which was his own. He groped for his harp. The stars on it had turned night-black. He swept his hand, or the knife-edge of a wind, across it. The strings snapped. As the low string wailed and broke, stone and illusion of stone shocked apart around him and began to fall.

Winds the color of the stones: of fire, of gold, of night, spiralled around him, then broke away. The tower roared around him and collapsed into a gigantic cairn. Morgon was flung on his hands and knees on the grass beside it. He could sense Ghisteslwchlohm and Eriel's power nowhere, as if the High One had bound them, in that final moment, to his death. Snow whirled around him, melting almost as soon as it touched the ground. The sky was dead-white.

His mind was reeling with land-law. He heard the

silence of grass roots under his hands; he stared at the
broken mass of Wind Tower out of the unblinking
eyes of a wraith of An at the edge of the plain. A
great tree sagged in the rain on a wet hillside in the
backlands; he felt its roots shift and loosen as it fell.
A trumpeter in Astrin's army was lifting his long,
golden instrument to his mouth. The thoughts of the
land-rulers snarled in Morgon's mind, full of grief and
fear, though they did not understand why. The entire
realm seemed to form under his hands on the grass,
pulling at him, stretching him from the cold, empty
wastes to the elegant court at Anuin. He was stone,
water, a dying field, a bird struggling against the wind,
a king wounded and despairing on the beach below
Wind Plain, vesta, wraiths, and a thousand fragile
mysteries, shy witches, speaking pigs, and solitary towers that he had to find room for within his mind. The
trumpeter set his lips to the horn and blew. At the
same moment a Great Shout from the army of An
blasted over the plain. The sounds, the urgent onslaught of knowledge, the loss that was boring into
Morgon's heart overwhelmed him suddenly. He cried
out again, dropping against the earth, his face buried
in the wet grass.

Power ripped through his mind, blurring the bindings he had formed with the earth. He realized that
the death of the High One had unbound all the power
of the Earth-Masters. He felt their minds, ancient,
wild, like fire and sea, beautiful and deadly, intent on
destroying him. He did not know how to fight them.
Without moving, he saw them in his mind's eye, fan-
ning across Wind Plain from the sea, flowing like a
wave in the shapes of men and animals, their minds
riding before them, scenting. They touched him again
and again, uprooting knowledge in his mind, breaking
bindings he had inherited, until his awareness of trees
in the oak forest, vesta, plow horses in Hed, farmers
in Ruhn, tiny pieces of the realm began to disappear
from his mind.

He felt it as another kind of loss, terrible and bewildering. He tried to fight it as he watched the wave draw closer, but it was as though he tried to stop the tide from pulling sand grains out of his hands. Astrin's army and Mathom's were thundering across the plain from north and south, their battle colors vivid as dying leaves against the winter sky. They would be destroyed, Morgon knew, even the dead; no living awareness or memory of the dead could survive the power that was feeding even on his own power. Mathom rode at the head of his force; in the trees, Har was preparing to loose the vesta onto the plain. Danan's miners, flanked by the Morgol's guard, were beginning to follow Astrin's warriors. He did not know how to help them. Then he realized that on the edge of the plain to the southeast, Eliard and the farmers of Hed, armed with little more than hammers and knives and their bare hands, were marching doggedly to his rescue.

He lifted his head; his awareness of them faltered suddenly as a mind blurred over his mind. The whole of the realm seemed to darken; portions of his life were slipping away from him. He gripped at it, his hands tangled in the grass, feeling that all the High One's hope in him had been for nothing. Then, in some misty corner of his mind, a door opened. He saw Tristan come out onto the porch at Akren, shivering a little in the cold wind, her eyes dark and fearful, staring toward the tumult in the mainland.

He got to his knees and then to his feet, with all the enduring stubbornness that small island had instilled in him. A wind lashed across his face; he could barely keep his balance in it. He was standing in the heart of chaos. The living and the dead and the Earth-Masters were just about to converge around him; the land-law of the realm was being torn away from him; he had freed the winds. They were belling across the realm, telling him of forests bent to the breaking point, villages picked apart, thatch and shingle whirled away into the air. The sea was rousing; it would kill Heureu Ymris, if he did not act. Eliard would die if Morgon could not stop him. He tried to reach Eliard's mind, but as he searched the plain, he only entangled himself in a web of other minds.

They tore knowledge, power from him like a wave eating at a cliff. There seemed no escape from them, no image of peace he could form in his mind to deflect them. Then he saw something glittering in front of him: his broken harp, lying on the grass, its strings flashing silently, played by the wind.

A strong, clean fury that was not his own washed through him suddenly, burning away all the holds over his mind. It left his mind clear as fire. He found Raederle beside him, freeing him for one brief moment with her anger, and he could have gone on his knees to her, because she was still alive, because she was with him. In the one moment she had given him, he realized what he must do. Then the forces of the realm shocked together in front of him. Bones of the dead, shimmering mail and bright shields of the living, vesta white as the falling snow, the Morgol's guard with their slender spears of silver and ash closed with the merciless, inhuman power of the Earth-Masters.

He heard, for the first time, the sorrowing cry a vesta made as it died, calling plaintively to its own. He felt the names of the dead blotted out like blown flames in his mind. Men and women fought with spears and swords, picks and battle axes against an enemy that kept to no single shape, but a constant, fluid changing that mesmerized opponents to despair and to death. Morgon felt them die, parts of himself. Danan's miners fell like great, stolid trees; the farmers from Hed, viewing a foe beyond all their conceptions, nothing their placid history had ever suggested existed, seemed too confused even to defend themselves. Their lives were wrenched out of Morgon like rooted things. The plain was a living, snarling thing

before his eyes, a piece of himself fighting for its life
with no hope of survival against the dark, sinuous,
sharp-toothed beast that determined the realm would
die. In the few brief moments of battle, he felt the
first of the land-rulers die.

He sensed the struggle in Heureu Ymris' mind as,
wounded and unaided, he tried to comprehend the
turmoil in his land. His body was not strong enough
for such torment. He died alone, hearing the crashing
sea and the cries of the dying across Wind Plain. Morgon felt the life-force in the king drain back to Ymris.
And on the battlefield, Astrin, fighting for his life,
wrestled suddenly with an overwhelming grief, and
the sudden wakening in him of all land-instinct.

His grief woke Morgon's again, for the High One,
for Heureu, for the realm itself, entrusted to his care
and dying within him. His mind shook open on a harp
note that was also a call to a south wind burning
across the backlands. Note by note, all tuned to sorrow, he called the unbound winds back to Wind Plain.

They came to him out of the northern wastes, burning with cold; rain-soaked from the backlands; tasting
of brine and snow from the sea; smelling of wet earth,
from Hed. They were devastating. They flattened the
grass from one end of the plain to the other. They
wrenched his shape into air, uprooted oak at the edge
of the plain. They moaned the darkness of his sorrow, tore the air with their shrill, furious keening.
They flung apart the armies before them like chaff.
Riderless horses ran before them; dead frayed back
into memory; shields were tossed in the air like leaves;
men and women sprawled on the ground, trying to
crawl away from the winds. Even the Earth-Masters
were checked; no shape they took could batter past
the winds.

Morgon, his mind fragmented into harp notes,
struggled to shape an order out of them. The bass,
northern wind hummed its deep note through him; he
let it fill his mind until he shuddered with sound like

a harp string. It loosed him finally; he grasped at another voice, thin and fiery, out of the remote backlands. It burned through his mind with a sweet, terrible note. He flamed with it, absorbed it. Another wind, sweeping across the sea, shook a wild song through him. He sang its wildness back at it, changed the voice in him, in the winds, to a gentleness. The waves massed against the shores of Hed began to calm. A different wind sang into his mind, of the winter silence of Isig Pass and the harping still echoing through the darkness of Erlenstar Mountain. He shaped the silence and darkness into his own song.

He was scarcely aware of the Earth-Masters' minds as he battled for mastery over the winds. Their power was filling him, challenging him, yet defending him. No mind on the plain around him could have touched him, embroiled as it was with wind. A remote part of him watched the realm he was bound to. Warriors were fleeing into the border forests. They were forced to leave their arms; they could not even carry the wounded with them. As far as Caithnard, Caerweddin, and Hed the noises of his struggle with the winds were heard. The wizards had left the plain; he felt the passage of their power as they responded to bewilderment and fear. Twilight drifted over the plain, and then night, and he wrestled with the cold, sinewy, wolf-voiced winds of darkness.

He drew the power of the winds to a fine precision. He could have trained an east wind on the innermost point of the cairn beside him and sent the stones flying all over the plain. He could have picked a snowflake off the ground, or turned one of the fallen guards lightly buried under snow to see her face. All along both sides of the plain hundreds of fires had been lit all night, as men and women of the realm waited sleeplessly while he wrested their fates, moment by moment, out of the passing hours. They nursed their wounded and wondered if they would survive the passage of power from the High One to his heir. At last, he gave them dawn.

It came as a single eye staring at him through white mist. He drew back into himself, his hands full of winds. He was alone on a quiet plain. The Earth-Masters had shifted their battleground eastward, moving across Ruhn. He stood quietly a moment, wondering if he had lived through a single night or a century of them. Then he turned his mind away from the night to scent the path of the Earth-Masters.

They had fled across Ruhn. Towns and farms, lords' houses lay in ruins; fields, woods, and orchards had been harrowed and seared with power. Men, children, animals trapped in the range of their minds had been killed. As his awareness moved across the wasteland, he felt a harp song building through him. Winds in his control stirred to it, angry, dangerous, pulling him out of his shape until he was half-man, half-wind, a harpist playing a death song on a harp with no strings.

Then he roused all the power that lay buried under the great cities across Ymris. He had sensed it in the High One's mind, and he knew at last why the Earth-Masters had warred for possession of their cities. They were all cairns, broken monuments to their dead. The power had lain dormant under the earth for thousands of years. But, as with the wraiths of An, their minds could be roused with memory, and Morgon, his mind burrowing under the stones, shocked them awake with his grief. He did not see them. But on Wind Plain and King's Mouth Plain, in the ruins across Ruhn and east Umber, a power gathered, hung over the stones like the eerie, unbearable tension in the sky before a storm breaks. The tension was felt in Caerweddin and in towns still surviving around the ruins. No one spoke that dawn; they waited.

Morgon began to move across Wind Plain. An army of the Earth-Masters' dead moved with him, flowed across Ymris, searching out the living Earth-Masters to finish a war. Winds hounded the Earth-Masters out of the shape of stone and leaf they hid in; the dead forced them with a silent, relentless purpose out of the land they had once loved. They scattered across the backlands, through wet, dark forests, across bare hills, across the icy surfaces of the Lungold Lakes. Morgon, the winds running before him, the dead at his back, pursued them across the threshold of winter. He drove them as inflexibly as they had once driven him toward Erlenstar Mountain.

They tried to fight him one last time before he compelled them into the mountain. But the dead rose around him like stone, and the winds raged against them. He could have destroyed them, stripped them of their power, as they had tried to do to him. But something of their beauty lingered in Raederle, showing him what they might have been once; and he could not kill them. He did not even touch their power. He forced them into Erlenstar Mountain, where they fled from him into the shape of water and jewel. He sealed the entire Mountain—all shafts and hidden springs, the surface of the earth, and ground floor of rock—with his name. Among trees and stones, light and wind, around the mountain, he bound the dead once more, to guard the mountain. Then he loosed the winds from his song, and they drew winter down from the northlands across the whole of the realm.

HE RETURNED TO WIND PLAIN, THEN, DRAWN BY MEMory. There was snow all over the plain and on all the jagged, piled faces of the stones. There was smoke among the trees around the plain, for no one had left it. The gathering of men, women, animals was still there, waiting for his return. They had buried their dead and sent for supplies; they were settling for the winter, bound to the plain.

Morgon took his shape out of the winds, beside the

ruined tower. He heard the Morgol talking to Goh; he
saw Har checking the splint on a crippled vesta. He
did not know if Eliard was still alive. Looking up at
the huge cairn, he stepped forward into his sorrow.
He laid his face against one of the cold, beautiful
stones, stretched his arms across it, wanting to encompass the entire cairn, hold it in his heart. He felt
bound, suddenly, as if he were a wraith, and all his
past was buried in those stones. As he mourned, men
began to move across the plain. He saw them without
thinking about them in his mind's eye: tiny figures
drawn across the blank, snow-covered plain. When he
finally turned, he found them in a silent ring around
him.

They had been drawn to him, he sensed, the way
he had always been drawn to Deth: with no reason,
no question, simply instinct. The land-rulers of the
realm, the four wizards stood quietly with him. They
did not know what to say to him as he stood there in
his power and his grief; they were simply responding
to something in him that had brought peace to the ancient plain.

He looked at the faces he knew so well. They were
scarred with sorrow for the High One, for their own
dead. Finding Eliard among them, he felt something
quicken painfully in his heart. Eliard's face was as he
had never seen it: colorless and hard as winter
ground. A third of the farmers of Hed had been sent
back to Hed, to be buried beneath the frozen ground.
The winter would be hard for the living, and Morgon
did not know how to comfort him. But as he looked
at Morgon mutely, something else came into his eyes
that had never been in the changeless, stolid heritage
of the Princes of Hed: he had been touched by mystery.

Morgon's eyes moved to Astrin. He seemed still
dazed by Heureu's death and the sudden, far-flung
power he possessed. "I'm sorry," Morgon said. The

words sounded as light and meaningless as the snow
flecking the massive stones behind him. "I felt him
die. But I couldn't—I couldn't help him. I felt so
much death . . ."

The single white eye seemed to gaze into him at
the word. "You're alive," he whispered. "High One.
You survived to name yourself at last, and you
brought peace to this morning."

"Peace." He felt the stones behind him, cold as ice.

"Morgon," Danan said softly, "when we saw that
tower fall, none of us expected to see another dawn."

"So many didn't. So many of your miners died."

"So many didn't. I have a great mountain full of
trees; you gave it back to us, our home to return to."

"We have lived to see the passage of power from
the High One to his heir," Har said. "We paid a price
for our seeing, but . . . we survived." His eyes were
oddly gentle in the pure, cold light. He shifted the
cloak over his shoulders: an old, gnarled king, with
the first memories of the realm in his heart. "You
played a wondrous game and won. Don't grieve for
the High One. He was old and near the end of his
power. He left you a realm at war, an almost impossible heritage, and all his hope. You did not fail him.
Now we can return home in peace, without having to
fear the stranger at our thresholds. When the door
opens unexpectedly to the winter winds, and we look
up from our warm hearths to find the High One in
our house, it will be you. He left us that gift."

Morgon was silent. Sorrow touched him again,
lightly, like a searching flame, in spite of all their
words. Then he felt from one of them an answering
sorrow that no words could comfort. He sought it,
something of himself, and found it in Mathom, tired
and shadowed by death.

Morgon took a step toward him. "Who?"

"Duac," the King said. He drew a dry breath,
standing dark as a wraith against the snow. "He re-

fused to stay in An . . . the only argument I have ever lost. My land-heir with his eyes of the sea . . ."

Morgon was mute again, wondering how many of his bindings had been broken, how many deaths he had not sensed. He said suddenly, remembering, "You knew the High One would die here."

"He named himself," Mathom said. "I did not need to dream that. Bury him here, where he chose to die. Let him rest."

"I can't," he whispered, "I was his death. He knew. All that time, he knew. I was his destiny, he was mine. Our lives were one constant, twisted riddle-game. . . . He forged the sword that would kill him, and I brought it here to him. If I had thought . . . if I had known—"

"What would you have done? He did not have the strength to win this war; he knew you would, if he gave you his power. That game, he won. Accept it."

"I can't . . . not yet." He put one hand on the stones before he left them. Then he lifted his head, searching the sky for something that he could not find in his mind. But its face was pale, motionless. "Where is Raederle?"

"She was with me for a while," the Morgol said. Her face was very quiet, like the winter morning that drew a stillness over the world. "She left, I thought, to look for you, but perhaps she needs a time to sorrow, also." He met her eyes. She smiled, touching his heart. "Morgon, he is dead. But for a little while, you gave him something to love."

"So did you," he whispered. He turned away then, to find his own comfort somewhere within his realm. He became snow or air or perhaps he stayed himself; he was not certain; he only knew he left no footprints in the snow for anyone to follow.

He wandered through the land, taking many shapes, reworking broken bindings, until there was not a tree or an insect or a man in the realm he was not

aware of, except for one woman. The winds that
touched everything in their boundless curiosity told
him of lords and warriors without homes in Ymris
taking refuge in Astrin's court, of traders battling the
seas to carry grain from An and Herun and beer from
Hed to the war-torn land. They told him when the
vesta returned to Osterland, and how the King of An
bound his dead once more into the earth of the Three
Portions. They listened to the wizards at Caithnard
discussing the restoration of the great school at
Lungold, while the Masters quietly answered the last
of the unanswered riddles on their lists. He felt Har's
waiting for him, beside his winter fire, with the wolves
watching at his knees. He felt the Morgol's eyes looking beyond her walls, beyond her hills, every now and
then, watching for him, watching for Raederle, wondering.

He tried to put an end to his grieving, sitting for
days on end in the wastes, like a tangle of old roots,
piecing together the games the harpist had played, action by action, and understanding it. But understanding gave him no comfort. He tried harping, with a
harp as vast as the night sky, its face full of stars, but
even that brought him no peace. He moved restlessly
from cold, barren peaks to quiet forests, and even the
hearths of taverns and farmhouses, where he was
greeted kindly as a stranger wandering in from the
cold. He did not know what his heart wanted; why
the wraith of the harpist roamed ceaselessly through
his heart and would not rest.

He drew himself out from under a snowdrift in the
northern wastes one day, impelled south without quite
knowing why. He shifted shapes all across the realm;
no shape gave him peace. He passed spring as it came
northward; the restlessness in him sharpened. The
winds coming out of the west and south smelled of
plowed earth and sunlight. They strung his wind-harp
with gentler voices. He did not feel gentle. He sham-

bled in bear-shape through forests, flung himself in
falcon-shape across the noon sun as it crossed his
path. He rode the bow of a trade-ship three days as
it scudded and boomed across the sea, until the sail-
ors, wary of his sea bird's strange, still eyes, chased
him away. He followed the Ymris coast, flying, crawling, galloping with wild horses until he reached the
coast of Meremont. There he followed the scent of his
memories to Wind Plain.

He found on the plain the shape of a prince of Hed,
with scarred hands and three stars on his face. A battle echoed around him; stones fell soundlessly, vanished. The grass quivered like the broken strings of
a harp. A blade of light from the setting sun burned
in his eyes. He turned away from it and saw Raederle.

She was in Hed, on the beach above Tol. She was
sitting on a rock, tossing bits of shell into the sea as
the waves splashed around her. Something in her face,
an odd mixture of restlessness and sadness, seemed to
mirror what was in his heart. It drew him like a hand.
He flew across the water, flickering in and out of the
sunlight, and took his own shape on the rock in front
of her.

She gazed up at him speechlessly, a shell poised in
her hand. He found no words either; he wondered if
he had forgotten all language in the northern wastes.
He sat down beside her after a moment, wanting to
be near her. He took the shell from her hand and
tossed it into the waves.

"You drew me all the way down from the northern
wastes," he said. "I was . . . I don't know what I
was. Something cold."

She moved after a moment, drew a strand of his
shaggy hair out of his eyes. "I wondered if you might
come here. I thought you would come to me when you
were ready." She sounded resigned to something beyond his comprehension.

"How could I have come? I didn't know where you
were. You left Wind Plain."

She stared at him a moment. "I thought you knew everything. You are the High One. You even know what I am going to say next."

"I don't," he said. He picked a shell bit from a crevice, fed it to the waves. "You aren't bound to my mind. I would have been with you long ago, except I didn't know where in Hel's name to begin to look."

She was silent, watching him. He met her eyes finally, then sighed and put his arm around her shoulders. Her hair smelled of salt; her face was getting brown under the sun. "I'm wraith-driven," he said. "I think my heart was buried under that cairn."

"I know." She kissed him, then slid down until her head rested in the hollow of his shoulder. A wave rolled to their feet, withdrew. The dock at Tol was being rebuilt; pine logs brought down from the northlands lay on the beach. She gazed across the sea to Caithnard, half in shadow, half in fading light. "The College of Riddle-Masters has been reopened."

"I know."

"If you know everything, what will we have to talk about?"

"I don't know. I suppose nothing." He saw a ship cross the sea from Tol, carrying a Prince of Hed and a harpist. The ship docked at Caithnard; they both disembarked to begin their journey. . . . He stirred a little, wondering when it would end. He held Raederle more closely, his cheek against her hair. In that late light, he loved to harp, but the starred harp was broken, its strings snapped by grief. He touched a mussel clinging to the rock and realized he had never shaped one. The sea was still a moment, idling around the rock. And in that moment he almost heard something like a fragment of a song he had once loved.

"What did you do with the Earth-Masters?"

"I didn't kill them," he said softly. "I didn't even touch their power. I bound them in Erlenstar Mountain."

He felt the breath go out of her noiselessly. "I was afraid to ask," she whispered.

"I couldn't destroy them. How could I? They were a part of you, and of Deth. . . . They're bound until they die, or I die, whichever comes first. . . ." He considered the next few millenniums with a weary eye. "Riddlery. Is that the end of it? Do all riddles end in a tower with no door? I feel as if I built that tower stone by stone, riddle by riddle, and the last stone fitting into place destroyed it."

"I don't know. When Duac died, I was so hurt; I felt a place torn out of my heart. It seemed so unjust that he should die in that war, since he was the most clear-headed and patient of us. That healed. But the harpist . . . I keep listening for his harping beneath the flash of water, beneath the light . . . I don't know why we cannot let him rest."

Morgon drew her hair out of the wind's grasp and smoothed it. He tapped randomly into the continual stream of thoughts just beneath the surface of his awareness. He heard Tristan arguing placidly with Eliard as she set plates on the table at Akren. In Hel, Nun and Raith of Hel were watching a pig being born. In Lungold, Iff was salvaging books out of the burned wizards' library. In the City of Circles, Lyra was talking to a young Herun lord, telling him things she had not told anyone else about the battle in Lungold. On Wind Plain, the broken pieces of a sword were being slowly buried under grass roots.

He smelled twilight shadowing Hed, full of new grass, broken earth, sun-warmed leaves. The odd memory of a song that was no song caught at him again; straining, he almost heard it. Raederle seemed to hear it; she stirred against him, her face growing peaceful in the last warm light.

He said, "There's a speaking pig being born in Hel. Nun is there with the Lord of Hel."

She smiled suddenly. "That's the first in three centuries. I wonder what it was born to say? Morgon, while I was waiting for you, I had to do something, so I explored the sea. I found something that belongs to you. It's at Akren."

"What?"

"Don't you know?"

"No. Do you want me to read your mind?"

"No. Never. How could I argue with you, then?" His expression changed suddenly, and her smile deepened.

"Peven's crown?"

"Eliard said it was. I had never seen it. It was full of seaweed and barnacles, except for one great stone like a clear eye . . . I loved the sea. Maybe I'll live in it."

"I'll live in the wastes," he said. "Once every hundred years, you will shine out of the sea and I'll come to you, or I will draw you into the winds with my harping . . ." He heard it then, finally, between the drift of the waves, in the rock they sat on, old, warm, settled deep in the earth, deep in the sea. His heart began to open tentatively to something he had not felt for years.

"What is it?" She was still smiling, watching him, her eyes full of the last light. He was silent for a long time, listening. He took her hand and stood up. She walked with him to the shore road, up the cliff. The final rays of the sun poured down across the green fields; the road ahead of them seemed to run straight into light. He stood, his heart opened like a seedling, hearing all over Hed, all over the realm, a familiar stillness that came out of the heart of all things.

The silence drew deep into Morgon's mind and rested there. Whether it was a memory or part of his heritage or a riddle without an answer, he did not know. He drew Raederle close to him, content for once with not knowing. They walked down the road toward Akren. Raederle, her voice tranquil, began telling him about pearls and luminous fish and the singing of water deep in the sea. The sun set slowly; dusk wandered across the realm, walked behind them on the road, a silver-haired stranger with night at his back, his face always toward the dawn.

Peace, tremulous, unexpected, sent a taproot out of nowhere into Morgon's heart.

People and Places

AIA   wife of Har of Osterland
AKREN   home of the land-rulers of Hed
ALOIL   a Lungold wizard
AN   kingdom incorporating the Three Portions (An Aum, Hel) ruled by Mathom
ANUIN   seaport in An; home of the Kings of An
ARYA   a Herun woman subject of a riddle
ASTRIN   brother of Heureu; land-heir of Imris
AUM   ancient kingdom conquered by An

BERE   grandson of Danan Isig; son of Vert

CAERWEDDIN   chief city of Ymris; seat of Heureu; a port city
CAITHNARD   seaport and traders' city; site of the College of Riddle-Masters
CITY OF CIRCLES   home of the Morgol of Herun
CORBETT, BRI   ship-master of Mathom of An
CORRIG   a shape-changer; ancestor of Raederle

DANAN ISIG   land-ruler and King of Isig
DETH   a harpist
DHAIRRHUWYTH   an early Morgol of Herun

DUAC   Mathom's son; land-heir of An

EARTH-MASTERS   ancient, mysterious inhabitants of
  the High One's realm
EDOLEN   an Earth-Master
EL ELRHIARHODAN   the land-ruler of Herun
ELIARD   the Prince of Hed; Morgon's younger
  brother
ERIEL   a shape-changer; a kinswoman of Corrig and
  Raederle
ERLENSTAR MOUNTAIN   ancient home of the High
  One

GHISTESLWCHLOHM   Founder of the School of Wizards at Lungold; also impersonator of the High One
GOH   a member of the Herun guard
GRIM MOUNTAIN   site of Yrye, home of Har of Osterland

HAR   the wolf-king; land-ruler of Osterland
HARTE   mountain-home of Danan Isig
HED   a small island ruled by the Princess of Hed
HEL   one of the Three Portions of An
HERUN   a kingdom ruled by the Morgol
HEUREU   the King of Ymris
HIGH ONE   sustainer of the land-law of the realm
HLURLE   a small trade-port near Herun
HUGIN   son of Suth the wizard

IFF   a Lungold wizard
ISIG   a mountain kingdom ruled by Danan Isig
ISIG PASS   a mountain pass between Isig and Erlen-
  star Mountain

KING'S MOUTH PLAIN   site of a ruined city of the
  Earth-Masters
KRAAL   port-city at the mouth of the Winter River

KYRTH   trade-city in Isig on the Ose River

LEIN   kinsman of the High Lord of Marcher
LUNGOLD   city founded by Ghisteslwchlohm; home of the School of Wizards
LYRA   the land-heir of Herun; El's daughter

MADIR   ancient witch of An
MARCHER   territory in north Ymris governed by the High Lord of Marcher
MATHOM   King of An
MEREMONT   coastal territory of Ymris
MORGON   the Star-Bearer, at one time the Prince of Hed

NUN   a Lungold wizard

OSTERLAND   northern kingdom ruled by Har

PEVEN   ancient lord of Aum

RAEDERLE   daughter of Mathom of An
RAITH   the Lord of Hel
ROOD   Mathom's younger son; brother of Duac and Raederle
RORK   High Lord of Umber

SEC   an Earth-Master
SUTH   an ancient wizard

TALIES   a Lungold wizard
TERIL   Son of Rork Umber
TOL   small fishing-town in Hed
TOR   a territory in Imris
TRISTAN   Morgon's sister

UMBER   Midland territory of Ymris

VERT   daughter of Danan Isig

Wɪɴᴅ Pʟᴀɪɴ   the site in Ymris of Wind Tower and a
ruined city of the Earth-Masters.

Yʟᴏɴ   an ancient King of An; son of a queen of An
and the shape-changer Corrig
Yᴍʀɪs   a kingdom ruled by Heureu Ymris
Yʀᴛʜ   a powerful, blind wizard at Lungold

PATRICIA A. MCKILLIP discovered the joys of writing when she was fourteen, endured her teen-age years in the secret life of her stories, plays and novels, and has been writing ever since—except for a brief detour when she thought she would be a concert pianist.

She was born in Salem, Oregon and has lived in Arizona, California and the England that is the setting for *The House on Parchment Street*. After a number of years in San Jose, where she received an MA in English from San Jose State University, she moved to San Francisco, where she now lives.

Miss McKillip has also written *The Throme of the Erril of Sherill*, *The Forgotten Beasts of Eld*, *The Night Gift*, *The Riddle-Master of Hed*, and *Heir of Sea and Fire*.